R

W9-BQL-748

# The
# Murderous
# McLaughlins

# The Murderous McLaughlins

## JACK DUNPHY

Thorndike Press • Thorndike, Maine

**Library of Congress Cataloging in Publication Data:**

Dunphy, Jack.
    The murderous McLaughlins.
    1. Large type books.  I. Title.
[PS3507.U6793M8  1988b]      813'.54–      88-29471
ISBN 0-89621-225-4 (lg. print : alk. paper)

Large Print edition available in North America by
arrangement with McGraw-Hill Book Company.

Cover design by Michael Anderson.

For Truman and Gloria
My Loves

*Cast your mind on other days*
*That we in coming days may be*
*Still the indomitable Irishery.*

−W. B. Yeats

# 1

"What do you imagine they could be thinking?" my mother would ask us. "What do you think they say to one another, when visitors have gone home, and they are alone in their cages? Does Horatio talk to Sinbad? Do the birds talk to the seals? I swear that if Sinbad could speak he would say, 'I'll meet you outside.'"

"That's what you tell us to do, if we get separated," I said, wanting to draw her attention away from Sinbad and back to the family, which I considered indestructible at the time, and eternal.

"Escape, escape," my mother had the nerve to tell Sinbad.

"Gert's gone," I said.

Matthew, in his carriage, howled at that, but my mother scarcely regarded us.

"Gert's outside the gate. Go get her. Make up some excuse to the guard. I'm sure he'll let her back in," my mother said, without taking her eyes off Sinbad once.

"Can I wheel Matthew with me?" I asked.

"Meet us in the lion house," my mother said, holding fast to Mattie's carriage.

Gert was standing on Girard Avenue crying to anybody who would listen to her that she was lost.

She always did that.

"Mister," I said to the guard at the gate, "can I bring my sister back into the zoological garden, please?"

"Oh, she's your sister, is she? What's she doin' out there on Girard Avenue, if she's your sister? She don't look like you."

"I can't help that," I said. "She's my sister, all the same. And, besides, she's lost."

"Is that her trouble?"

"Yes, she's always getting lost. It's a way of calling attention to herself, my mother says."

"Well, for God's sake," said the lady in the ticket office. "I never heard of such a thing. Lands."

"Can I go get my sister and bring her back into the zoological garden, sir?"

"Go ahead."

The lady in the ticket office stood up in order to see us pass. She said she never would understand how some people raise their chil'ren.

8

My mother was standing in front of the king of the jungle when we got back to her.

"Horatio isn't hungry, today, and I don't blame him," she told us.

We used to save Horatio for last because he was noble and plainly superior to his captors, my mother said.

One of them threw Horatio a big piece of meat, which he disdained.

"That's right," my mother said.

"You said Horatio wasn't hungry, Maw," I told her, "and he wasn't."

My mother steered Matthew proudly into the birdhouse, always a sign that we were on our way home.

I did not like the zoological garden anymore, but since my mother enjoyed going there so much, I would hurt her if I said so. Anyway, winter was on us, according to her. Pretty soon we would not be going to Fairmount Park, summer being for roaming and winter for staying home, she said, though I was not all that much home when it snowed, and I told her so.

"Well, it's not here yet," she said, and she took off her leghorn straw hat with its wide band of pink ribbon and fanned herself with one hand, and wheeled Matthew in his carriage across Girard Avenue with the other.

"All the same," I said, "I hope Horatio eats

tonight. I'd hate to see him have to lean against his bars to stand up."

"Why, what a thing to say," said my mother. "Horatio would sooner die than let himself go to pieces like that."

Our street was a riot when we got to it. Johnny Ervine's wagon had been run over by the milkman's horse and lay shattered in the middle of Ingersoll Street, much to Johnny's joy, though he pretended to be sad as anything.

When the milkman said he would buy him another, Johnny burst into tears, he was so happy. It was for that reason he almost got up the courage to go into the water at the swimmies that evening.

It was a lovely evening. It rained a bit to cool us off, and to settle the dust down, my mother said, then the sun came out again so that we could see it set in the west beyond the playground.

The swimmies was in shadow behind red-brick walls at the corner of the playground on Master Street. The water in the pool looked like ink, and Johnny said it was, and he wouldn't go in and come out blue as a nigger for all the money in the world.

Aunt Frances said Johnny was a coward, but that was because she hated all kids but me, even Gert.

10

Aunt Frances was my dearest friend and first in all the world to me, but I did not let on especially, at least not to my mother.

Johnny watched me enviously as I swam and floated in a swarm of other kids as if I was alone all by myself in the swimmies, my own private backyard pool, when all the time it was the property of the municipality and belonged to all of us.

"Suppose my new wagon's there when I get home?" Johnny yelled, having found the courage to actually kneel on the wet pavement beside the pool.

He was all right, even if he was a coward. Even if he was, I don't think it mattered. And I did not see why it should have mattered to Aunt Frances. Suppose in her heart of hearts Aunt Frances thought I was a coward? I was sure that if she did, or that if I did something base to make her think I was, she would love me just the same, the way I did Johnny.

Johnny got carried away so by the thought of a new wagon that I laughed when two kids pushed him off the wet pavement into the inky blue water, because I was sure he thought he would come out dyed.

He came up making more white water than three boys his size, and his eyes looked as they

11

should have when the milkman's horse ran over his wagon.

"Don't worry, Johnny," I said, "I'm coming."

The first thing he did when I reached him was to scratch me straight down the side of my face from my eye to the corner of my mouth, where his fingers stopped between my teeth. Then he climbed on me, as if I was a pair of steps. His knee struck my chin. I felt one of his feet after the other trying to dig a foothold into me. I thought of Horatio, and what he would do, and my mother at our funerals, and of Aunt Frances staying away because she blamed it all on Johnny Ervine's cowardice. By the time the lifeguard's shrill whistle dominated every other noise in the bathhouse I had died. I came to to a heaven of faces encircling Johnny and me and Johnny saying I had made him go into the inky blue water over his head. He was crying when I crawled through a puzzle of skinny bare legs to our locker and got dressed.

The sun had gone long ago and Master Street was in shadow on our way home swinging our trunks, both wet for a change.

"Mammy," I sang, "Mammy. The sun shines east, the sun shines west, but I know where the sun shines best. Mammy, Mammy, I'd walk a million miles for one of your smiles, my M-a-a-a-a-mmy."

# 2

The cream in the bottles of milk on the front doorstep had shot up frozen stiff six or so inches from their ordinary place, at the same time maintaining the round cardboard caps on their tops just as they did when the cream was liquid, which it would have been had it not snowed last night.

"Maw," I sang out, "I can't even see across the street to Johnny's house because of the hill of snow."

Just then I coughed, or something. I felt funny, anyway. Too funny to eat breakfast.

"Come over here, by the stove, and sit down," my mother said, looking at me, as if she could feel what I felt.

I would rather have sat by the stove in the kitchen, so I could see out. Here, in the dining room, I felt cut off from bliss.

"Don't move," my mother told me, getting into her coat. "And don't wake Mattie, or Gert. They'll sleep late because of the quiet."

13

"Where are you going, Maw?"

"I'm going to get Doctor Reiner for you."

"Can I have some of the frozen cream before it melts?"

"Yes," my mother said, "but I'm in a hurry."

I could hardly swallow the cream because of my sore throat. It wasn't worth trying, no matter how much I liked it at other times.

"I knew it," my mother said. "You've got something."

The stove in the dining room was round-bellied, but not yet red, as it would be later on in the day. I watched around it, after my mother went out, to see what I could of the world outside. But the snow looked threatening now. I did not know why until my mother returned with Doctor Reiner.

"What have we here?" Doctor Reiner asked when he saw me, not expecting an answer from anybody but himself, since he looked into his bag and pulled out two little black hoses connected to a silver medellion and stuck the end of the hoses into his ears and the medallion against my chest. He seemed to make me sicker, as doctors do at first, and my throat grew dry and sore by the minute, by the second, maybe quicker.

"He can't stay here with the rest of you. Not home," said Reiner. "We'd do best to send him

14

to the Municipal Hospital. You'll be in and out before you can say Jack Robinson," he told me, shoving his hairy face close to mine, and pressing back the flesh over my eyes so that he could see my brains, if I had any.

"Why, what's wrong with him?" my mother asked, as if it were all my fault.

"Scarlet fever," replied Reiner, sounding to me as if he had it for breakfast every morning, he loved it so. "I'll have the ambulance here in a jiffy. And a sticker on your door to warn your neighbors away in less time than that."

"Don't let Johnny Ervine come near me, Maw," I said, when we were alone, and she was shoveling coal into the stove in the dining room.

The flames made me love the house and her, but I hoped I would be like Horatio and not cry. After she closed the door to the stove she sat down and looked at me. "It won't be for long," she said. I guess I loved her more than anybody, even Aunt Frances.

"Jim!" my mother called out to Dad from the foot of the stairs, "you better go down to your mother till the sign's off the door. He's got scarlet fever and is on his way to the Municipal Hospital. There's Reiner with the sticker at the door now."

"Why wasn't he sick before?" she said to

15

Reiner. "Not even last night."

"He'll be sick enough soon," Doctor Reiner told her.

The bad things Doctor Reiner said did not necessarily turn out to be true, but the good things he said were mostly fake and meant to fool you. I knew better than to say Jack Robinson, but all the same I found myself praying his name, in the belief (that I really did not believe in) that it would get me out of the Municipal Hospital and home again before the hill of snow between Johnny's house and mine melted.

When they shaved my head and said it was for my own good, I did not believe them, but thought, rather, that it was for their good that they did it, to save them the work of washing it. I watched my hair fall into the towel they put on me and I tried to convince myself that it would never grow in again and my mother would be sorry she had sent me away. At night the long shadows cast into the ward by the light in the hall fell across my bed like railroad ties.

I was hardly sick a day in the Municipal Hospital, but jumped up and down on the bed with two other boys who first saw me do it, then copied me. If we did not do that, we called for Miss Prunes, the nurse, who came,

16

finally, but when we least expected her, and without making a sound, because of the crepe-soled shoes she wore.

Miss Prunes liked us, she said, because we were only three, where as we might have been ten, there being seven other cots in the ward, all empty. Ben Potatoe was the boy in the bed on one side of me, near the window, and Steven Crossley was the other boy. Ben wasn't like his name at all, his last name, Potatoe, but lithe and wiggly, like Chinese writing — only Ben was the color of cocoa.

Steven was a Catholic. He wore scapulars and slept on rosary beads, and he had a missal he couldn't read full of holy cards. Miss Prunes said that Steven had just about everything you need to ward off evil except a strong body and a good appetite. It was so bad that he gave his ice cream to Ben Potatoe, who said he would never forget it.

But at night a cloud of loneliness would roll over our heads, only to be denied next morning, especially if it was a sunny day outside.

Ben said he was going home first, and Steve said that he was, but I was telling myself, in secret, that I never wanted to go home again, especially not without hair, so I said nothing.

Ben said he was going to be a baseball player when he grew up, and he was always posing like a pitcher on the mound. His favorite place to pose was on the windowsill, which was strictly forbidden. Ben was up there, anyway, throwing hot balls across an imaginary home plate when he stopped and said there was a lady outside. I looked and saw it was my mother, but I was so ashamed of my empty head that I got a towel from the bathroom and climbed up on the windowsill with Ben wearing it like a turban.

I liked dressing up and had a flare for it, but Ben Potatoe was unimpressed.

"How do you expect your mother to know you with a towel around your head?"

"One thing she won't do, and that is take you for me, Ben," I said, and we laughed and put our arms around one another, standing there on the windowsill, as if my mother had come to photograph us.

We must have been three floors up and my mother stood out on a just-shoveled road between two high banks of snow. The day was gray and her hair showed up redder than it was. From where we stood we could never have made out her freckles, which were pale anyway, and not like mine. Before I knew it Ben had slipped the towel from my head and was wiping my tears as fast as they fell.

# 3

"Who was the little colored boy standing with you on the windowsill the day I came to see you?" my mother asked when she came to take me home.

"Oh, that was Ben Potatoe, Maw. He's going to be a baseball player."

Just then Ben came along with his mother, who was so large that if she ever sat on him Ben would not be anything but a smudge of himself, to say nothing of being a professional baseball player.

"Good-bye, Ben," I said.

Ben looked at me as if he thought I was crazy, talking to him so familiarly.

"Say good-bye to the little white boy, honey," Ben's mother told him.

But Ben would not. He did shake my hand, though woodenly, when I offered mine, but only because his mother made him.

"I'll write you, Ben," I said, as he turned away, for we had promised, back in the ward with the seven empty beds, that we would.

"You better not," Ben now told me.

"Pick up yoh feet, you lil' ole grouch," Ben's mother commanded, pushing him ahead of her.

All the same he grinned at me around her before they turned the corner in the Municipal Hospital's hall.

My mother brought along a hat for me to wear home, knowing I would hate to be seen bald. I hoped Aunt Frances would not be at her window when we passed her house next to the corner of Ingersoll Street, but she was. She pushed up her window as soon as she saw us.

Her eyes rested on me a minute before she spoke.

"Well," she said, in her dry way, "home comes the sailor, after weathering many a storm. Feeling better?"

"Oh yes. I feel ready to take on the world."

"Well, we've got pretty grown up, haven't we, since being in the hospital?"

My answer rubbed Aunt Frances the wrong way and she shut down her window without another word to either of us.

"Mrs. Fitzgerald has her good days and her bad. She's grieving today for times past, before Mr. Fitzgerald and her daughter were taken away from her," my mother told me as we continued up the brick sidewalk to our door.

The hill of snow between the two-story row houses on Ingersoll Street had melted, and in its place stood Johnny Ervine's new wagon.

"I hope," my mother said, "that you're not going to take a wagon that's not yours."

"I don't think Johnny would mind if I tried it out."

"Don't you want to come into the house first? If it's not one thing with you it's another. You're excited about being home."

"Just across Twenty-fourth Street and back."

"Yes, and be killed in the bargain. Traffic's not what it was before you went away. It's fierce. Besides, what do you think Johnny will say when he comes out of the house and sees his wagon's gone?"

"That will be all right. We swore to share everything alike."

"You did, did you? Well, go ahead. But don't get killed. I'll be in the house."

I crossed Twenty-fourth Street and went out Morris Street to the swimmies and came back to Ingersoll Street just as Johnny Ervine came out of his house.

"Thief."

"But, Johnny, I thought we'd agreed to share everything we have in common."

"Not since you've become contaminated. And get out of that wagon. It's probably contami-

21

nated now too. I really ought to make you buy it from me."

I was glad Aunt Frances came out to sweep her steps, but hurt that she did so and went in again without a word to me.

"I suppose you know your father left home?" Johnny said to me when we were alone.

"He didn't. He's staying with my grandmother. Now the sign's off our door he'll be back."

Johnny walked off pulling his wagon, and Aunt Frances looked past me through her windowpane at Twenty-fourth Street.

Contamination being what it is, I wished I was back in the Municipal Hospital again with my own kind.

# 4

In those days the seasons flew like the furled pages of a picture book, and it was summer before you knew it and time to go back and see how Sinbad and Horatio were doing. It was warm for May and the budding trees did not cast the shade they would later on. Matthew still relied on his carriage for distance. In all this time my father had not returned home, and this is what my mother talked about.

"He might as well wait now, that is if he ever intends to come back to us at all."

"Why should he wait?"

"Why, until the baby's born," she said, speaking very frankly to me in lieu of having anyone else to talk to.

"Oh yes," I said, as if I understood everything, "he better wait. You're right."

"And, afterwards," my mother said, "I think you'd better go down and get him."

"One thing," I said, "I'm glad he didn't see me without my hair."

23

"Walk Mattie into the lion house," my mother said. "He's too much of a load for me in his carriage now."

I picked Mattie up and carried him into the lion house, but near dropped him in surprise and disappointment when I saw Horatio was not in his cage.

"What do you think happened, Maw?"

"He probably asked for a transfer. I have heard that in Buenos Aires zoo animals walk free."

"Even lions?"

"I don't suppose the lions do — yet."

Still, it wasn't the same without Horatio.

"Something's gone out of the zoological garden for me since I know Horatio's not here," my mother said.

"Me too, Maw. Suppose Sinbad's not here?"

He wasn't. There was a sign explaining why, on which some wit had written in chalk: *Gone home.*

"Maybe we've grown up from the zoo," my mother said, in the birdhouse, on our way out. "Maybe we'll have to look for other things somewhere else, things to admire, things to look up to, like we did Horatio."

That night we were awakened by the sound of a parade without music, a parade of giants. Or so it seemed from the sound of it. People were running down the middle of Ingersoll Street to Twenty-fourth Street, some of them in their nightgowns.

"It can't be a parade, that's silly," my mother said, though she had said it was in the beginning.

Whatever it was, it was more like a movie than real life, with everything happening in the dark, with only flashes of white. Kids were in bare feet, though not all. Johnny Ervine came out of his house looking as if he was dressed for winter and began shouting something about a stampede, since he always exaggerated, no matter what. He seemed to me to be afraid to leave his front steps, while other people were passing him to the corner three and four at a time.

"What's up, Johnny?"

"It's a stampede, and everybody's going to be stampeded. Don't come out."

But I did.

I squeezed through the crowd and took my place beside Aunt Frances, who must have been first out, because she had the best spot to see everything, right on the edge of the curb.

Before us herds of cattle were being driven down Twenty-fourth Street by rough-looking men brandishing sticks, who had to run to keep up with them. They could have scattered back to our houses had any broken away from the

25

herd, but none did. They stayed close to one another as possible, wanting more than anything, I felt, to get the thing over with.

They were black and brown, but the mass of them hurrying by gave an impression of blackness, of a river of tar.

The sounds they made, besides the tapping of their hooves on the asphalt street, were those of creatures under stress, talking to one another in captivity, and only every once in a while exploding out in gruff protest against it.

"Where are they going?" I asked.

Nobody seemed to know except Johnny Ervine, who had finally found nerve to make it to the corner with the rest of us, babies in their mothers' arms, dogs on the leash. Two sweaty dogs worked with the trotting men to keep the cattle on their way, but there was no need of this. The beasts jostled one another as if they were improperly glued together. It seemed to pain them to be parted, as if they were so many mothers and sons, in a holiday crowd at a carnival, adjuring one another to keep close.

"They are being taken to a slaughterhouse," Johnny Ervine shouted, as if he knew, when he didn't, not for sure.

People began to remember their appearances, and to go back to their houses that they had left in their curiosity and excitement. Once the

26

sensationalism of the scene had worn off, which was soon enough, the sight of the be- devilment of creatures with feelings like themselves for commercial purposes held no more interest for them. None would even think of it tomorrow when they bought beef. Soon Aunt Frances and I were alone with the traces the animals had left behind them.

"That Aunt Frances sure cares about animals," I told my mother later on.

She seemed surprised.

"Why, who's Aunt Frances?"

"Why, Mrs. Fitzgerald."

"Well," my mother said, "you must be pretty close, is all I can say."

"We're not, though."

"You're not?"

"No, since I've been home from the hospital I haven't been in her house once."

"And you were before? I didn't know that."

"Yes, but no farther than the vestibule, mostly."

"Ah yes, when she gave you a touch of her dandelion wine. That must have been when she said you could call her Aunt Frances — during your drinking sessions together. Was it?"

"No it wasn't."

"When was it then?"

27

"I don't know. It just happened. It just came to me, like reading."

"You learned to read at school, didn't you?"

"No I didn't. I never learn anything at school. I learned to read from you."

"Well, now," my mother said, pleased.

It was a great compliment, since she had trouble even reading the funnies to me, as she would readily admit, I guess.

Now that I could read them myself, I realized how much she had made up when she came across a word she did not know. Her words were better, and her pronunciations too.

The funnies were funnier when my mother read them to me than when I learned to read them myself.

# 5

On Fourth of July Johnny Ervine said he would commit suicide if his mother would not let him shoot off fireworks, but she would not.

"How's your mother?" Mrs. Ervine asked me in her drawling way.

"She's all right, Mrs. Ervine," I replied, but I did not think so.

My mother was walking around holding on to too many things to suit me.

"Well," said Mrs. Ervine, "she must have known she was being talked about, because there she is at her front bedroom window. Go up and take care of her. Now that your father's gone, you're the man of the house."

"Go on," Johnny cried, forgetting all about his firecrackers in his concern for my mother, even though it was only a game to him, like everything else.

I couldn't wait to tell my mother what Mrs. Ervine said about Dad not being home, but when I got upstairs to her it slipped my mind, there being so much else to do.

"Run get Reiner, but before you do, here help me make the bed."

After we made the bed I ran out through a forest of firecrackers and crossed the porch at Doctor Reiner's house and rang the bell.

"He's out in the yard with his flowers," Mrs. Reiner told me. "What a time to choose to have a baby. The Fourth of July. And your father not home yet, either, is he?"

"My mother said hurry, Mrs. Reiner."

Doctor Reiner came out by the side yard in his shirtsleeves.

"You come here," he said to me, taking me by the hand.

He led me through the dark, cool, heavily furnished house to the kitchen, where he poured me out a glass of cold milk and cut off a slice of a big chocolate cake for me.

"Another one in the world," Mrs. Reiner shouted at her pots and pans.

Reiner watched me eat as he got into his shiny blue serge jacket. He took my hand again, and I hoped we would ride, but we did not, we walked.

"Hair's all grown back in, I see."

"Oh yes, it grew like anything, Doctor Reiner. One thing I'm glad for, is that my father didn't see it."

30

"He's not home yet, huh? I thought he was due back from your grandmother's when the sign came off the door."

"I'm supposed to go get him someday, my mother says, Doctor Reiner."

"He must send you something. He's got to."

"Yes he does, but I'll be going down to get him soon."

"Will he like that?" Reiner asked, stopping and looking down at me, all smiles.

I did not see what was funny. Besides, we were at the house.

"You better go up right away."

The doctor looked at me again, but this time seriously, with an impatient shake of his head.

"Why, yes, I mean to," he said.

I followed him upstairs and watched him go into the front bedroom. He looked at me before closing the door and shook his head again, but in bewilderment this time.

The next thing I heard was a baby cry, then the front door opened and Gertie came in with Matthew. I went down to them and asked if they were hungry. They said they were, naturally.

And all the time the new baby cried.

Gert, who tended towards a melodramatic interpretation of all things, especially our doings, fell back against the cold stove in the

31

dining room when the new one cried. It did not sound as if it felt wanted to me. It wasn't.

"Not another one!" Gert said.

Reiner came downstairs and looked into the dining room at us from the hall.

"There's too many little people in this house, and not enough big ones to take care of you," he said.

"We're all right, Doctor Reiner," I said, feeling my mother would not have liked to hear him talk like that to us, as if we were the children of beggars.

When someone knocked smartly at the front door Doctor Reiner opened it before I could, though I was right behind him.

"Yes?" I said to the figure on the doorstep. "What is it you want?"

The person paid no attention to me, but addressed herself to Doctor Reiner in a breathless sort of way, looking up and down Ingersoll Street as she spoke, as if she were being sought after by all the city, though for as long as she stood there nobody came near her that I could see.

She was of an intriguing dark complexion, with great flabby red cheeks and floppy red lips, much too red to be real.

I wondered what it could be that she was selling from door to door and was surprised to learn that it was no less a commodity than her swarthy self.

"Here I am, Doctor Reiner. Is this the house? Well, it must be, since you're here, as your wife said you'd be. Now there's a woman. No wonder you're all smiles, despite your treacherous work, knee-deep in disease and no care for yourself. It's because you've got a good home, and a good girl to go home to."

Doctor Reiner seemed to be highly amused by her, which was more than I was.

"Well, Ruth," he said to her, "I think the least you could have done was to wash your face. These are plain people here. They won't know what to make of you."

"Let them make of me what they will. Do I get the job or don't I? Do they need help or not? Judging from the crowd peering out from around you I'd say they do."

"Keep your opinions to yourself until I go up and explain to her who you are," Doctor Reiner directed her. "It may be that she won't want you."

"Or can't afford me. If that's the case, I'm off."

"Well, wait a minute. God knows they need somebody."

I ran up the stairs after Reiner and blocked his way in to see my mother.

"We don't need her, Doctor Reiner. We're all right by ourselves. Besides, she's awful."

"She is that," Reiner agreed. "But let's try her. If things get too bad you can always come tell me."

He was in and out of my mother's room in a minute. "Go on up," he told the woman at the door. "But wash your face first. You look like something out of a sideshow."

"There's nothing wrong with the way I look. I've never had complaints before."

"You've never looked this bad before. You're enough to scare the wits out of a body."

She looked in at all the doors to the rooms before she went upstairs. "Not a stick," she said.

"I'll leave you now," said Reiner, and he was off.

She took an age to climb the stairs, so long, in fact, that even Mattie, crawling on his hands and knees, was able to keep up with her.

"How are you doing?" she asked, sitting down on the edge of my mother's bed, making the springs creak, and my mother wince. "Not s'good, huh?" She snatched up the new one. "Don't weigh nothin', does he? Well, if anything happens to 'im, you have this crowd t'fall back on. I hope they're good. Are they? I don't take sass. Now, I wancha all *out!*"

34

She pushed herself up from the bed and shooed us, but to no avail. Seeing that she could not scare us, she hiked her shoulders and left the bedroom in a huff.

"I think you should go get your father," my mother told me, when we were alone with her.

"I couldn't leave you with her, Maw."

"Why not? We'll be all right. She's not so bad. If only she didn't sit on my bed."

"My name is Ruth Bee," she told us at dinner.

"Ruth B. what?" I asked.

"Never you mind, impertinence."

And that was that.

"If you're good I'll bake youse an apple pie."

She did, but she ate most of it herself. After three days of her sitting on the edge of the bed my mother had enough of her and got up and washed and dressed and told her to beat it. All the same we missed her when she went. She said she had been a nun and everything.

"All lies," my mother said.

"I don't think she was on the stage, either, do you, Maw?"

"Lord no. What stage? I didn't hear that one."

"She said she was in the lineup at Keith's and showed us her legs and even did steps."

"Well, we're rid of her now. You better get Dad."

"Doctor Reiner asked me if he'd like it if I went down to get him. What do you think?"

"Why, I don't know what to think. I'd say he'd be glad to see you."

"The sign's been off the door so long. There's nothing contaminating about me now, is there, Maw?"

"I think you should go down. Whatever you do, if you do go down, don't say a word about the strawberry festival at Johnny Ervine's church to your grandmother. Or that you ever went to church with Johnny."

"I can still go, though, can't I, to the strawberry festival?"

"I don't see why not."

# 6

The strawberry festival was a big fake. It was the one thing I agreed with my grandmother on. There wasn't a strawberry from one end of that churchyard to the other. There were chocolate cakes for sale for the benefit of naked savages in a faraway place across many bodies of deep ocean, the preacher at Johnny's church said. Then they sang. Then they prayed standing up. Then they sang again before going out in the yard under Japanese lanterns where I expected to be stuffed with strawberries because Johnny said they would be thick as raindrops in a summer shower. No wonder my grandmother was furious when she heard.

How she heard was a puzzle.

"And we'll never know the answer to it, not exactly, anyway," my mother said, adding that it must have been something that your father let out at dinner, or playing cards, down there.

My mother lifted the new baby, whose name was Mark, up out of his crib and looked at him, holding him out at arm's length.

"Sometimes I feel this baby's all mine."

"Well he *is*, Maw."

She laughed then, but I didn't see what was so funny.

I got over being mad about the strawberry festival, but my grandmother didn't. She gave orders that I was not to go to Johnny Ervine's church again, which suited me perfectly, except that she found a church not far from where we lived that she thought I should go to, strawberries or no strawberries.

I was sent off by myself, which was often the case, so I was used to it, though I was still only eight years of age.

I went through streets new to me, and passed houses I had not seen before. I adopted a crowd, betting it could only be on its way to church, the day being a Sunday, and allowed myself to be swept towards a tall building of gray granite, and up its stone steps through pinewood doors into a marble vestibule, where nerve failed me and I seemed to turn to marble myself.

People filed by me in great numbers, so that from being cold, I turned hot and began to perspire.

To each side of me were wide wooden staircases that turned out of sight, but might offer me refuge, I hoped, out of the embarrassment and confusion that had overcome me since entering the place, embarrassment and confusion that were to be augmented by the sight of an object close enough to me to touch, but that I had not until now fully taken in because of the press of worshippers, and the bad light.

Before me, shielded by a glass box without a top, which both contained and protected them, were two life-sized figures carved from white marble, a hooded woman supporting a limp and naked man lying across her lap. Much as I longed to, I could not go up either staircase and hide somewhere until the crowd had come out of the church and all gone home, but must stare at the figures behind the glass, horrified at the possibility that they might be mother and son.

From being sad and human, they began to look frozen and inhuman. What first held me now seemed to thrust me away. What was rather understandable when I first came on the couple grew to be so exaggerated in my mind that I was torn between laughter and tears.

Finally, I felt I was not supposed to see them with their grief so wretchedly exposed. From feeling sorry for them I began to feel ashamed for them and ashamed of myself for watching them.

Since the stairs were an equal distance from the sufferers, I had little to choose between them, but flung myself up the flight I felt was nearer to me. I arrived in a loft which smelled of dust and dry wood, and contained nothing else in it that I could see but two chairs and a piano.

Over the piano was suspended a mirror, the size and shape of a pencil box, in which I was able to see the reflected backs of many of the people who had thronged by me downstairs in the vestibule. Before them was what I took to be a stage, all white and red and new to me, since I had not yet been to a theater, a living theater, only movies. But this was theater as I learned about it from picture books and stories my mother told me of the playhouses in town. The Garrick, the Chestnut Street Opera House, and the Walnut. Though ignorant of all that went on inside them, I felt, as I turned away from the mirror for the *real* thing below, that I was seeing here something like what my mother talked to me about.

All it wanted was music and song, and I got these soon enough.

Approaching footsteps on the staircase that I had just taken did not budge me. I was much too entranced by what was going on below to be frightened. When an intense-looking little man entered the left and made a dart for the piano stool, all the while massaging his fingers in great eagerness to be at the thing (the object of his life, it seemed to me), and seated himself and began to play without noticing me, I experienced a feeling of such satisfaction that I could have honestly sworn that I had not *lived* till then, so much was I overwhelmed by what I heard and saw.

When I told my mother that the man in the choir loft also sang, though he did not *look* as if he could, or would ever want to, not in the public way, anyway, not for people, my mother said that he was probably a different man when he sang.

"Mrs. Leslie Carter was one woman on the street, and another altogether on the stage," my mother said. "I know, because your father and I waited for her at the stage door of the Walnut Street Theater, and when she came out to go home, she was ordinary enough. Without the lights and the music she could have been any one of us, not what she had been on the stage at all."

As she talked she seemed to be living it all over again. She smiled, but a tear stole down her cheek all the same and struck Mark, who seemed to like it, since he put out his tongue for more.

41

"Oh look," I said, knowing I should not, somehow. "Mark got a grown-up tear on his face before he's grown up."

"Don't say that," my mother said, wiping the baby's face. "He hasn't even been christened yet, and never would be, as far as his father's concerned."

"Do you want me to go down and get him?" I asked, what I nearly always said when my father was brought up. I was pleased to see I had made her laugh, something she had not done much of lately. "What's funny, Maw?"

"You. The way you're beginning to say, 'Shall I go down and get him?' As if you're older than you are, and bigger than your father."

"Oh," I said, "Dad's not so big."

My mother closed her eyes. My fooling tired her. She put Mark back in his cradle and went upstairs. By the time she had come down again Gert had come home with Mattie, and all three of us regarded my mother with eyes full of appreciation.

She had combed her hair and changed her dress. It was not often we saw her in high heels. "Don't worry," she said, surprising us, even hurting us, "I'm not going anywhere. I'm not going anywhere, because I have nowhere to go."

All the same she stepped out of the house and walked quickly down the street without once looking back at us.

We were in bed when she came back, or I thought she had come back, though after a few seconds I realized it did not sound like her at all. The footsteps were not hers. They were heavy, as well they might be, since they belonged to our grandmother, who asked me right away, "Where's your mother?"

"To the store."

"The store? At this hour? What store?"

"A special store."

The more I lied, the more I felt my mother was under attack.

"Where's the new baby?"

"Upstairs with us."

"Show him to me." She laughed at me for hesitating. "Don't be afraid, I won't eat him."

She moved heavily up the staircase while I stood below in the downstairs hall ready to warn my mother of her presence in the house should she come in while our grandmother was upstairs.

But she did not come in, and our grandmother came down and went home with a picture in her mind of how we lived with so much left out, all the truth.

"For God's sake tell your mother to have that baby baptized before it dies and goes to hell," she told us on the doorstep.

43

"What's hell?" Gert wanted to know, after watching her trundle over the brick sidewalk and disappear around Hampton's grocery at the corner. "And what's baptized?"

"Baptized is something we better have done to Mark before he dies."

"And goes to hell?"

"Yes, and goes to hell."

"Is he going to hell then?"

"Not yet. At least I don't think so. He's too small yet to die."

"Were you baptized?" Gert suddenly asked me. "I feel you were. And that I wasn't, and Mattie wasn't."

Mattie, who understood he missed out on something, began to cry.

"He's crying because he's going to hell," Gert said. "Don't cry, Mattie," she told him, "I'll be with you."

# 7

My mother put me up to ask Aunt Frances to stand for Mark, but Aunt Frances said she was of another persuasion.

"Please, Aunt Frances. They're all ready for us at St. Elizabeth's. They don't care what you are or who you are there. They let me in. I don't see why they won't let you in, too."

I was talking to Aunt Frances through her front window screen that had a view of hills and dales painted on it, and it gave Aunt Frances a black eye and green hair, but I could still make her out.

"If it was my baptism you'd stand for me, wouldn't you?"

"Why sure I would. Only it's not yours, it's the new baby's, Mark, and I don't know him, or even if we'll get along. Besides, as I say, I'm of another persuasion."

"Aunt Frances, you're kidding me."

She laughed and asked Happy if she was kidding me or not. Happy kept coming and

45

going, as was his way, walking miles after work and on his day off, up and down the house until it was time to eat and go to bed.

"Happy never takes sides," I said to Hap's cigarette, gleaming out to me from the dusky, cool parlor, before Hap turned and continued his promenade.

"Happy's Mrs. Fitzgerald's star boarder," my mother said, adding that what goes on between them only the walls knew.

She put on her leghorn straw hat and took up Mark and told Gert to mind Matthew and that we would bring them back something.

"Something like what?" Gert demanded.

"Something like a slap in the face, if you're so fresh," my mother replied, her spirits low because of Aunt Frances's refusal to stand for Mark.

I was about to say I'd better go down and get Dad when she rallied.

"Well," she said, with a laugh, "if Mrs. Fitzgerald won't stand for you, Mark, you'll just have to stand for yourself."

Aunt Frances stopped us as we were going by her house, which was one from the corner, next to Hampton's grocery. The Hamptons caught us passing and came out of their store to see Mark. Everybody wanted to see the new baby, even Aunt Frances, though she was cool with

46

Mr. and Mrs. Hampton, as she was with nearly everybody on Ingersoll Street but me. She walked us to St. Elizabeth's and said she would gladly come in with us if it wasn't for the fact that she was of another persuasion.

"Which persuasion would that be, Mrs. Fitzgerald?" my mother asked, with a smile, I was glad to see.

"Why, none at all," Aunt Frances replied, adding that she had never been persuaded by any of them. "I walk my own way," she said, with a tilt of her chin, her warm brown eyes targeted right in on heaven, it seemed to me, which was right above wherever she was, and always is, when I think of her, which is often.

"In that case, Mrs. Fitzgerald, I don't see why you can't walk in with us."

"I don't either," replied Aunt Frances, and she put on her black straw that she wore when she went into town, but which I had not even noticed she had been carrying in back of her until now, when she put it on and climbed into St. Elizabeth's with us, where I rushed her up to the left to see the piano.

"That's no piano, that's an organ," she told me, running her fingers over the silent yellow keys.

"Can you play, Aunt Frances?"

"Sure I can," Aunt Frances replied, sitting

47

down at the keyboard. "Get under there and pump those boards for me."

I did as she said. I got down on my hands and knees in the dust and worked the big foot pedals of the organ for all I was worth while music ran like wildfire through the empty church.

When we went downstairs the priest who was to baptize Mark asked Aunt Frances if she was the musician. She admitted that she was. "I hope you don't mind. It was too tempting to resist," Aunt Frances told the priest in a voice and manner that I had not heard her use before. I was awfully proud of her, but then I really always was.

"Mind? I loved it," the priest told Aunt Frances. "What was it you were playing?"

"Anything that came into my hands" was Aunt Frances's reply, which seemed to both puzzle and please the priest. "Are you," he asked Aunt Frances, "from a musical family?"

"My father had a voice," Aunt Frances replied with so violent a toss of her head that I feared her straw hat would come off and tumble into the basin before us.

# 8

Aunt Frances's look of satisfaction with her life was never more evident than when she was looking at Happy. The day we saw him in town at Fifteenth and Market in his American Express truck he might just as well have been piloting an airplane over the mountains of Peru for all the look of Aunt Frances's face. She walked on air for the rest of the day in town, especially when we took the side entrance into John Wanamaker's department store, telling me, "This is the way the blue bloods used to come to Wanamaker's in their carriages, driven by sometimes as many as four horses."

I couldn't imagine anybody more "blue-blooded" than Aunt Frances.

Even when she looked at precious jewels sparkling in their glass cases under powerful electric lights, Aunt Frances looked as if she could afford them, or had the right to wear them.

My mother was altogether different when she

looked at things she wanted but could not afford, or would not have you give them to her on a silver platter.

My mother would pass by these things with a furtive look and a light step, urging me to "Come on," while I dragged behind, casting a backward glance at things we could not afford, things beyond our reach.

In Aunt Frances's world nothing was beyond one's reach. That is why she was such a stimulant. Yet, miraculously, her simple life with Happy contented her, for she felt it was rich, and she considered much of the world poor in comparison to what she had. So did I. Our house was empty compared to the house, one from the corner, that Aunt Frances shared with Happy.

"Aunt Frances, why do you love Happy so much?"

"Why, because he's the man in the house. A house without a man has a hollow ring to it."

"Is that what's wrong with our house, Aunt Frances? I thought it was because we have no furniture."

"No, it's because —"

Aunt Frances put her arms around me, which my mother never did. It is what I liked about Aunt Frances most, when she drew me to her and told me things I did not always understand, but promised myself I would someday, only I never have. How fathom the depth of those brown eyes, their temerity that dared me on to worlds as yet unconquered?

"I don't see why I don't go down and get him myself, Aunt Frances. She can't. Not and always having babies. Don't you think I should go down, Aunt Frances? I do. I know the way."

"Sure you do."

"All you do is take the number 7 trolley on Twenty-ninth Street."

"That's right."

"And get off at Tasker Street."

"And you're there."

How drab life on Ingersoll Street was to me after projecting myself on a voyage everybody but Aunt Frances seemed to assume I would never make. Besides, wretched Robert Morris school was opening. No wonder there was a rail around that granite building. It was a prison. The thought of going back to it again made me want to run away. Johnny Ervine could not wait to get back there to give the teachers hell.

"The leaves are turning," Aunt Frances said, giving me a glass of wine she made and Johnny Ervine said she sold. "Now's the time of year when birds fly south and bears search a good warm tree to sleep in until winter is over."

"Is that what bears do, Aunt Frances?"

51

"Yes, they hibernate."

Because I looked blank, Aunt Frances took out the dictionary she kept locked in the bottom of the sideboard in the dining room and read to me Daniel Webster's definition of hibernate: "To spend the winter in close quarters in a dormant condition, as certain animals."

"Aunt Frances, you look so cute in glasses. You look like Mamma Bear."

"No," Aunt Frances replied to me, "I could never hibernate. I like to be able to go out in all weather."

"Me too, Aunt Frances. Imagine being on the number 7 in a blizzard, when the motorman would have to *clang* his bell all the way down to Tasker Street."

I stopped talking, suddenly, and my enthusiasm for distant places appeared to me to have evaporated, dried up, taken off, never to return. Even when Aunt Frances offered me a penny for my thoughts I could say nothing.

She lifted my chin up from my chest with the tips of her cool fingers. "Now what's the matter? Don't tell me your courage has failed, and that you have given up all thoughts of the trip."

"Aunt Frances, suppose they don't know me when I get there? Suppose they take me for another boy?"

"That will never happen so long as you

52

remember yourself and your mission."

"My mission, Aunt Frances?"

Out came the dictionary. On went the spectacles.

"Mission," Aunt Frances read to me: "an assigned or self-imposed duty or task; a sending or being sent for some duty or purpose.

"Missionary," Aunt Frances continued. "A person who is sent on a mission. That," she said, locking the dictionary away again in the sideboard, "is what you'd be, if you went down."

Happy called me the little missioner after that, though who would guess he had been listening to us? I wouldn't.

"Why, I never heard of such a thing," my mother said, but pleased, really, when I told her of my mission.

"I hope I don't lose the two of you in the bargain."

"What do you mean by that, Maw?"

"You won't stay, too, will you, down there? There's school to be thought of. I don't want the truant officer all over me about you."

Instead of giving me carfare and seeing me off, my mother took off herself, in her high heels, as was her way now, leaving us bewildered and a bit frightened, only this time, after reassuring Gert I would be back, and back with her, my mother, I took off after her, leaving Gert entranced by the whole idea of the thing, since she told me she was sure that Maw had "somebody on the outside."

I guess I wanted to lose her, since I was ashamed of myself for following her. I could not blame her for passing the Fairmount. There was nothing playing that we would have liked. She was always pretty good at hiding her surprise, and that is what she did when I went right up to her when she stopped outside the zoological garden.

"I wouldn't want to go down for him myself (not that I'm afraid) and, maybe, disgrace all of us," she said. "This way I can still hold up my head."

There was no one outside the gate of the zoological garden. The dry fall-sound of leaves could be heard, but the flags had been put away, and the gate was locked.

So this was where she came when she left us. To stand outside the gate of the zoological garden, as if Horatio was still there.

"Remember when we used to visit him?" she said, looking into the zoological garden the way she used to look at Horatio in his cage.

I felt my old jealousy of him, so I tried to change the subject.

"Sinbad was something too," I said.

54

"Well, yes, they all were," my mother said. "But all that's over now," she added. "All that was for when we were very young."

"All the same," I said, wanting to please her, "I wish Horatio would come back, if only for a summer."

"I need someone. I feel I have no one," my mother said.

"To tell you whether to go down or not?"

"No, I know I shouldn't go down. I could never go down and keep my head up. Still, I'd like to know what to do. I must do something."

"I'll go down," I said. "Horatio would go down, if it was *his* father."

More than anything she wanted to reach a decision tonight, I felt. So that when someone came toward us from the inside of the zoo, she started expectantly. It was only a guard. He cast a sorry shadow compared to Horatio, but still my mother saw fit to try and make use of him, even though his keys sounded as if they weighed more than he did. He approached us sneakily, and even timidly, even though he was protected by iron bars an inch thick.

"It's disgusting what's put in there to mind their betters," my mother whispered to me.

Well, we had a good laugh. The guard was really comical. He jumped with fright when my mother beckoned to him. She was doing

55

something at last and it made her look better. "What happened to the lion, the great lion, you used to have in there?" she asked the guard, who relaxed when he answered her, and even smiled, though in a lugubrious way.

"He died," he said. "He had some roar on him. He hungered and died."

We walked away over the dry leaves. It was really very sad. It was like the end of the most beautiful story, hearing about Horatio that way in the dark, with the flags rolled up and the gate closed, but all the same my mother took heart before we reached home and asked me if I really thought I should go down, and when I said I did, she said, "All right, then go."

# 9

"Stay away from me. You're contaminated," my father said, as soon as he saw me, making me furious.

"Now you've made him mad, Jim. Don't make him mad," my grandmother told him, laughing in that grim way she had. They were very much alike. They both had a sarcastic laugh, and sarcasms always ready.

"Well, now, Jim," my great-uncle Chauncey said, "they've come to lasso you home, so make the most of your freedom while you have it. There's a card game tonight, your night off from the paper, so let me get a bottle and some smokes, and get Tom down. I'll tell them across the street that I'll tend no bar for them tonight. Let them go thirst in hell for all I care."

"There goes another job up the flue, Chauncey," my grandmother told him. "You should be more like your brother Tom."

"My brother Tom is it? And have another ladies' man in the family, is it?"

"He is that," my grandmother agreed, "and each one is worse than the last. He's free at the moment of all of them, thank God, and can call his soul his own, which is not often the case."

"We must get Little Bottle in, too," said Chauncey. "He'll be fun and won't cost us a penny, because he'll lose everything he's got, which is never much, God knows, poor shell shock."

Little Bottle was already primed when he arrived. He was by way of being a tailor, hiring himself out to sweatshops, or bringing home piecework, but the men of my family never mentioned Little Bottle's trade to him, as if they felt it was something the poor "shell shock" should be ashamed of. He was a dancing little fellow with arms and legs that seemed to be made of rubber. He dropped his cards on the table, and my father said he had never seen anything the likes of Little Bottle at a card table.

Little Bottle gave me a nickel and told me to stand by him for luck.

"Now, nobody can do that for you but the Blessed Mother," Chauncey told Little Bottle, who replied that he did not believe in anything like that, and that if Chauncey didn't like it, Chauncey could lump it. At which Chauncey took out a little pistol from his pocket and made everybody jump but my grandmother, although she did look up from the book she was reading in her rocker in front of the kitchen stove.

Not everybody smoked at first, but it was like the plague and caught on. Soon all the grownups were smoking but my grandmother, who seemed to me to like her kitchen disguised as a gray cotton vessel with no sound coming out of it but the chink of coins and the shuffling of cards. Soon she nodded and fell asleep. There was a muffled crash when her book slipped from her hands and struck the brick pavement around the stove. I was forgotten.

I should have known enough to let well enough alone, but I did not. Instead, I picked up the book, and was about to waken her, when she startled me by demanding that I read to her. I did so, fumbling over the big ones, but I saw I had impressed her, as well as the men, who had stopped their game to listen to me.

"That's bravely sung," said Little Bottle.

"He likes to read, and that's half the battle," my grandmother grudgingly admitted.

But Little Bottle was carried away, as he was by nearly everything. His mother still beat him, as though he were five, not fifty. And he had no wife. "Why," he cried, forgetting cards and game and everything but me, "he sounds

59

t'me like a priest or a missioner. God knows," he went on, in his rollicking way, throwing his cards to hell, "he could do worse than to become one or the other of them, though he'll be scalped for sure with that redhead of his if he goes down amongst the Amazonians, where they're wild as monkeys, the papers say, and have no more time for religion than I have, God bless them."

"I am a missioner, Mr. Bottle," I said, talking out of turn, which my grandmother never liked, though she did not seem to mind it now, and despite the censorious regard my father cast my way. "I've come on a mission to take my father home."

"And with a missioner's zeal at that," cried Uncle Tom, laughing his gold-toothed laugh, and everybody but my father laughing with him.

"Get on with the game," my father said, but since the front doorbell rang just then, no one paid attention to him.

My grandmother took her book back from me as if I had my nerve with me, after all, reading from it, though she had as much as commanded me to do so, and went to answer the door.

"It's for me," said Chauncey, just as crestfallen as could be. "Jenkins has the DTs, as he

60

does at this time nearly every night, and, as nobody can control him, they've sent for me. Drat that Jenkins."

"They want you across the street, Chauncey, but not for long," my grandmother said, sweeping into the kitchen, bringing the relief of some fresh air with her. "It's Jenkins. They can't do anything with him, and they know you can. So go over, but not with your gun."

"What's he doing with a gun, anyway?" my father asked. "It's totally out of character."

"It's not at all," said Chauncey, miffed. "I don't know that any of you here know my character, come to speak of it, not my true character."

"Whatever it is, it hasn't anything to do with guns. Give the gun here, Chauncey," Uncle Tom ordered him.

"All you see," Chauncey went on, in a moody way, "is a man come down to bartending, when, with a little luck, he could have been almost anything else."

"Be that as it may, give up the gun," Uncle Tom persisted.

"Or don't go across the street at all," said my grandmother.

"I will. I have to," Chauncey answered her, rocking on his little round feet in their soft high black shoes, and he was out of the kitchen

61

and out of the house before anybody could stop him — with his gun.

"Now, he shouldn't have taken his gun," said Uncle Tom.

"No matter. He doesn't know one end of it from the other," Little Bottle put in.

"True," said Uncle Tom. "He's like a fat boy with a kite. Too lazy to get the thing aloft."

"Play cards," Dad told them, with a look at me, as if he secretly wished the two of us were out of this, and home on Ingersoll Street.

My grandmother had hardly settled back in her rocking chair by the stove with her book when the doorbell rang again and she said she wondered who in the name of God that could be.

"It's some kid practicing for Halloween," my father said, but I could see he did not believe it any more than I did.

Instead of resuming the game everybody waited until my grandmother came back into the kitchen after answering the front door. When she did come back she was throwing a shawl over her shoulders, and the men half-rose from the card table at the sight of her.

"Now I don't think it's anything," my grandmother said, attempting to control everything as usual, even now when she was almost as ignorant as the rest of us were about what happened.

"Of course nothing's happened," said Uncle Tom.

"At any rate, the wind's blowin' up a gale," my father said. "You left the front door open, Mom."

"Did I? I didn't mean to," my grandmother replied, at a loss what to say or do for the first time that I had known her.

When the doorbell rang again, this time with the front door wide open, she threw off her shawl and thrust out her chest at the expected intruder, who failed to appear.

Instead Chauncey came in demanding why the card game had come to an end, and with no idea at all, apparently, that he had left the front door open behind him.

"I should have thought you'd close the front door behind you, at least," said his brother Tom. "Sit down."

"Go close the door," my father told me. "And pick up your grandmother's shawl from the floor," he added, as if everything was my fault. Only the thought of my mother and my mission made me hold my tongue in my own defense.

But I could not close the door, because there were so many men lodged in it at once, all trying at one and the same time to enter the house, but afraid to, or too shy to, my grandmother being what she was. So there they were, all stuck there, between the front steps and the vestibule. They pulled themselves out, some even falling into the vestibule across the white tiles, when a "red devil" pulled up at the curb in front of my grandmother's house and two cops got out of it and slowly climbed our steps between the lines of men.

Again the noise of the front doorbell sawed through the house, only this time everybody came to answer it, including Chauncey, who said he wondered just who the cops thought they were, ringing people's doorbells in the dead of night.

"Shut the door!" Chauncey shouted at my grandmother, who was at the head of the party. She turned to him as if she realized it all, not only that his job was up the flue, but that all was lost for him, at least for a while.

She seemed more relieved than not when the cops carted Chauncey off, which they did not do without him telling the men in the vestibule, and those lining the front door steps, that it was all a frame-up.

"Jenkins always hated me. Now he's got me where he wants me, saying I shot him, when I didn't, when I left my gun behind, at home, as any of my family can tell you I did."

64

He stopped on the pavement, turning on the balls of his little round feet.

"There they are!" he shouted, much to my grandmother's shame, I could see. "Ask them. Ask any of them, if I didn't leave me gun behind when I went across the street tonight. Go ahead. Go on and ask them. Ask my sister, if you don't believe me. Go on, go on. Ask her."

Of course they did not, since it was such a lie. But I wondered, had she dared speak, if my grandmother would have lied, too, in defense of him, her brother, her little brother, and against all else she believed in, especially decency.

She didn't, though. She refused to open her mouth. She let them take him.

"At least he didn't kill Jenkins," she said to the men lining her front steps, the men in the vestibule having long joined them out there.

"No such luck," said one.

"It was no more than a scrap, if that," said another.

"Not that Jenkins didn't put up a howl and a holler, he did," said still another. For the thing was all pent up in each of them and they were dying to talk and had no place to go now but home, where they would be told by their wives to be quiet because of the kids. The saloon across the street was closed and dark now in the garb of respectability.

"Well, go home now," my grandmother told them. "Don't run on about it," she added. "Stick to the truth of the thing as best you can. It's bad enough as it is. There's no sense making it out worse."

# 10

We ran into Jenkins the next day when she took me shopping with her on the Lane. He was shaking all over, and dirty as well, but there was something cocky about him for all that. He had taught school in the past, and had yet to outgrow the habit of lording it over others.

"I'd serve his time for him, if only for your sake, Missus," Jenkins told her, with a wink at me.

"You're lucky you didn't lose your life, and my brother's lucky he didn't take it from you," my grandmother told Jenkins.

I felt sorry for her. All she needed now, I thought, would be for Uncle Tom to turn against her, which is just what happened. He stood outside the house saying he would not come in because she had turned against her brother.

"She could have saved him, and she didn't," Tom told passersby. "She could have talked, but she did not."

"Come in here, Tom," my grandmother whispered to him through the half-open front door. "Tom, come into the house, and stop making fools of us before the neighbors."

When all was quiet and he had gone away, we settled down for a peaceful night with just ourselves by the kitchen stove. She returned to the story in her book, smiling and sighing over it, and only glancing at me from time to time, to see if I was still there. We were in bed when my grandfather and my father came in together from work. My grandfather was a night watchman at Strawbridge and Clothier's Department Store; Dad was a linotypist on the *Morning Ledger.* They talked lightly of Uncle Chauncey going to jail as they climbed the stairs, and parted in the hall for their separate rooms. I was in Chauncey's old room, while my father slept in the room next to it. Grandpop had the room next to the bath at the end of the hall, as far away as possible from my grandmother, it seemed to me, who kept to her own room in the front of the house during all this, either sleeping or not, it would be hard to tell, though her presence was felt, of course, no matter what it was she was doing. She was everything, but that is not to say that Gramp was nothing. He wasn't as grown up as my grandmother. He was more like me.

"Well," my grandfather was saying out there in the hall to my father, by way of good-night, "I for one am glad that I won't be seeing him for a while. I wish they'd give him loife."

"I don't know what he was doing with a gun in the first place," my father said, repeating what he had said last night. "It's totally unlike Chauncey to have carried a gun."

"Well, he'll be taken care of, something he's always wanted. He'll be missed, of course, but not by me. *She'll* miss him."

I could see Grandpop nod in the direction of my grandmother's room as he said that.

Soon I heard the whole house snoring and I had to admit to myself, now in the dark, that my mission had failed, and that I'd do better to return to my mother, rather than leave her alone, as I was doing, enjoying the excitement, while she only had Mark and Gert and Matthew to talk to. I had not even been able to tell anyone why I'd come down, except when I made a joke of it, as I had done during the card game last night. And when I remembered Happy calling me the missioner I felt ever so ashamed of myself, for I had not turned out to be a good one.

So I decided to leave my grandmother's house right there and then, middle of the night or not, even if I had to walk home, and I supposed I would have to, since I hadn't a penny.

My grandfather was going into the bathroom, having just turned on the electric light in that room, when he saw me, suddenly illuminated, about to leave the house, which I had decided to do after the failure of my mission.

"Now what the deuce are you up to?" he demanded of me in a hoarse whisper, which he endeavored to keep low so as not to awaken my grandmother or my father, but which, in any case, was never much higher than a low whisper, all voices being muted, as everything else seemed to me to be, in that house.

"I'm going home, Gramp."

I had a little bag in which I had packed my shirts, underwear, socks, and an extra pair of pants. This and all it contained I hugged to my chest, as if I feared its being taken from me along with my determination to reach Ingersoll Street sometime tomorrow.

"You're not going to stop me, are you, Gramp?"

My grandfather threw a look up the hall in the direction of the front bedroom while carefully hiking his braces back on his shoulders so they would not jangle down around his knees when he walked, and motioned me ahead of him down the stairs, where he donned his derby and overcoat, and hid his thin bare neck in a scarf.

"Good-bye," I said, slipping out of the house ahead of him, determined to go as I had come, alone and penniless and unexpected, like a missioner, albeit a missioner who had failed.

My grandfather came out of the house with me, and, after trying the front door to make sure it was locked, he followed me down the steps.

"Good-bye," I said to him again, breaking out in a cold sweat at the thought of the long journey before me in the dark.

"Good-bye yourself," my grandfather gruffed behind me. "Where d'yuh think you're goin'?"

"Why, home, Gramp."

"And you mean t'walk?"

"Yes, I mean to walk."

"Why?"

"Why, because my mission failed."

He gasped at that, though I did not see why, and trailed me up Twenty-fourth Street.

"What're you missionaryin' on, anyway?"

"My father, Gramp. I came down to get him to come home to us, but failed."

He was still behind me when I turned into a square where we sat down on a bench in the dark and the two of us fell asleep. I woke up first and was surprised that I had been sleeping with my head in his lap.

A noisy crowd of three people came by, either not seeing us or not caring. A priest haranguing a drunk home, and a woman behind the two of them. "I keep hearing the shot that almost killed me last night, Father," the man with the priest was saying, while the woman behind the two of them shouted him down.

"Would to God that it had gone home and took us all out of our misery," she cried.

"Don't say that, Mrs. Jenkins," the priest pontificated. "You know you don't mean it."

"I do mean it. I wish he was in jail, like the bartender who attempted to do him in."

"I'll tell you one thing," said Jenkins, "I'm not drinking till he comes out and we can drink together again. I've sworn off. My conscience couldn't take it, knowing I'd brought it all on myself, and on him. Hooch is behind me, Padre. At least till Chauncey McLaughlin gets out of Moymensing and is back behind the bar again."

"Thanks be to God for that," the priest sang out in the square. "Why, the shooting's a blessing in disguise."

That didn't say much for Chauncey's predicament, I thought, but a lot they cared. Mrs. Jenkins cried and thanked heaven, and so did

Jenkins. Then he knelt down in the leaves, and so did she, and the priest gave them his blessing. They did not notice us. It was as if we weren't there, and maybe we weren't.

Maybe I dreamed it. The next thing I knew I woke up in Chauncey's old room and my grandmother was demanding if I wasn't famished for breakfast, because she was. I followed her downstairs and she grinned at me as we ate, but not sarcastically.

Afterwards she guided me through streets that had taken on the appearance of winter, and in and out of the baker's and butcher's, as if she was half wondering what to do with me, give me the heave altogether, and send me home, or take me to her bosom as a confidant, the last thing she would ever do.

Schoolchildren passed us sleepily with their books, which they were obviously unused to carrying. After they went by my grandmother seemed to be on to something. Something had excited her. There was always something or other that interested her. She had a new project and I was it, though I did not realize I was until we were seated before a wooden-faced old nun at St. Ursula's school out on Morris Street, where my grandmother had taken it into her head to enroll me as a student without consulting either my father, my mother, or me. Her action was so powerful that I found myself watching and listening to her as if she was speaking about another little boy, and not me at all.

"I don't blame you for giving him the stare, Sister. It's your job to mistrust all and sundry. But it's only Christian to take him in. He's been running with Lutherans and is as like them as they are to themselves. He's bright enough when he has his wits about him, but he's been held back in one way and given too much leash in another. Take him. You won't regret it."

"Can he count?" asked the nun.

"I'll tell you one thing about him, he's head and shoulders above other people his age in reading. It's a talent we all have on his father's side of the family. He'll learn to count well enough when he has something to count. What good's it to a beggar to count? None at all. But with libraries everywhere, and all of them free, it's reading that counts, Sister (surely you can see that), not counting. Why, there's not a clerk that can't count his way around the block. Where does it get him but home again, back where he started, and is doomed to die. Reading, Sister, carries a man to the stars."

"Can you count?" the old nun asked without

looking at me. "What's two and two?"

"Four, Sister."

My answer filled my grandmother with pride in me, and the way she showed it was to look on the poor old nun as if she considered her a fool.

She got back at us soon enough when my grandmother left me alone with her. "Two and two makes four," she hissed, mimicking me, I assumed. "Anybody knows that, even a baby."

Mark didn't, I wanted to tell her, but I did not. I knew better. I was already entrapped. "Have you prayed for your uncle yet, the one who killed a man last night at Oyster's Bar? Have you lit a candle? Have you knelt and begged forgiveness for being related to a common criminal?" All this with her finger in my back "guiding" me to further torture through dark, cold halls past classrooms from which poured idiotic mass chants, or the nasal voices of teachers blasting knowledge into heads that longed for peace and solitude as mine did, even as I joined them.

The horror of those tallow faces, their look of malnutrition. I thought of Chauncey in his tomb in Moymensing Prison and envied him. At recess I was surrounded by boys asking about him. Proud though I was having an uncle incarcerated for attempted murder, my

75

little classmates' impromptu questioning concerning him took all the swagger out of me.
Soon they said I wasn't related to the "killer" at
all, and I let it go at that, determined never to
return to the school again. All the same I did.

When they decided to dump me at St. Ursula's Father Stienhagen came to the house to
break the news to my grandmother. Matter of
fact he walked me there. He seemed a kindly
man, but too zealous to see particular cases and
to handle them in a particular way.

"He does not fit in," Father Stienhagen told
my grandmother. "It may be he will never fit in
anywhere. The Lutherans got him too early."

My grandmother acted as though everything
the priest told her about me took her breath
away. It gave her time to think and to strategize.
She was like an actress in a play that I was
seeing for the first time. I did not know what
she would do next. She looked different. She
looked better. She was my first theater.

"Well, Father," she said, drawing me to her,
and away from him, as it were, though I knew
for a fact that neither was crazy to have me,
"you may be right and we've lost him, as a
missioner, to the other side."

"Missioner? Who vants to pe a missioner?
*Him?*"

"So he has said. Where it came from, or how,

I have no idea. He threw it at us during a card game."

"He plays cards, too? and he vants to pe a missionary? Come, my dear voman, there is a limit, and you haf gone beyond it. You haf been very kind, very generous. You bought me a chasuble. That, how can I forget? But now to tell me that your grandzon has a wocation is too much for me to take."

My grandmother pushed me out of her way and stood up, her arms out to Stieny, who cringed, thinking, perhaps, that she intended to embrace him.

"Vocation's the word, Father," she told him. "Vocation's what I've had in mind, and lacked the nerve to come out with."

Father Stienhagen's mouth hung open. So did mine.

"Vhere do you mean to take him?" he demanded, quivering with greed at the possibility of losing me, questionable though my worth had been to him until now. "I hope," he managed to bring out, with a stutter, "that you are not thinking of returning him to th – th – the Lutherans?"

"Why not?" my grandmother blandly replied. "Didn't they bring him out? Didn't they give him strawberries?"

"Strawberries? Vhat in the name of Gott haf

77

strawberries to do with it?"

"Everything," said my grandmother, closing her eyes, as if she felt she saw more that way than she did with them open, and, considering the way she was talking, maybe she did.

"Vell, maybe you're right about him. You know something? I think you are right," said Father Stienhagen, with sudden grand enthusiasm, the idea of another chasuble from her crossing his mind, perhaps.

Afterwards, as she trundled the crowded, comfortable house, she made me think of what my mother had said about seeing Mrs. Leslie Carter come out of the stage door, and how ordinary she was compared to how she had looked onstage.

Her sister came in from Westchester and they sat mumbling stories of their childhood in Ireland, where Chauncey had been the light of their young lives, and now look at him, gone up for nearly killing a man, and sitting with an unopened Bible in a dark, damp cell in Moymensing Prison, that was as like an Egyptian tomb as Egyptian tombs were to themselves, maybe worse.

But that night, as I lay in her feather bed with her, she told me stories of Galway and carrying Chauncey on her shoulders, the two of them looking seaward, even the little boy.

For she shared her dreams of far places with him, as she was doing with me, and I probably understood her no more than Chauncey had, though I tried. I tried to tell her that I was only missionarying for a father, and not for the whole wide world, but I could feel how carried away she was by the idea of me paddling up the Amazon, bearing the cross to savages, and I was sorry for all her other disappointments, so I said nothing.

# 11

What I wanted more than anything was to go home – with my father. My grandmother's house wasn't all that big, but you would have thought it was, the successful way we kept our distance from one another. I hardly ever saw Dad, except when he took off for work, his nights off, and even these last he began to spend elsewhere.

I heard more of his snores in the room next to mine than anything else about him. When he would get by me, after I had let a perfect opportunity to speak to him slip by, I would feel like such a traitor to my mother that I would then make a point of dodging him for days afterwards.

Then I slipped into his room without thinking.

"Dad," I said, acting a familiarity that I did not feel.

"What is it?" he asked. "If you want a nickel, take one out of my coat, hanging on the hat rack, in the downstairs hall."

Sunlight streamed around the edges of the green blind at the single window. The room was so stuffy it made me breathless. Besides, it was considered a crime to wake a night worker before his time to get up, so I left.

"What are you doing, skulking on the stairs?" my grandmother cried, almost falling over me. "Go on out and play, or do your homework. There's lots to be done besides trying to waylay your father. Hasn't he got enough to do, earning a living to support you all? I'll say he has. Now be off!"

If she meant me to go, she did not act it. Instead of letting me go downstairs, where she had only directed me, she bent and grabbed me to her. She was a dark woman, and high feelings brought a flush to her face that made it even darker. Besides, except for light coming through the glass transoms over the closed doors to the right and left of us, the hall was dark.

"What's lassoing a father, to lassoing the world?" she whispered to me. "Think of it. Oh, if I were a boy, I'd show them. I'd cross the burning desert. I don't know what I wouldn't do. I'd go around the world, for one thing. I'd find villages that no white man had ever seen before. I'd bring services to the poor, vaccines

81

to the sick. Don't you know what you have?" she whispered, on her knees before me, and shaking me violently with her every word. "You have a *vocation*, you little devil. A vocation, you hear? What priests and cardinals pray for, you have."

"But Mr. Bottle as good as said they would scalp me, because of my red hair, if I went amongst the savages."

"Little Bottle's a fool. Don't listen to him. Listen to me —"

My father saved me. He came out of his bedroom in his nightgown and bare feet and asked my grandmother what I'd been up to this time.

"Nothing, Jim. Go on back to bed. You've got a good hour's sleep ahead of you yet before your time to get up and go to work."

"Yes, but what did he do?" Dad persisted, not wanting to know, really, not wanting to know anything that might bother him, distract him from his betting, his card games on his night off, and whatever else he might be doing on the outside.

My grandmother held me for fear I would fly to him, perhaps, and beg him to come home with me; that we were lonely without him, at least my mother was.

"It's school," my father said. "He hates

82

school, any school. The truth is, he's unteachable."

"It's not true!" My grandmother flared up, shocking my father, so that he fell back into the green light and stuffiness of his bedroom, where she pursued him. "How dare you say the boy is unteachable? It's what you said about yourself, when I pushed you, urged you, dreamed for you. It's what Chauncey said about himself, and Tom said about himself, all of you content with the ignorance you were born with. Let me dream with this boy at least. Let me alone with him. Go home, if you want. I don't need you now. You were never interested in my dreams for you. You were full of scorn for them. Well, now, I'm full of scorn for you."

"You don't mean that, Mom."

"Of course I don't. You know I don't. All the same let us alone. Let me alone with him. Let me dream again on somebody, Jim. I won't be here for long."

"Don't say that."

There was a shout from my grandfather's room at the end of the hall, followed by a string of curse words. "I would have never brought him back the night he ran away if I thought you were going to act this way with him," my grandfather shouted.

"Well you did," my grandmother shouted back at him, "and it's the best thing you ever did."

"He's only an ordinary boy," my father quietly remarked of me.

"He is not!" my grandmother as good as shouted at him, too. "He said so himself he's not, his first night here, during the card game. He won't be like the rest of you, disappointing me at every turn to my face."

"You're not the woman I married," my grandfather shouted from his bedroom.

"Of course I'm not," my grandmother shouted back. "Did you expect me to stand still as all of you have? To have learned nothing? To have seen nothing? No, when I crossed the Atlantic —"

"You're damned," my grandfather cried, making a great thing of hopping from his bed. "Damned, damned, damned," he chanted, opening his bedroom door and slamming it closed behind him. "Damned!" he yelled down the hall, before going into the bathroom and slamming that door, since no door in my grandparents' house on Twenty-fourth Street was ever allowed to stand open.

"Malediction of the blood" were my grandmother's words for what ailed us. I did not know what that meant, but it had a fine, gloomy ring to it, and I liked it. It made me feel there was something wrong with us, but also that we were somehow superior to others. It was a sort of home plate of our being: Touch it and achieve something; miss it and go down to ignominious defeat. Nearly all of us were down, as far as my grandmother was concerned, but she had hopes for me. It was my own fault for speaking up as I had during the card game.

# 12

My life at St. Ursula's was a disaster. Most of my tallow-faced classmates did not speak to me, and some seemed not to be able to — yet. These last Father Stienhagen addressed in German on his rounds. Then their poor little gray faces would wake up and light up and they would smile and "yah yah," but it made me feel I had been sent to learn things at the North Pole.

But I was brought home with a bang to all that was familiar when Little Bottle would be waiting for me outside the schoolyard, clinging to the cold iron gate, rain or shine, dying to tell me the story of his life, which he did, bit by bit, day after day, that autumn.

"I was a good soldier, that is, I went where they told me, and stayed there, without running away, and no questions asked. I was stronger then, and quick on my feet, as I still am — sometimes."

"Did you kill anybody, Mr. Bottle?"

"I don't know. I'm not sure. I believe I did. I don't like to think about it."

"It was the big guns, then, and not you, that did the dirty work?"

"That's right! That's right! Oh, it was fine, in a way, and I'll never forget it."

He squeezed my hand he was holding, and looked down at me.

"I can't forget it," he said, shaking his head. "It's lodged in here, between my two ears, and it goes off like it did then."

"An explosion?"

"Yes, a terrible explosion that put me out of kilter for a while, and still does, but I'll be all right."

"Sure you will, Mr. Bottle."

He squeezed my hand again.

"No one calls me Mister but you. You have a way of drawing me out like I never expected anybody could anymore."

"I do? Drawing you out from where, Mr. Bottle?"

"Where? Why, from my secret secretest self is where. I like it when you do. It makes me feel I'm traveling, crossing the Atlantic again, with the American Expeditionary Forces."

"That must have been wonderful."

"Why, you know," said Little Bottle, with some wonder in his voice, "it was."

"Don't let people see you with Little Bottle," my grandmother told me. "It doesn't speak well for me, nor my house."

"I don't see why not," I replied to her with some heat, which seemed to surprise her but not displease her. "I like Mr. Bottle. I like his stories. He tells me he was once a strong young man, and I believe him."

My grandmother smiled grimly, but did not touch me. "You're right," she said, turning away to the back kitchen, where I heard her blowing her nose.

She read to me from the first book of Dickens. "What you don't understand, don't worry about. What you do understand, think about." There was a knock on the front door, which made her jump. Not a ring, a knock. That was unusual at this hour of the night, or any hour. "It's nothing but a beggar," she said. She looked at me. She was always looking at me as if I had said something to her when I had not. "We're all beggars," she said then, before going to answer the door.

While alone in the kitchen I picked up the book and read it myself. "It was a beggar. I was right," she said, coming back and settling herself by the stove. But when I attempted to give her the book she ordered me to read it to her, which I did, stumbling over the big ones, which made her restless, I thought, but I was wrong. It was the beggar.

"I should have asked him in," she said. "There's soup, there's leftover chicken. We have so much, and I didn't ask him in. He left his card, though."

"Then he wasn't a beggar."

"Sure he was. There wasn't a pick on him, God forgive me."

"Will he come back, you think?"

"Why should he? Read to me. Don't worry about the big words, they'll come to you in time. Then where will I be? Out in Holy Cross pushing up the daisies." She closed her eyes, flung herself violently back in her rocker, and rocked. "I don't care," she murmured, clenching and unclenching her false teeth. "You've given me a hint of what you mean to do. That's almost enough." She rocked harder and harder, showing the tops of her high laced black boots, which she seldom did. Her apron flew about her legs, giving the impression that she was running. She stopped dead when the doorbell rang this time. "It's the beggar again," she said. "Somehow I knew he'd be back."

"Are you going to ask him in?"

"I didn't say I was. You sit there and read. Go over the big words. You're not so smart."

She smiled as apologetically as she could,

which was still not very much, hardly at all, really, and said ever so softly, "Yes you are." Then she charged me, almost touched me, and whispered, "Don't let me down," before going to answer the door.

It was all my fault for saying I'd come on a mission, which I had, but I was sorry that I had now. I would have given anything to be back home again in our bare little kitchen on Ingersoll Street talking about Horatio, and how we must be like him, upstanding and courageous in spirit, and not run and hide from things, the way Dad did, from me being contaminated to babies being born.

"It was him all right," my grandmother said, coming back into the kitchen after answering the front door. "He wanted to know if he had forgotten to give me his card or not. Imagine the gall? If he's begging, why doesn't he beg in a straight-forward manner, instead of posing as a —"

It was not her nature to hesitate. I asked her as a what?

She gave me the "beggar's" card for an answer and picked up her book and began to read aloud to me as if we had not been interrupted in the first place. But the "beggar's" card fascinated me. I could not help but read it, and when I did, I could not help but think of

90

it in spite of everything. Here is the card:

**RICHARD MCQUEEGLY**
PORTRAIT PAINTER
*Pets a Specialty*

"He cleans, too," said my grandmother, looking up from her book. "That's probably what he's all about. Imagine a dusty boyeen like that calling himself a painther. Glory be to God, what next?"

"Was he dusty?"

"No he was not. He was neat and clean, and thin as two pencils. His coat sleeves ended at his elbows, and his trousers had long lost the acquaintanceship with his ankles. I would be afraid to see the soles of his poor shoes, since I'm sure I could see through them to the heart of his problem, poverty and pride, for he held himself like a prince."

She closed Dickens as though it was all his fault, with a bang.

"Help yerself to a piece of me apple pie and hie yerself t'bed," she said, reverting in her speech to years back, when she was a girl from Galway, and had no jet-black beads jigging on her ears and cascading down her front, like a gypsy.

"I can't help seeing you doing the same,

begging as he's begging, from door to door, thrustin' yer card at people, as he's thrustin' his at us. What will it say, fer God's sake?"

"Runaway Fathers Brought Home to Their Loved Ones," I yelled, catching on to the thing, which I thought great fun, though my grandmother did not, though she had started it.

The next day Little Bottle was clinging to the schoolyard gate, waiting for me, despite the rain. "Guess what," he said, "we're having our house cleaned."

He couldn't get over it, but then he was greatly in awe of his "house" and everything about it, including his mother, or especially her.

"Mom's having it done at a price, but it's not like we had a maid, it's a man, a guy, a young fellah, who says he's a painter besides."

"Did he leave his card?"

"He did, and Mother invited him in. He's there now, if you'd care to see him."

The Bottles' house was on a side street with crooked brick pavements and crooked white marble steps, three to a house. We stepped up the Bottles' three into such busyness as I had not seen before. Everything was upside down, including Bottle's little old mother, whose bottom alone was visible, the rest of her being well tucked away into the depths of the kitchen oven, while a slight young man, with bright yellow hair, urged her to go in even deeper, then forgot her, and threw things at us, brushes and mops and goodness knows what all, thinking we had come to help.

"It's a wonder we don't throw Clancey at us, but I guess he's afraid to," said Little Bottle, referring to their taciturn parrot, whose perch having been taken from him in all the hustling, clung as best he could to the cord of the kitchen window shade. "We'd better get out" was Little Bottle's opinion, and mine. "Now you've seen him, what do you think?" he asked me outside. "Do you think he's a painter, a real painter, an oil painter, or not?"

"Mr. Bottle, I don't know what to say. How do you expect me to know what I feel about him? You better go back home and see that your mother gets out of the oven. That Richard is sure excitable. He might forget she's in there and bake a cake and bake your mother with it."

"Say," said Bottle, "that's a good one. Shall I send him around to your place, after he gets done with us?"

"Sure, I'll tell my grandmother he's coming."

But I didn't. I waited for his knock on the door, and when it came, I went with my grandmother to answer it.

"Who would knock at this time of day?" my

93

grandmother said. "It was different at night and the person not being able to see the bell."

She stopped at the sight of him.

"It's you, is it?" she said, as though they had known one another forever. She sounded ever so pleased, though she did her best, as usual, to hide it.

"Well, come in, come in," she said, pushing me away, so as to make room for the painter, house cleaner, beggar, whatever he was. Whatever he was, he was sure nosey, poking his head into the parlor, and feeling the velvet curtains on the door, and even checking the lamps on the sideboard, as we passed through the dining room on our way to the kitchen, to see if they lit up or not. When they did he looked disappointed, as if he would have had them out of order, so he could make them right.

He was nice, though. He stood with his poor wet shoes together and his eyes lowered when he came into the kitchen. He had the goldenest hair I had ever seen, and my grandmother looked on him from her rocker, Dickens in her lap for a defense should she need one, which she did not, as if she had been waiting for him ever since she left Galway.

"Well, do I get the job or not?"

That's the way he was, very much to the point.

But he relaxed soon enough with a piece of apple pie and a steaming hot cup of coffee and told us the story of his life and his ambition to be a painter the way shy people will — suddenly, as if there is nothing being held back. The three of us huddled at the kitchen table, the door closed, as usual, but something seemed to happen to the old house, something new. It seemed to have taken off, as though it were a boat, but who was doing the piloting, and who our captain was, we were too absorbed in one another to ask ourselves, or to much care.

The sound of footsteps stirred on the floor above us as my father and grandfather prepared to leave the house at five o'clock for work. Ordinarily they dressed and came downstairs and waited in the parlor reading the paper until they were called to their meal. But today they skipped the parlor and hurled themselves into the kitchen, pushed by curiosity.

Of course they pretended not to see Richard, who stared at them as if he had never seen their likes before.

"Sit where you are, Richard," my grandmother directed him, as he attempted to remove himself as far as possible from the two grouches who had descended on him from above. "We'll continue with our business after I get these two off." Here Gramp made an awful noise with his throat, which caused Richard to jump up out of his seat at the table, which was what it was supposed to do. My father followed my grandmother into the back kitchen, and so did I. "Who's the guy with the bleach job?" he demanded of my grandmother.

"If you mean the young man I've hired to clean the house, his hair is as natural as yours and mine, Jim. Don't be jealous."

"It may be natural and his own, but it's still dyed. Where'd he wander in from, anyway?"

"He petitioned from door to door for work, and found it, but his real job's painting."

"Painting what, for God's sake?"

"Why, yerself, if yer willin', Jim."

"Mom," said my father, grinning, "I think you've lost your mind."

"On the contrary, I've found it — with him."

"But, Mom, haven't you got enough with us?"

Grandpop opened the back kitchen door and asked what did they mean leaving him alone with a stranger? My grandmother put twelve pork chops in a pan and did not answer him. She mashed boiled potatoes and put the coffee on. We were, of course, very crowded in the back kitchen. Besides, the floor slanted, throwing us at one another.

96

"I'm not going back in with him. Get my coat, my hat, and my scarf, you chump, you," Gramp said to me.

"You can't go to work without eating, Gramp," I said, laughing at his anger and anxiety. "Don't be afraid of Richard. He's really awfully nice."

"You ought to be home helping your mother," my father said to me.

"I am helping her," I said, meaning that I was trying to get him to go home to Ingersoll Street with me, though I did not say so, because I did not dare. He knew what I meant, and looked to his mother for help with me.

"Mom," he said, "where is he picking up his fresh talk? I don't want him hanging out with Little Bottle."

Gramp made a bolt for the door to the backyard, meaning to go to work without his hat and coat, but my grandmother stopped him with a bowl of mashed potatoes. "Carry this in, and stop making a spectacle of yourself. What'll the young man say of us when he's attending the Academy of Fine Arts?"

"I don't care what he says about us," cried Gramp. "Why should I care for the opinions of strangers?"

"Go in, the lot of you," said my grandmother, handing Dad a tureen of gravy, and me some peas. She carried the chops in herself. "We might as well all of us eat together," she said. "Sit down, Richard. Do you like coffee with your meal, or do you want it after?"

Richard sat down without a word, having doubtlessly heard much of the dispute about him from the back kitchen. He looked too hungry to leave the pork chops, though, no matter what people felt about him, and fell on them ravenously.

My grandmother was so certain that Richard was attending classes at the Academy of Fine Arts that she called there, only to be told that they had no one by the name of Richard McQueegly.

She emerged from the telephone booth in the cigar store at Twenty-third and Tasker with a pale face and a tottering step. She was like a prisoner awakening from a dream of freedom only to find himself still behind bars.

"It's all a dodge," she said to me. "He's not what he claims to be."

She was so upset she hardly recognized Little Bottle's mother skipping towards us down Tasker Street, glad to be on equal terms with us about something, which was not often the case. She was so short, and so used to looking up to people when she talked to them, that she even looked up at me — that is, over my head.

"I was so surprised," she said, "that you coulda taken my eyes for nothin', they stood that far out of their sockets, when that kid knocked at my door (knocked, mind you) and asked could he clean for me. I'll tell you what I said to him. I told him t'mind his own business about my house is what I said. I said it was as clean a house on Bannister Street is what I said, and I'm sure you said the same, Missus —?"

My grandmother replied nothing to this chatter, but moved past Bottle's mother with her eyes closed, and her jet-black earrings jigging, as if she were passing through a cloud of gnats.

When we turned the corner on Twenty-fourth Street there he was ringing our bell for all he was worth. He did not recognize us when we climbed the steps and were nearly on top of him, but exclaimed impatiently, "What do you imagine happened to the people of this house?"

"I'm the lady of the house," my grandmother told him, hurt, I could tell, that he no more recognized her than he did me.

When we got inside Dad and Gramp were hanging over the bannister in their nightclothes.

"There she is, there's the gallivanter, and she's got that scallywag with her, that cleaning woman in disguise," cried my grandfather.

99

"Mom, we thought the house'd burned down, and firemen were at the door," my father complained.

There was a letter for me from my mother in the vestibule under the letter-drop, but my grandmother did not care about that, now that she had Richard. She wanted us all away, even me, even my father, to say nothing of Gramp, so she could be alone with him.

"Go back to bed, the two of you," she called up to Dad and Gramp. "And you get going back to school," she said to me. "Don't let those Germans up at St. Ursula's shame you with their punctuality. Anybody can be on time. It's what you bring to it that counts."

She wasn't talking to us, to me or my father, or to Gramp, but to Richard. She was showing off her good sense to him. She was as good as telling him that she was not from Bannister Street, or any other *little* street. Not that he noticed. "There's an awful lot to be done here," he said. "I should have brought my wife along with me. I will next time."

"You'll do no such a thing," my grandmother said, pushing me out the door to school with my letter. She seemed to be hurt beyond anything that Richard had somebody beside herself. "He no more has a wife than you do," she was to tell me, and she was right.

100

# 13

My mother's letter only said they were all all right, nothing about me, except to hope I was too, or my mission.

All the same I could not put it away in my pocket or take my eyes off it, not even walking the streets, not even in the classroom.

"What have we here? A letter? A letter from home?" my teacher asked, startling me, for I had not noticed her proximity, mesmerized as I was by my mother's letter. I rolled it up and stuffed it under my desk. "No, no, that won't do at all," she said. "Give it here."

The tallow faces regarded us. A wave of envy washed over me from all sides. Nobody got letters, except begging letters from Germany. What was this Irisher doing with a letter?

"It's because she wants letters herself that she took yours," my friend, Peter Shultz, told me at recess.

I moved away from him, sickened by his smell.

"You think so, Shultzie?" I asked, keeping my distance.

"She wants love letters herself," Shultzie told me, adding that he did not believe Hildebrande was a nun in the first place, but a flapper in disguise.

Shultzie's father drove a Hellmann's mayonnaise truck, and, from the look and smell of him, Shultzie lived and slept in the truck. He had no mother, only a sister and a brother, both older than he was. Elf, his brother, had taught Shultzie to talk in a grown-up way about grown-up things he no more understood than I did. We had a great common interest in Nick Carter, whose paperback books, the property of his brother, Elf, Schultzie brought me from home by the half dozen. His eyeglasses were covered with his fingerprints, and his clothes and face were oily. He was the dirtiest boy I ever knew, and the nicest.

"It ain't bad enough you're going to be a missioner when you grow up," Schultzie said, throwing an arm around me and drawing me to him. "Now Hildebrande has to go and rob you of a letter from your mother. What's your mother look like, anyway? Do you even remember her?"

"Sure I remember what my mother looks like, Schultzie. What kind of a dope

102

do you think I am?"

I held my nose so as not to smell him, but he was all right, really.

"How come your mother and father are separated, anyway?"

"I got contaminated and he had to leave the house because of his work."

"And he never went back? Why?"

"Why, because he still thinks I'm contaminated, Schultzie."

"He ain't got somebody else?"

"No, it's me. Even at my grandmother's he keeps his distance."

After class Schultzie went up to Hildebrande, who kept her distance from him as I did, and demanded my letter back. I remained at my desk, determined to stay there the night if I did not get the letter.

"You be on your way home, Peter Schultz," Sister Hildebrande ordered Schultzie, who backed away from her as if he had been shot. "And close the door behind you," she called after him, with a smile on her freckled face.

Sister Hildebrande was not like other nuns. She was pretty. You could tell she was slim, because her habit did not touch her anywhere but at her shoulders and the tops of her boots. Sometimes, when Hildebrande turned from us to write on the blackboard, it was as if she was going into another room – to dance. One day she touched my hair and I felt she was sorry she had cut hers. As my grandmother waited for Richard McQueegly to show himself to her, so I found myself waiting for Sister Hildebrande to show herself to me, which she did every school day, of course, but I meant really.

After Schultzie left me alone in the classroom with Sister Hildrbrande I experienced an instant sense of intimacy with her, though she did not look my way, scarcely seemed to be aware of my existence.

She busied herself at her desk, then rose and adjusted the window shades so that they were all at the same level. When she had finished, she scanned the classroom to make sure all was shipshape, and then she came to me with my letter. "There you are," she said. "You didn't think I'd keep it from you, did you? Did Peter Schultz say I would? Poor Peter. Half the time he does not know what he is talking about. I don't know what he will be like when he grows up, because he believes he knows everything now. Maybe he does. Maybe he knows as much now as he'll ever know. He'll probably live and die in this neighborhood, where he was born, without seeing any more of the world than he does now. There are such men. I believe Peter Schultz is going to be one of them."

She bent over me, so that the scarf of her hood hung between us, hiding us from one another.

"Yet he took your side, just now, Peter did, he championed you," she said. "He played squire to your knight. That was very beautiful, very touching. Something entered him that was bigger than himself, bigger and more important than Peter will ever be. For a minute he gleamed. He didn't even smell anymore of Hellmann's mayonnaise."

Sister Hildebrande pushed back her veil that had fallen between us and looked into my face and laughed.

"Look at you!" she exclaimed. "You haven't understood a word I said, and I don't blame you."

The classroom door was opened and Sister Hildebrande turned to it like a young girl in her first long dress — expecting praise. Instead she faced Father Stienhagen, with his fixed smile that was no smile, and the understanding look in his eyes that was not understanding at all, but presumptuous.

"Need any help, Sister?"

"No thank you, Father. Not right now."

He closed the door all the way and came into the classroom.

"Is it a matter of discipline?"

"No, nothing like that."

He looked around the room, whose very orderliness seemed to push him to where he might demand: Then why are you here? Why aren't you at your washing, ironing, scrubbing, sewing?

For they were slaves, their brains parked in the world outside, with whatever talent they might have had. Hildebrande's hands were rough, and not as they should have been, and probably had been, before their betrothel to Fels Naphtha soap.

"Sister, you often seem to me to be on the verge of tears. I hope it is not for home, Sister. I hope it is not homesickness. Vhere Gott is, is your home."

He was a liar, and I felt like telling him so, but I held back for Hildebrande's sake. She had to live here, maybe till she died. I could always go *home*.

"You can go," Hildebrande told me.

As I took my leave, she flew to the windows like a prisoner-bird and let fly the blinds she had only a few minutes ago lowered, flooding the schoolroom with late afternoon light.

"Wait, come back," she commanded, as I was about to close the door on the two of them, the witty young nun and the middle-aged peasant-priest. "I want you to help me carry these across the schoolyard," she said, loading me down with potted plants and taking up an armful herself. "They need air," she explained to Father Stienhagen. "More than they are getting here. I'm sure after a few nights outside on the porch they will be much refreshed. Otherwise, what good are they? I'd rather have no plant at all than a sick plant in my classroom, Father. Good-night."

The walk across the schoolyard was short. In no time we had put the plants down on the open porch of the house where the sisters lived, and I faced the schoolyard gate, where Little Bottle waited for me, as usual, clinging to the rails like a pet monkey, his angst-ridden eyes watching my every move. "There's your friend," Hildebrande told me, as if she knew everything about me. "I must say your choices are disreputable. What made you pick Little Bottle, to say nothing of Peter Schultz?"

"It just happened, Sister. Sister Hildebrande, how is it you seem to know so much about me?"

"Curiosity, because you are an outsider here."

"Are you an outsider here, here at St. Ursula's, too, Sister?"

"Yes."

"Do you want to go home, too?"

"Yes, but it is not a sign of sickness, but of health, that I want to. Father Stienhagen has it all backwards, as usual."

Sister Hildebrande picked up a bowl of cactus and spoke to it lovingly, spitefully pricked though it was.

"Here's where I come from, me and my freckles, from where cactus grows, desert lands, flat, heartbreakingly flat, but guarded all around by our mother, the mountain, Sierra Madre."

"Indians, too, Sister Hildebrande?"

"Soft-eyed Indians, not driven Germans, though we're all God's children."

"What keeps you here, Sister?"

"Duty, decency. The fear of having to tell people who believe in me that I failed in what I feel I am meant to do."

She took hold of my hair and gave it a tug.

"Don't look so worried, I'll survive."

"You will?"

"Well, won't you? Won't you get what you want? Don't you feel you will? Isn't there something that tells you not to be satisfied with less? Haven't you something, someone you look to for guidance? Someone you're ashamed to let down?"

I thought of Horatio, but I didn't dare tell

her, any more than I would have told my grandmother. All the same it made me feel very close to Horatio again, when he was alive and roaring, and we used to save him for last.

# 14

The green-and-red curtains were down. The rugs were rolled up. And *he* was in the kitchen, sitting *on* the table, talking a mile a minute. No wonder he coughed.

Suddenly he got up and unscrewed the cellar door from its hinges, and fixed it back on so that it opened into the cellar instead of into the kitchen, as it used to do.

"Why," said my grandmother, when he had finished, "it gives me all the room in the world. Now, there's a difference, and you're to be commended, Richard. Sit down and rest and stop coughing. I'm sure it's just a nervous tickle you get in your throat from overexhaustion. You drive yourself too much."

"I don't. I don't do half what I want to do." He looked at me.

"Well, you're back, are you? What did you learn? That the oceans are deep and the skies high and the moon's yellow and the sun's hot, that the grass is green and water's wet, and sand sandy and mud muddy – or didn't you learn none of those things? Come, tell us what you learned. We are so dumb, and you look so full of knowledge. Tell us just a little thing."

"Oh, he's a stone for silence when it suits him," said my grandmother. "I wish I could say the same of the two birds above," she added, casting a rueful eye up at the next floor, where my father and Gramp were at their ablutions.

"They'll be down on us before you can cross yourself. So be off with you, Richard McQueegly. What a funny name."

She slipped him a shoe box full of good things to eat, which he held up to his nose, while my grandmother blew her own, remorsefully, because she had not given him enough. "I'll never forgive myself for not asking him in the first night he called," she told me, after closing the door on him. "No, I'll never live it down."

A truck came for the rugs and the curtains, and, afterwards, it was as if we were in the process of moving. Gramp walked across the wooden planks of the parlor floor as if he had not stepped on bare wood before and might fall. My father was as bad. They never rode to work together, my father slipping out of the house first, as though it were a thing long agreed on, though nothing had ever been said about it, and nothing ever would. When I walked Gramp to Twenty-third Street to his trolley he asked me what she got for the rugs and the rest of the stuff she sold to bail her bum of a brother out of Moymensing Prison.

"It's a terrible thing t'find the savings of a loife's time pulled out from under yer feet with the curtains on the door, everything gone to the high-flier sonsabitches who take yer money at the prison's gate to let those out who ought to stay in, and keep those poor basthards in, who by all roight's ought to be out. I'm sorry I ever married an' don't you do it or you'll never get another nickel from me. No, nor the roller skates I promised you, neither."

He hadn't, though he saw me looking at them covetously each time I walked him to his trolley stop, the toy store being on the corner, and the roller skates displayed in the window.

"I tell you what," my holy little grandfather said, eliciting a wicked promise from me, "if you promise never t'marry I'll buy them for you. I'll buy them for you, though I'm a poor man with a crazy wife, who has sold up all we have, and given her money to bail men."

"I promise, Gramp."

"Now, what are you afther talkin' about?"

"I promise never to marry if you buy me these roller skates in the window."

"I'll be late for me work, then what? No matter, let's in."

We bought the skates, taking all his dear money but his carfare, but he still would not go to work, letting trolley cars pass one after another up Twenty-third Street.

"I want to see you use them. I want to see you skate. I don't trust you. I think you're the marryin' kind, afther all, and have screwed me good and proper, leaving me with nothing but me fare to and from me job. You saw the rugs were up, didn't you? You saw me threadin' me way through the splinters on the floor, didn't you? Show me if you can skate or not and give me a reason for ever comin' to this godforsaken counthry. You can't. You're a bail man like all the rest."

"I'm not, Gramp. I'm really not," I said, struggling as fast as I could to get the skates on me and to get him off before he was so late for his job that he lost it.

"Well, go on, go on, let me see you skate."

When I did, he took off his derby and waved it each time I passed him by. He caught me by the hand and swung me to him. I flung my head back. There were stars.

"Oh, my little missioner," Grandpop cried, making me nearly feel like one for the first time.

113

# 15

I skated past my grandmother without her knowing who I was, though she had come to her front door looking for me. "Why, I hardly recognize you with those things on. What did you do, win them or what? It's wonderful what you can do, once you set your mind to it. I bet you outspelled those Germans up at St. Ursula's t'beat the band. Cut a caper for us, you're that light on your feet, you get it from your mother."

I was skating over the bare floors of the dining room and parlor when Chauncey came into the house with two men who said they had stood bail for him, and was it safe to leave him with my grandmother till his trial came up.

My grandmother stood before them like Christ before Pilate, with her hands crossed in front of her, and her head bowed in sorrow and shame, while Chauncey rocked back and forth on his little round feet, in a peevish way that implied it was all her fault, and that is just what he said as soon as the bail men had gone and left him with us.

"I don't know that I should have come back," he said. "Tom told me I shouldn't, and that I should go with him, but he has company at present, and three's a crowd."

It was as far as I was concerned. I was sorry he was out.

"I don't know what this kid's still doing here," he said, meaning me. "Wasn't it bad enough that he was born out of wedlock, without having him flaunted in the faces of respectable people? Tell me I'm to share my bed with the son of a whore and I'll leave. I'll go throw myself on the mercy of my bondsmen."

"He'll sleep with me," my grandmother told him, drawing me to her, skates and all.

"Yes," said Chauncey, screaming over the din I made, "but he has already slept in my bed, and no holy water will cleanse it. I'll not follow him there. I'll sleep on the floor."

At that he noticed for the first time that the rugs were missing. He rushed hysterically from room to room, missing this, missing that. You would have thought the things were his, the way he carried on.

"You're movin', aincha?" he cried. "You were set to leave me behind, weren't you? Lettin' me rot in jail while you did the midnight flit on me."

"Chauncey, go to bed," my grandmother told him. "You're tired and overwrought. You'll be bether in the morning, and afther, when all this is behind you, and you c'n start life anew."

"I need a drink," Chauncey replied, matter-of-factly, and he turned around on the balls of his little feet and left the house for Oyster's Bar across Twenty-fourth Street.

Afterwards my grandmother sat before the kitchen stove and ordered me to bring various covered dishes to her from the icebox in the unheated back kitchen. "I'm tired," she said, slipping the dishes I brought her into the oven, "I'd go anywhere with Richard, though. Arizona'd take his cough away. He'd be fit enough in Arizona." She closed her eyes, rocked back and forth. "I'd send him there. I'd feel good, knowing he was betherin' himself."

Soon the aromatic odors of her casseroles filled the big kitchen. Kidney beans and cottage ham, and pickled red cabbage, with slices of black bread and sweet butter, and cups of strong, red-hot, mahogany-colored tea.

We were eating by the fire, like gypsies, she said, when Chauncey came in and went up to his bed without a word. At his trial he was given a year in jail, and all but his brother,

116

Tom, wished it had been more.

The rugs came back and Richard laid them as if they were his own. He took great pains with everything. But sometimes he would slip down on the parlor floor and just lie there as if he were figuring something out on the ceiling.

He asked me if I liked him and I said I did, but he did not seem to believe me, so I told him I used to be jealous of him, but that I wasn't anymore.

"There you go," he said, pleased with me for leveling with him.

The house was different with Richard, not only cleaner, but more together and purposeful, as if it had somewhere to go, now that Richard had come into my grandmother's life.

After a great deal of coaxing on her part, and honest reluctance on his, he brought her some of his drawings, which even I could see plainly disappointed her, though she pretended otherwise, so he brought her more.

Evenings she would tire herself poring over them, to find merit where her instinct told her no merit was. Dickens was forgotten. I did my lessons and went to bed and was asleep when she got upstairs. Sometimes she woke me with her tortured soliloquies concerning the work she had been poring over all by herself down in the kitchen in her rocker by the stove, shaking her head yes, then no, her black jet earrings jigging from the ends of her ears, nearly covered by her ever-whitening hair.

"Arizona would do wonders for him and his work," she would murmur to herself while undressing. Then, one night, she told herself she would even give him up, pay his way, stay behind herself, since "My journey's done, Lord."

If it was she didn't act it when Richard sent word by Little Bottle that he would come to clean no more. She thrashed about the house finding clothes fit to wear on the street and got into them any old way, telling me to come with her.

"Can I bring my skates?"

She shook her head yes, as if she were admitting to herself that we were going on a fool's errand, anyway, so what did it matter how much noise I made alongside her.

We found his place, an empty room without even a bed in it, in a rundown boardinghouse on Race Street, owned by a Chinaman who said he had not seen Richard in days. There were things pinned to the walls, nothing finished, nothing of value, but my grandmother begged the Chinaman for them, giving him something in return. We carried them home to Twenty-fourth Street. I don't think my gandmother ever looked at them again.

She let the house go as well, as if she felt in her heart that Richard would return, but he never did. Such was her spirit that she picked up reading Dickens again, listening for a knock on the door, not a ring, a knock.

Halloween someone did knock on the door, but we did not answer it, knowing it could only be kids. My grandmother hated Halloween, and taught me to distrust it. We sat in the kitchen imagining all sorts of things going on outside in the surrounding streets, where masked children begged from door to door. We heard cries of anger and pain as the bigger boys slugged one another with stockings, the toes of which were often filled with hard coal. It was a disagreeable holiday, men in women's clothes, and women in men's clothes, while small children in sheets and stark black-and-white masks streaked by in the dark as ghosts.

Taught as I was to have a purpose, I saw no fun in this carnival. Shultzie called earlier in the evening, masquerading as a pirate. A lot of good it did him. I would have smelled him out anywhere and as anything. He begged me to take him upstairs to see Chauncey's bedroom. Chauncey was more infamous than ever in the neighborhood, and especially at St. Ursula's, now that he had been sentenced, and his trial

119

noted in the back pages of the newspapers.

We roused my father, who slept in the room adjacent to Chauncey's, and he came out into the hall in his nightgown and bare feet, wanting to know what all the noise was about. He was even more irritable than usual, but he did not faze Shultzie, who forgot all about being a pirate at the sight of him.

"Is this your father?"

I said it was with an air that more than implied that Dad was as good as I could do, which was still not very much.

"He's not like I imagined him to be," said Shultzie, puffing through his mask, which was as crazy and unconvincing a face as I had ever seen.

"Why, what did you think I'd look like?" my father wanted to know.

"Well, for one thing," said the "pirate," "I didn't expect you to be wearing a *nightgown*. I wish I could meet your Uncle Chauncey," he said to me. "You're lucky he didn't shoot you when he was free. Did he ever try?"

"Only once or twice," I said, making my father wince disapprovingly.

"Well," said Shultzie, "at least he didn't kill you. He almost did kill Jenkins. Jenkins'll be famous for that for the rest of his life."

"What are you supposed to be, anyway?" my

father asked Shultzie, wanting to get even with him for denigrating his nightgown, but Shultzie acted as if he thought it would be beneath him to reply, and pushed rudely past us and went downstairs, where I followed him.

"Your uncle's room is neat," he told me ever so gratefully when we were outside on Twenty-fourth Street. He put his arm around me, what he always did, and drew me to him, despite my resistance, for he was strong. He reeked, though. He just couldn't help it. "I especially like it that you didn't wash the bloodstains off the walls," he said.

"Bloodstains, Shultzie?"

"From your uncle stabbing himself to keep from going to prison. You don't think I missed them, do you? You don't think I thought they were fingerprints, do you? I'm no jackass," Shultzie shouted to me through his pirate's face. "That room's a horror chamber. I'd give anything to spend a night in it. Will you invite me sometime? I'll give you *all* my Nick Carters if you do. How about it?"

"I'll have to ask my grandmother, Schultzie."

"That target he made in the ceiling to shoot at."

"That's no target, Shultzie. That's the mark where the old gas fixture used to be."

"What about the bullet holes around it?"

"Flies, Shultzie."

"They aren't. Don't you think I know fly-marks when I see them? What are you afraid of? That I'll tell?"

"No, Shultzie. I know you'll keep my uncle's room a secret."

"Know something? I think I saw Sister Hildebrande tonight dressed as a Chinaman. Matter of fact I *know* I did."

"You did, Shultzie?"

"Yes, and you know what she did when she saw me? She ran up an alley, meaning me to follow her. But you know what?"

"No, what?"

"I didn't."

He made off with his wooden sword to join a gang of disinterred dead and their exotic companions, ambassadors from Old Venice, and their musicians and monkeys. They were tough bunches, the bigger ones, brandishing their black stockings containing hard coal. Little kids, like Shultzie, twittered around their edges like birds around cattle.

When I got home my grandmother lowered her parlor shades all the way on the celebrants and we withdrew to the kitchen, where we shared a pumpkin pie after dinner. I had hung orange-and-black crepe paper from the Tiffany lamp over the kitchen table, and glued a witch on her broom to the side yard window. That was as near as the holiday got to us, as much as we partook of its harvest madness. We had a real pumpkin on the table, though, and when my grandmother set the things for supper, her strands of jet-black beads brushed over it, making a picture.

I could not forebear listening to the shouts in the alley as the marauding kids overturned slop buckets and cried to one another to see the havoc they had wrought. Something about it all called to me, something young and alive, something wild. I kicked my legs under the table as though I were running with Shultzie under a full moon over vacant lots where things stood up against the sky and played hell with your imagination. I jumped when I heard a knock on the front door, and so did my grandmother, but she hid her excitement as well as she could, but I did not.

"It's Chauncey," I cried. "He broke out, I'll betcha anything he did."

"He didn't at all. Chauncey hasn't the gumption to break out of a paper bag. If it was me that was in, or you that was in, we'd break out. Richard would break out."

"It's Richard. It's his knock."

"It's not," she cried, the tears streaming down her dark, sallow cheeks, surprising and shock-

123

ing me. "It's not," she howled. "Why do you torture me, saying it is? What power have you got over me, you, a little boy?"

"I have no power over you."

"You have. I expect great things of you, which has put me at your mercy. I'm afraid you'll let me down before I die, and that I'll leave the world crying, as I cried when I came into it."

"Why would you do that?"

"Because you would have let me down, like all the rest, like Tom and Chauncey, like your grandfather, your own father, like Richard. It seems I blight, weaken, and ruin whoever I set my hopes on. Go home, little missioner. You should never have come here. I've made a prisoner of you, haven't I?"

"No you haven't."

"You want to go home to your mother, though, don't you?"

"Yes."

She answered the door herself, passing me roughly by, and did not seem to know me when she came back into the kitchen with Jenkins. "Go to bed," she said to me. I heard them whispering about Chauncey as I went through the dining room, where I missed the brass candlestick lamps on the sideboard for the first time. The next morning my grandmother received a pawn ticket in the mail for them and took me into town with her to redeem them, but more to garner what news she could of Richard McQueegly.

"My last bad penny, so don't you be," she said, suddenly making up with me, outside the pawnbroker's on Thirteenth Street in midtown. "Saying you want to go home to your mother. You don't want to do anything of the kind, do you?"

She swept me into "Uncle Bill's" before I had readied my answer, a lie, because I knew I could not tell her the truth anymore. This made me very sad, because, though I did not love her, I respected her. I looked up to her. She was distinct from other people. She was more interested in things than they were, and her interest was not a passing thing. It was a matter of intelligence. She was very bright.

"Race Street's the last address he gave me," the pawnbroker told her, when she questioned him as to Richard's whereabouts. "Yeh," he said, referring to a dirty copybook, with his dirty hands, while he chewed the end of a dirty-smelling cigar, "here he is, Race Street. But you c'n bet your brass candlesticks back, and lose them to me, that he'd be there."

"You seem to know him?" my grandmother lightly asked as if it meant nothing to her, when it meant everything.

"Oh, I've known McSqueegly off and on since he came to town from the sticks for years now. He was ambitious then. He seemed healthy enough. Weak blood. I even bought a drawing of his he made of my cat. It brings her back to me, I'll say that for it, though it's no great shakes as a drawing, I've been told by those who should know."

The pawnshop wasn't all that far from Ingersoll Street and my mother and Aunt Frances and Johnny Ervine that I couldn't find it if I took my courage in hand and made a run for it, but I did not. I could not.

It would have been different had she been somebody broken, as well as old, but she wasn't. She was too proud to pity, she would have cast my pity back in my face with a sarcasm. How did she look, with her white hair parted strictly down the middle and her straight short nose with its nervous nostrils, her mouth with its downward, negative droop, her jigging eardrops and swoops of black beads, her heavy ankles, and her fine, freckled hands? Why, she looked to me like the goddess of the harvest, her arms laden with the bright goods of the season, the brass candlestick lamps she had just gotten out of hock.

She put them down in a pew in St. John's, in

back of Wanamaker's, on Thirteenth Street, and lit a candle, for Richard, I thought. "No," she told me, giving me a burden that I could have fallen down with, it was that heavy, "I lit it for you, little missioner." She was like a gambler with nothing left her in the world to gamble on now but me, and I had only myself to blame for that.

Uncle Tom was waiting for us on the front steps of the house on Twenty-fourth Street when we got back with the purloined candlesticks.

"Well, I must say, Mary Ellen, you look a sight, carrying the goods of your house about the streets with you. Who is it you don't trust, now that Chauncey's gone? Poor Chauncey," Uncle Tom said, winding up his tirade, which had begun as a joke, but ended somewhat like a funeral oration. "I suppose you've heard?" Uncle Tom added, apparently referring to the news Jenkins had brought her last night, but which she had refused to let me stay down in the kitchen to hear, because I had hurt her by admitting that I wanted to go home, something she would not, or could not, understand.

"Well, let us go into the house," she said, her first concern being the neighbors, who were hanging outside their houses, some pretending to dust, some to wash, all of them having been

127

alerted by the presence of Uncle Tom, whose last turn on the street, when he had denounced my grandmother for not lying to the police about Chauncey's gun, might now be matched, if not beaten. Angry doors slammed, disgusted windows banged down when the three of us went indoors, disappointing the lot of them.

"Why, he could get life now, and no money this side of Mellon-money could ever get him out," said Uncle Tom.

"Well," said my grandmother, with a look at me, "I've got other things on my mind than Chauncey."

Uncle Tom's eyes, following my grandmother's proprietory gaze, stopped at me too.

"You mean the little missioner? How is he getting along, for God's sake? They talk about him everywhere."

"Where's 'everywhere,' Tom?"

"Why, everywhere I go, Mary Ellen."

"You mean across the street at Oyster's Bar? That's hardly everywhere, Tom. Keep him out of your conversations over there."

"But the boy is nearly as much mine as he is yours, for God's sake."

"He is not. You have nothin' to do with him. Nor has anybody. Nobody but me, if the truth be known, and you want to know it."

"Jesus, Mary, and Joseph, Mary Ellen, what's

got into you, girl?"

"Disappointment and heartbreak's got into me, Tom McLaughlin. I'm afther bein' weighted down with the lot of you. The boy's mine. At least till I die he is."

She took hold of me with her cold bare hands that were so fine to see.

"Aren't you?" she asked me.

I shook my head yes, seeing that Uncle Tom was as baffled as I was. He coughed, to clear the air as well as his throat, I thought.

"Be that as it may, Mary Ellen. I should think you'd show some feeling for Chauncey. You don't seem to understand that he has killed a man in prison."

"I do, but I can't take it in, Tom, and that's the truth. If I feel anything at all, it's relief when I remember where he is; in jail, and not out on the street; locked up, where he can't tear us down to his level; somewhere where I won't hear him, and don't want to hear him, and where I won't see him again, God forgive my wrath."

"Well, I can't say I blame you, Mary Ellen. I know how much faith you put in all of us. Had you been a man now —"

"Had I been born a man I wouldn't be standing here talking. I'd be commanding legions. I'd be on the bridge of a ship."

"I'm sure of that, Mary Ellen, but Chauncey isn't all I've come for. You're right to forget him. He's not worth the candle."

"I did not say that!" my grandmother shouted, slapping the kitchen table, and making our pumpkin from last night jump. "I have never let anyone down before they let me down first. I'd be outside the jail, living there, if need be, if I thought he was the least bit trustworthy, but I don't, not anymore."

"Nobody's worth you, Mary Ellen. I admit that. Nobody but this boy. One thing's certain," Tom shrewdly added, drawing an appreciative light from his sister's keen hazel eyes, "he ain't about to disappoint you, like we did, because you'll be gone before he can. It's a great thing you have in him, Mary Ellen. Myself, I think he's a reward for all you've done for the lot of us. Why, we'd never be in this counthry at all, without you pushin', drivin', dreamin'. There's been little return for you until now. You can leave with your ship coming into port."

"I know," his sister reluctantly admitted, not wanting to share what she felt about me with anybody, or not daring to, perhaps, for fear she might lose it, whatever it was.

"Mary Ellen," said Tom, taking out his pocket watch and staring at it while he talked, "I'm through with Chauncey. I'm through with

Oyster's. I'm about to set out on a new course, Mary Ellen."

My grandmother raised her head and sniffed the air like an old dog in the chase. Something was up. Something she had not counted on. Something that would have roused her to action in the past, but now —?

"I'm getting married. I'm leaving you, Mary Ellen. Don't you think it's about time?"

He slipped his watch into his vest pocket and fell on a chair, his face in his large hands, and wept hard tears for himself, for it was perhaps the biggest step, his only step that counted, and he had taken it without her, without consulting her, almost as if she were already dead.

"What's her name?" my grandmother asked, obviously feeling that all she needed to know of the girl, her race, her religion, her relations, would be contained in that awesome handle.

"Cissie Networth," Tom whispered.

" 'Cissie Networth.' Let's wait and see what her net worth is" was my grandmother's comment before the smoke of Uncle Tom's Havana had left the house with him.

Gramp and my father were already up and stirring above even before Tom left. "What was he doing here?" Grandpop asked, rushing down into the kitchen as soon as he felt sure the way was clear. "He's a brother to the killer and is as

131

like him as two peas in a pod, and has no right comin' to this house, bringin' the newspaper headlines with him."

"It's not as if we're alone here, Pop," my father said, indicating me. "There's others to consider besides ourselves."

"Oh, he's heard so much about killin', he'll be able to write a book about it someday," said my grandfather, shoving me out of his way as he took his place at table. "He's a regular authority on murder and murderers, and is probably known at school for just that. And furthermore, looked up to − or shunned," he dismally added, with a questioning look at me. "Which is it?" he asked me.

"Both," I answered, and they all laughed, even my father, who remembered himself to say, "He should be home. I don't know that this neighborhood's all that it was when I was a kid, Mom."

"It's a melting pot, and he'll be all the better for it," my grandmother replied. "To be Irish amongst the Irish is dull going."

"Well, maybe so, but I didn't think much of that boy he had upstairs the other afternoon. I didn't like the castigating way he referred to my nightgown."

Gramp banged his knife and fork down on his plate. "There's no need to talk of nightgowns at table," he gruffed. "Or anyplace else, in decent society," he said, turning his head and looking for a place to spit on the floor. It was a dirty habit of his, and though my grandmother put up with it, she never got used to it. Both my father and grandmother winced at the sight but said nothing, since they knew how "pigheaded" Gramp was and lost to correction of any kind. My grandmother even made a joke after he had done it.

"You do look a sight in your nightgown, Jim," she said, because my mother made it.

"The kid thought so. He seemed to feel I should be dressed like a sport, even for bed."

"Well, I'll buy you pajamas, if you like. They'll be warmer, and, certainly, you'll look better in them."

"Who's gonna see me? Besides, I'll be goin' home."

"Don't say that, Jim."

"Why not?"

"I mean, not just now, what with the scandal about Chauncey — and Tom marrying."

"Tom marrying? Really? Good for him. It's about time."

"Toime my eye," said my grandfather, raging. "He's old enough to have dropped ideas of marrying long ago. God help the poor tramp he's trapped."

"Tom'd go for anything, and that's the truth, what with Chauncey gone from him for keeps," my grandmother said. "I suppose we one of us, or all of us, should visit the prison. It isn't as if we were in another country from him."

"I am," said my grandfather, "and I've always been. If it weren't for you, I wouldn't have known them, swells though they think they are, I hope he gets loife. What else can he get, knifin' a man with somethin' made out of tin cans?"

"He must have got the moods and saw black and went mad," said my grandmother.

"Well, he's gone from us, and we'd be better home, especially the boy," said my father, elating me, for I saw my mission ended, accomplished, at last, but when I made to take his hand he pulled away from me. "Get back," he cried, with a laugh. "You don't think you're over being contaminated yet, do you?"

"Then you don't want the pajamas, do you, Jim?" my grandmother asked.

"Sure I do," he said, going out with her into the hall to get into his overcoat and hat and gloves, leaving me alone in the kitchen with Gramp, who regarded me in a fixed sort of way, as if he was about to say something mean, but he did not.

Instead he brushed bread crumbs into his

hand and threw them back on the cloth again, to see where they would go, I guess, one here, one there. He always did that.

# 16

The kids at St. Ursula's mobbed me at recess, wanting to know about Chauncey, but Shultzie wasn't amongst them. Shultzie had been struck on the head by a black stocking containing hard coal the night he himself had been masquerading as a pirate. He was still in costume when I came into his bedroom, but not altogether in his right mind, which he seldom was, anyway, as far as I understood it. He was being attended by his doctor, a gloomy man, and nursed by his sister, who smelled of mayonnaise, just as Shultzie did. He was delighted to see me.

"I'm dying," he said.

"You're not at all," his sister corrected him.

"He might be," said the gloomy doctor, and Shultzie began to cry.

"I don't want to die," he sobbed.

"Well, perhaps you won't after all. Let's see your bandage," the doctor said, pulling Shultzie's head to him in such a rough way that it made me hurt, but didn't seem to bother Shultzie, who was sweet-natured as anything.

"Say, you were right about your old man keeping his distance from you," he said, while the doctor was mistreating him. "I noticed that when you showed me your uncle's bedroom. How's he getting along at Moymensing? Did he kill anybody there yet?"

"Yes he did, Shultzie, and now he's in for life."

"What a family you come from."

"Keep still and stop raving," said the doctor. "You stop raving too," he told me.

"But it's true," I said.

"What's true? Do you think I was listening to your nonsense? I have enough to do. Besides, nobody pays me," said the doctor, turning and looking with begging eyes at Shultzie's sister.

"We'll pay you, Doctor Fishman," she said. "My father is an honest man."

"Can I get up, Doctor?" Shultzie wanted to know.

"You can get up, but don't go crazy."

"But he will, Doctor. He'll jump around like the devil. You don't know him."

"Then he better stay in bed."

"I think I better, too," said Shultzie. "I wander in my head since I was hit," he told me.

"Yes you do, but don't brag about it, Peter," his sister told him. "You want to get well, don't you?"

"I don't know," Shultzie told her. "I liked wandering in my mind. I imagined all sorts of things."

"Then maybe you better get up," said the doctor, getting up himself, and spilling things all around him. He seemed to me to be related to the Shultzes in sloppiness. He wore his overcoat, hat, and scarf all the time he was there. "Are you going to pay me, Anna?" he asked Shultzie's sister, who told him she couldn't, but that their father would be home any minute.

"Maybe you would like to go downstairs and wait for him."

As the doctor went downstairs a loud voice filled the small house, and a huge man in striped overalls came into the room and embraced Shultzie. They kissed and hugged as if they had not seen one another in years.

"Father, this is the Irisher whose uncle wounded a man and killed another."

"Wunderbar!" Mr. Shultz shouted, and everybody laughed, even the gloomy doctor, even me, though I had no idea what "wunderbar" meant.

"Doctor Fishman wants to be paid, Father," Anna said. "Also, he has ordered Peter to remain in bed."

"Nonsense," Mr. Shultz said, and he bent over and picked Shultzie up and set him out on the floor in his pirate suit.

"Where's my sword?" Shultzie asked, concerned as anything.

Mr. Shultz picked him up and carried him downstairs, where he put two sticks together and made Shultzie a better sword than he had before.

Then the doctor was paid and sent off and we all sat down at the kitchen table to dinner, since Anna would not hear of me going home without some food in me. "Winter's coming on, and we must all be healthy enough to beat it," she said. Mr. Shultz dished out dumplings and potatoes and chunks of boiled lamb.

Shultzie's big brother, Elf, came in and asked Shultzie what he was doing downstairs, and if he thought he was ready to go out on a date with some girls, because, Elf said, "I gotta extra tonight." Elf unhooked his carpenter box hanging by a leather strap from his shoulder and washed his hands at the kitchen sink and sat down with us. Mr. Shultz said grace and crossed himself, as we all did. Every once in a while something fell on the floor, a knife, a fork, but none of the Shultzes troubled to pick them up, reaching for another instead. Afterwards, they pushed back their plates and coffee cups, and sang in German. I walked home with the tunes in my head, tunes without words, since I knew the meaning of none of them, unless one word bound the lot, one word, one feeling. I thought so. I thought the word was love. I never did see a display of feeling such as the Shultzes showed for one another.

There was singing coming from Oyster's too. Shadows cast on the saloon's back room windows weaved and gesticulated in an exaggerated way, as if drink made people bigger as well as bolder. When the side door opened and trapped me in its shaft of light, I stood as though transfixed, gazing into the interior.

"What in the name of God have we got here?" asked a tall man with a small head and very long arms from within the back room, and with that he jumped through the open door and caught me by the fur collar of my little winter coat, sizes too small for me now, before I could take off, which I tried to do, sorry now that I had stayed as long as I had rubbernecking into a place that was no business of mine. "I know you well, me lad," the man detaining me let me know. His dirty hands could have snuffed the life out of me in a second. "You're one of the murderous McLaughlins."

"I'm not," I said, "I'm a relation, that's all."

"That's enough," said the man.

"I wouldn't brag about it, if I wuz you,"

somebody else called out from the back room. "Put him in here, Sweeny. Call Tom from the bar. Little, go get Tom."

"I won't," said Little Bottle. "I won't at all," and he came to me and took me protectively by the hand. "You've got your nerve, Sweeny," he said to the man with the small head and the long arms, "pullin' a kid into a lousy back room."

"What's lousy about it?" Sweeny asked, finally letting go of my collar, and taking a bit of the fur with him. "I'll tell Larry Oyster what you said about his establishment if you're not careful, Little Bottle. If you're not careful, I'll bounce you. I think I'll bounce you anyway."

With that the big brute sent poor Little Bottle rolling under the tables, where he lay as if dead.

"He'll never get home now," said a young girl, kneeling beside Little Bottle. She was pretty enough, but sad and used-looking. "You shouldn't have done that, Sweeny," she told the monster, who replied that he'd give her the same, if she didn't shut up, and he moved toward her as if he meant to carry out his threat.

"Move away, Cissie. You know the rotten likes of Sweeny when he starts thrashing. There's no stopping him," a woman with a big flat face advised Cissie, who said it would take more than the likes of a big moron to scare her. "Go get Tom," she said. "Tell him I want to go home. I wasn't meant for this sort of life, if anybody was."

Cissie looked like a nice girl to me. I hoped she wasn't the one Uncle Tom planned to marry, because, if she was, she was too good for him.

"I'll take Mr. Bottle home," I told her. "I know where he lives."

At that the habitués of the back room at Oyster's saloon cheered me so loud that they nearly knocked me off my feet.

"How do you like that for a little missioner," said Sweeny.

"It's a wonder how it's come true what's been said about him," said a man with his bare, dirty knees showing through his pants.

"Is this Jim's boy, then?" Cissie asked. She put her arms around me. "Don't tell me I don't feel like your mother," she said, "because I do."

"Now enough of that, Cissie. Let him alone. He has enough of trouble, considering the family he comes from," the flat-faced woman said, and she stood up, pulling her sweater over her housedress. "Anyways," she said, "I see nothin' unusual about offering to see a man home. Why, if I did it, I'd be held *suspect!*"

Here everybody but me and Cissie broke into cheers, and the flat-faced woman sat down and took up her glass, much pleased with herself, and held it aloft.

"Where's the boy?" Little Bottle asked, coming to. "Did I hear him say he'd see me home?"

The flat-faced woman stood up again.

"No, it was me who said I'd see you home, Little. How about it?"

After getting the laugh she expected, she remained standing and sang "I'll Take You Home Again, Kathleen," at the end of which a repentant Sweeny helped Little Bottle up from the floor and said he was sorry.

"I hardly know where I am, which ain't the first time," said Bottle.

He was coming toward me when Uncle Tom came into the back room from the bar and told Cissie it was time to go home.

"It is, is it?" said Cissie, as changed with Tom as could be imagined. She was almost another person. "It's about time you came to pick me up. I thought you'd forgotten all about me. Maybe I hoped you had."

"Now what's the matter with her?" Tom demanded of the company. "What have I done this time but asked her to marry me? Maybe I shouldn't have. What's got into her, will you tell me that, Stephanie?" Tom inquired of the

143

flat-faced woman who sang so well. "Will you tell me what more a man can do for a woman than ask her to marry him?"

"Ask your nephew, if you don't know," said Cissie.

"What's my nephew got to do with it?" Tom asked, over the silence his girlfriend's remark had created. "What is she talking about Jim for, Stephanie?"

"Not Jim, Tom," Stephanie whispered. "The kid they call the little missioner. That nephew."

Uncle Tom turned and took me in at last. "I'll ask you to leave my nephews out of this," he said quietly. "They have nothing to do with any of you here."

"A lot you know about it," Cissie told him.

"Why don't you tell me I'm used up and old and that's why you don't want me, and stop bringing up my family, Cissie?"

"You're all right," Cissie grudgingly complimented him.

"But not for marrying?"

"That's right, Tom."

Uncle Tom squeezed me to him for a shield against the onlookers and said nothing. There was something babyish about Tom, as there was about Chauncey. There was something boyish about my grandfather, too boyish, though charming and good. Gramp was terribly good to me in his way. My father was boyish and irresponsible as well. Was it my grandmother's fault that all her boys were such *boys?* I didn't know. I wished I did, standing there in Oyster's back room with my Uncle Tom, after Cissie Networth had jilted him in front of everybody.

I led him outside, but at the corner of Twenty-fourth and Tasker I remembered Little Bottle and went back to get him. Stephanie was up again, singing "I'll Take You Home Again, Kathleen." By the time I reached the corner with Little Bottle, Uncle Tom had gone. We could hear his machine. It had to be his, because it sounded as if it wanted to forget everything it had left behind, it went that fast, this way and that, up Twenty-fourth Street.

"Are you all right, Mr. Bottle?"

"Yes, but I don't want you rememberin' what Cissie said about your father."

"She wasn't talking about my father, she was talking about me."

"No, it's your father she loves, not Tom, don't you see? Now what am I afther tellin' you? You'll forget it, like a good boy, won't you?"

"Sure, Mr. Bottle. Are you all right?"

"I'm fine when I'm with you. I'm young and strong again. Don't, though, whatever you do, remember what I said about your father."

"That Cissie's his girl?"

"Yes, but you won't remember or tell, will you?"

"Shall I walk you home, Mr. Bottle? No, I won't tell."

"You'll keep it to yourself. Promise?"

"I promise. Good-night, Mr. Bottle."

"Good-night, little missioner. But what am I afther doin', sendin' you off with the weight of the world's wickedness on your shoulders? Come in, come in, and say hello to Mom."

"We'll talk about it later," said Mrs. Bottle to her parrot as I came into her kitchen with Little. That done, she gave her attention to me. "Chauncey," she let me know, as she seated me in her minuscule kitchen and put on the teakettle and rattled cups and saucers, and lit the gas jets, there being no electricity yet on Bannister Street, "Chauncey, as I was saying, ain't killed anybody at all at Moymensing, as he has every right to do, I'm sure, poor man. Not that I'm callin' Chauncey a thug, but he *is* amongst them. No, he'll be home, the pigeon-bellied little bastard, before you know it. Now how does that make you feel?"

Terrible, and my grandmother felt the same. "I've never wanted so much to go back to Galway," she said. "I'd like to see the sea from there once more. The sea has always given me courage."

The next day Gramp made a face when Uncle Tom appeared at dinner, though my father was airy enough. "Well, Tom," he said, not knowing what he was in for, "what are you doing down this part of the woods at this hour of the day? No funerals, no wakes, no weddings?" he asked, referring to Tom's cars, which he rented out for such occasions.

Tom's usually cheery face was clamped closed as a heat stove in August. "Speaking of weddings," he said, jumping right into the fray he had come for, and which his soft life had made him all too unused to, "mine's off."

"Off, Tom? How come?" my father nervously inquired, causing my grandmother to regard him as if she had never seen this side of him before.

"Well, Jim," she said, "it has nothing to do with you. You're all nerves, Tom," she said turning on her brother. "You'd be enough to upset a saint. Who cares about your girls? This one or that one. You'll get somebody else. Don't worry."

"I don't want anybody else," said Tom. "I want my own back. And I want Jim to give her to me."

"Jim give her to you?" said my grandmother,

giving herself time to think, I could see, and so could everybody, since it was her way. "Since when has Jim got anything of yours?"

"He knows what he's got of mine," Tom said.

"Well, for God's sake," my father chanted, making time, too, but which seemed to tell my grandmother, and Gramp too, the truth just as if he had spelled out his affair with Cissie Networth in so many words for the two of them, for they both of them looked older by years, and they both of them were looking at me, reaching for me, reaching hard, though they did not make a move toward me.

Dad left the table and went out to the hat rack in the hall to get into his coat for work. Tom followed him. When Tom began to curse my father in a low voice, to which Dad said nothing, my grandmother and Gramp looked so forlorn — so little, so tiny, as if they wanted sweet things to eat, and toys to play with, and Christmases forever, that I went to them, my arms out. It was nothing so bad as they thought, if they only knew, but they didn't. They did not know the great thing about my mother, how she had Horatio.

I was greatly tempted to go home that night, and both my grandmother and Gramp seemed to suspect I might. They came into Chauncey's old room where I slept and sat down one at a

148

time on the edge of the bed and talked about things they thought would interest me, but they didn't, really. All I thought about was my mother and the kids, of Mark learning to talk and me not being there. How awful. It rained, too, and the rain seemed to be coming in on us, I kept getting up, in my anxiety, to make sure my window was closed.

Dad looked in on me when he came home from work, something he had not done before that I was aware of, though he might have. The last to come in was my grandmother, who told me all this would pass, not even asking me whether I was awake or not.

Gramp shook me roughly awake, like Shultzie would have done, when he came in. "I hope you don't think you understood what was talked about in the kitchen between your father and your Uncle Tom, because you don't, do you?"

"Of course I do, Gramp."

"Well, then, I'll tell you something, you chump, you," he raged, in his dear, sweet way, "I'm sorry I ever gave you the pair of skates."

"You're not, you're not at all, Gramp."

"Well — I almost am."

# 17

My grandmother bought the pajamas for Dad and a new overcoat for me, but I preferred to wear my little coat with the torn fur collar. Uncle Tom came to the house now with a long face, which did not suit him. He was best loud and jovial, however fake. He bought another limousine, and then another, and was reckoned well off in that neighborhood, and for those days. He was ever so pious, and devoted all the time he used to give to girls to Chauncey, working to spring him, everybody hoping he would not, even himself, perhaps. All the same he did, and was noted ever afterwards, in that neighborhood, as a master of graft.

Chauncey lost tons in prison, but he was hardly out a week before he began to look like his bouncy old self again. He hated me, but invited me to share his bed with him anyway, which I refused to do at first until the entreaties of my grandmother made me renege and I did.

"Now we're going to do something I learned in prison and is quite the fashion there," he whispered to me in the dark.

I thought he was an awful old bore, but especially now. I had skated hours after school with Shultzie and I was tired.

"Why, what is it?" I asked, rather peevishly, sorry I had come to his room after all. "I hope you don't have to turn on the light."

That seemed to tickle him. He shook all over.

"Not at all," he whispered, his breath coming fast, "it's best done in the dark."

"Well, what is it?" I asked, sitting up, which displeased him no end, since he slapped me down.

"Ouch!" I said. "That hurt."

"Well, then," he said, "behave yourself."

"I don't want to behave myself. I want to sleep."

"You're a disagreeable little son of a whore."

"I'm not," I said, "whatever it means, I'm not."

"You are, and it means your mother gave herself to every Tom, Dick, and Harry, like your father's new whore does, Cissie Networth."

"My mother didn't do that, Chauncey. You take that back."

"I will if you're quiet and lie down and be a good boy."

"No, I don't want to be a good boy. I want you to take that back."

"Well, I won't, so you can get out, if you want."

"I mean to," I said, hopping out of the bed, "but not before you take that back."

I turned on the overhead light and took up his hairbrush from the bureau. The big man cringed when I held it over him.

"You'd wake your grandmother wouldn't you?" he whined.

"Take it back."

"Why, what was it I said? Of course I take it back. Now get into bed and we'll play the game I was afther tellin' you about. Now where're you goin'?"

I turned off the light and went out into the hall and closed his door behind me and leaned against it, breathlessly, as though I had run uphill. I was frightened as well, and stole downstairs and hid in a closet, where I fell asleep with Chauncey's hairbrush in my hand for protection, in case he should come and want to play the game they play in prison.

The next day Chauncey attacked Cissie on Morris Street as she was coming from work and Shultzie and I caught the fight. The entire population from Oyster's Bar surrounded them. Stephanie, of the big flat face, said, "It was a sorry day when Cissie Networth decided to have anything to do with the McLaughlins."

"Cissie Networth decided to have something to do with the McLaughlins is it?" said Chauncey. "It was the other way around, and an act of mercy at that, when my brother Tom picked her up afther Elf Shultz dropped her cold with half his kid in her, and Tom pays for the abortion."

Hearing his adored brother, Elf, talked about, though far from understanding why, Shultzie charged through the crowd with his tender head and kicked Chauncey smartly in the shins, to the delight of the crowd.

"There's a brave little fellah."

"Oh, my God, ain't he a gem."

"Sticks up for his own and why not? Who else have we got, when we're downed by the world, but our own?"

Chauncey returned Shultzie's kick with a blow on the head with a stout stick he carried now instead of his gun. Shultzie fell down and lay still and I slid down on my knees beside him, telling Chauncey that I hated him, which wasn't exactly true. The crowd did, though. It moved in on him and would have hurt him had it not been for Sweeny, who held them back.

"Give him to us, please," begged the man with his knees coming through his pants.

"I won't," said Sweeny. "You'll only get yourselves into trouble."

"Help me with this kid and don't be so wild for vengeance," Cissie cried, falling down on the pavement with me beside Shultzie, who opened his eyes and asked if he was dead or not.

"Here comes his brother, Elf," someone out on the edge of the crowd cried, "Now you'll have someone your size to answer to, Chauncey."

"Come here, Elf!" people called. "Come here, Elf!"

"Why, what's the matter?" Elf asked, striding up to the crowd with his workbox on his shoulder.

"It's your brother. He's been hurt, Elf."

At that Sweeny drew Chauncey away, and Chauncey went willingly.

Elf shouldered his way to the center of the crowd and took off his box and dropped down on his knees beside Shultzie.

"Elf, am I dying?" Shultzie asked. "If I am, come with me, Elf. I don't want to die without you."

"You're not doin' no such thing, you little crazy, you." Elf laughed. He picked him up and

154

stood up himself and held out his big hand to Cissie and helped her up too.

I went home with the three of them, carrying Elf's toolbox for him, which was pretty heavy, but I didn't mind, though I had to stop a lot to put it down. After they had bathed Shultzie's head, Elf looked at Cissie and told her it looked to him as if they were together again.

That night Mr. Shultz and his daughter, Anna, called on my grandmother with Shultzie, his head bandaged again. Instead of expostulating with her, they begged my grandmother not to worry. "It has all worked out for the best," Anna said. "Now Elf and Cissie will get married, which is the way it should have always been."

An ironical expression played on my grandmother's face. It would not have been her way of interpreting the fight. Besides, she did not like to see Dad lose anything, even a girlfriend.

Shultzie took the opportunity to explore Chauncey's room again, which he found more gruesome and bloodstained than ever. "It's worse than I remember it. I'd give anything to sleep here a night. I know if I did, that I'd have the most terrible nightmares. Do you, when you sleep here?"

"Do I what?"

"Find it gruesome."

"Oh yes, terrible."

# 18

As I slept downstairs on the parlor sofa, I could tell from the sound of him that my father was unhappy, the way he came in from work in the middle of the night with Gramp. It used to be that he joked over nothing, but now all the jokes were on Grandpop's side. Chauncey's room being at the head of the stairs, Gramp took to slapping his door as he passed it on the way to his own room down at the end of the hall, causing the former prisoner to tumble out of bed, thinking he was back in Moymensing Prison again. To make sure that Chauncey did think he was back there, Gramp would yell, "Fifteen thirty-three, up." It was all the funnier since 1533 was the number of our house on Twenty-fourth Street. "Up on your feet, fifteen thirty-three."

My father liked this at first, but his mood having changed for the worse, he begged my grandfather to call halt.

"I hope we don't have to expect the same tonight, Pop."

My grandfather would do it, anyway.

Rap-rap-rap.

"Prisoner fifteen thirty-three, up on your feet."

Gramp's antic met with my grandmother's approval.

"Now you shouldn't, Jack," she told him, clearly meaning that he should. Gramp swelled with pride as a result of this compliment, however indirectly given. My father having already left the house for work, I took advantage of their good humor to suggest it was time Dad left for Ingersoll Street.

"How come?" my grandmother demanded.

"Well, he's lost his girlfriend, she's marrying Elf, so he hasn't any business being down here anymore."

Since marrying made the whole thing respectable in his eyes, Gramp took my side, not that he let on in front of my grandmother. "You're roight," he said, giving me a nickel out in the hall as he got into his overcoat, and telling me not to tell "her," my grandmother.

"What did your grandfather say to you?" she wanted to know.

"Nothing," I replied, "except that he agrees that it's time Dad goes home."

"Oh, I do, too," she let me know. "But not you. I'd be lost without you now. What do you think of that?"

As I put my head down and remained silent, she entreated me to answer her, but I could not.

"It won't be for long," she said. "Before you know it, I'll be out in Holy Cross pushing up daisies. I'd kidnap you first!" she said, breaking off her self-pitying speech and becoming hard and driving, but not frightening me a bit.

After all, I could always leave, walk north if I had no money, ride there if I did. Why did I stay? Well, for one thing there was the wedding. It hurt my father. "It makes me feel old," he said.

"It doesn't, Jim," my grandmother told him, since that would make her older, when she often said to me she wanted to live now, to see what would happen to me, making me almost wish for her death.

"It makes me feel I'm no fun anymore, Mom."

"Well, you're not!" Gramp let him know. "You're nearly double the girl's age."

"Well, Pop, you seem to know a lot about it. Going to the wedding?"

"We're bound to be invited," said my grandmother. "The Shultzes are fine people, very upstanding."

"Well," said my father. "Shultz better be upstanding, since his bride is very demanding, as I happen to know."

Gramp put his knife down, breaking his plate, in his anger. "There's this boy who's come to get you, because your wife considers it beneath her to do so herself, and I don't blame her."

"Are you telling me to get out, Pop?"

"I'm telling you to pay your way."

"He does, he does, Jack," my grandmother protested.

"He doesn't, and you know he doesn't."

"I do when I have it, Pop."

"You do when you give in to her begging, making her work her wiles on you, like a common — I don't know what," poor Gramp ended, with a look at me.

"Gramp," I said to him, as I would have had we been alone, "I never heard you talk so long before. You don't sound like yourself. You sound different and grown up."

I threw my arms around him, hid my face in his thick head of hair, that felt so boyish to me even now.

"Now we're all upset, Jack," said my grandmother. "And it's you who's done it. All

159

because of a wedding, for God's sake. A German wedding. Well, there'll be beer. Beer beer beer and more beer. And, oh yes, sauerkraut."

There was. There was sauerkraut and pigs' feet and hasenpfeffer and sauerbraten, there was smoked sausage and white wine. There was strudel and noodles. And after all that was eaten and drunk, there was music and dancing. And after that tears and good-byes. For not only were Elf and Cissie going away, but so were all the Shultzes.

"I was wrong about Peter Shultz," Sister Hildebrande told me the day of the wedding. "I said Peter was the sort of boy who would never see any more of the world than the streets of his old neighborhood."

"And now he's going west," I said, lugging her plants back into her classroom for her after school.

"So there's hope for all of us," said Hildebrande, laughing at my dejection.

"How come, Sister? You mean for you and me? I'm stuck here. I don't know about you."

"You're only a little boy, and you already talk like an old man. Go home and put on your roller skates, and come back and we'll talk through the rails."

I did as she told me and was back in a jiffy, but Hildebrande was nowhere in sight. I skated around the schoolyard until Father Stienhagen tapped on a window in the rectory and signaled me to be off. So I skated in front of the school where he couldn't see me. He heard me, though, since he came to the door of the rectory and ordered me still further away. After he closed his door I took off my skates and went and knocked on the door of the house where the nuns were quartered. Sister Hildebrande herself answered the door. She wore a blue gingham apron and her sleeves were rolled up. On the floor at her feet stood a scrubbing brush and a pail of dirty water.

"I forgot all about you. You're a sticker, aren't you?"

"Where's Minnesota, Sister?"

"Why, west. Where did you think it was?"

"Far west?"

"Far enough for you not to think of walking there. Well, have a good time at the wedding tonight."

She put her bucket between us, then dug in the pocket of her habit and came up with something which she handed to me across the dirty water. I backed away without looking at it. Hildebrande closed the door. Soon I heard the sound of her scrubbing brush knocking the door as if Sister was nailing herself in. I put the medal she gave me into my pocket without looking at it and went to the wedding.

"I suppose you know we're going to Minnesota," Shultzie said, winking me to follow him into their little outside kitchen, which we had to ourselves, away from the rest of the wedding. "I'll tell you one thing," Shultzie said, sliding a tumbler of beer toward me across a little table covered with flowered oilcloth, "I don't want you to get drunk. Watch me, and you won't."

"Why," I said, watching him, "is that all there is to it?"

"There's more to it than you think there is."

"It's only drinking, Shultzie. Anybody can drink."

"They can't," said Shultzie. "Elf can't drink. My father told him if he ain't careful he won't be able to do nothin' with Cissie tonight."

"I'm hungry, Shultzie."

"Wait here," he said. "I don't think you can trust yourself on your feet. Can you?"

"Sure I can," I assured him. I stood up and sat down, then I stood up and sat down again.

"You're like me," said Shultzie, after watching me with intense approval. "You can drink. Did I tell you we were going to be farmers? I'll tell you one thing, I can see you coming out there to see us someday."

"Oh, Shultzie —"

"Well, I can. I see you on a horse."

"I can't, Shultzie. I can't even ride a horse."

Shultzie got up and turned his chair around and got on it with the back against his chest. "There," he said, "that's riding a horse. Nothing to it. Let's have some more beer."

When Shultzie came back with the beer Cissie was behind him with food for us. "You kids will be making yourselves drunk, drinking all that beer and not eating." Cissie looked different and was different. Well, for one thing, she was married. She kissed the two of us and went back to the party.

"That Cissie can't keep her hands off me," Shultzie said. "I hope she don't think she married me too. I got enough to think about."

"Like what, Shultzie?"

"Well, like Minnesota. What else do you think? This house is sold, but the people who bought it ain't going to come into it for a while, so it'll be empty."

It was. I used to pass it and wave, first making sure nobody would notice, but it wasn't the same as when Shultzie was there to wave back.

# 19

Little Bottle told me that Minnesota wasn't so far, and that if I thought about it enough, I'd probably wind up there someday. The Bottles' parrot was named Clancey, but he never said a word, though he listened to what everybody else was saying with great inquisitiveness. Whenever I came to the house Mrs. Bottle would turn to Clancey, after having greeted me, and say, "We'll talk about it later, Clancey." This had the effect of making me curious.

"What is it your mother and Clancey go on about, Mr. Bottle?"

Bottle was aghast at my ignorance. "You ought to know Clancey doesn't talk," he said.

"I know that, Mr. Bottle, but it is as if he did. Do you think he might, but not in front of you?"

"It would be most insulting to me if it were true. You know something? I think it just might be true."

"What's that you're carrying, Mr. Bottle?" I

asked, for the little man was loaded down with a heavy pile of brand-new woolen cloth.

"Why," he said, with some pride, "it's me piecework. You know I'm a tailor, I hope? I learned it in the government hospital after the war. I couldn't get my full of sewing until one day a nurse said to me, 'Why Bottle, you'd make a tailor, you know,' and I stopped sewing there and then, but I became one all the same."

"Do you think we'll ever catch your mother and Clancey talking together, Mr. Bottle?"

"Now you stole me thoughts roight out of me mind, you have, little missioner. I was thinkin' the same thing."

"Don't call me that, Mr. Bottle."

"Why not?"

"Well, because I'm not one, really. I'm not doing anything. I'm not going anywhere, while everybody else is."

"Don't lose your courage now, just because you've lost a friend. You've still got me, if you want me. And Mother. To say nothing of Clancey. Let's go in the back to see if we c'n catch them at it."

"Talking together?"

"Well, as you say, they just might be in cahoots."

We went up the back alley, sidestepping the buckets of uncovered slop, pushed open the Bottles' unbolted gate, crossed the yard with its ghosts of old cabbage plants, and stepped up a wobbly wooden step into Mrs. Bottle's kitchen.

"We'll talk about it later, Clancey," said Mrs. Bottle to the parrot, before giving her attention to us.

Now, though Little Bottle must have heard her say this a thousand thousand times in the past, today it made him furious.

"What's wrong with you?" his mother asked, making fists.

"I'm sick of you and your secrets, and that bird, and his secrets."

I had never seen Clancey look so curious as he did then, cocking his green head to a side, and adjusting himself on his perch to better follow the upcoming battle.

"Clancey," replied Mrs. Bottle, very much on her dignity, "is no bird, if you please, but a gentleman, which is more than I c'n say for some. Put down yer piecework and go wash yer hands and come to the table. How about you, little missioner? Have you an appetite? There's nothin' but beets and potatoes and corn beef and an old onion I steamed, but yer welcome. Didn't I," she told Bottle, "tell you to put down yer piecework?"

"I will," said Bottle, "if you'll tell me what you and that bird talk about all the time."

166

Here Mrs. Bottle assumed a pugilistic stance in the middle of her kitchen floor and cordially invited her son to defend himself, which he was preparing to do when the doorbell clanged and my Uncle Chauncey appeared in the Bottles' kitchen begging the combatants to lay off one another and help him.

"You know yerselves that a man's nothin' without a change of clothes," he said.

"Especially yerself. You're a dude when you want to be, and the spirit moves you," Mrs. Bottle flattered him.

"Well," replied Chauncey to that, "I ain't got a stitch, except the rags on me back, that Mary Ellen ain't got."

"Why not send yer little nevvy here for them?"

"What nevvy? I don't recognize him or them. Anyway, it's a gun I'm huntin', and only a man c'n find it, and you're the man, Little Bottle."

"Your gun's been confiscated by the police, Chauncey," I said. "Don't pretend we have it, when we don't."

"Am I in me roight mind, or ain't I?" Chauncey demanded of the Bottles, who told him he was and gave me a look to be quiet and behave myself.

"Hop around the corner with him, like a good boy, Little, 'n' see if you can't get her to give up his clothes. Here, give me yer piece-work t'hold for you until you get back. Chauncey, you've as good as got them back. Yer gun as well."

"But, Mrs. Bottle," I said, after the men had gone, "my grandmother hasn't got Chauncey's gun, the police have it, and the only way he can get it back is through pull."

"Of course she ain't got his gun, little missioner. I just wanted to get rid of him. Sit down and let me feed you."

"How about Clancey?" I asked, as we ate. "Aren't you going to feed him?"

"Clancey eats all day, for God's sake."

"And talks all day, too, I'll bet, doesn't he, Mrs. Bottle?"

"I don't think yer grandmother feeds you enough," she said, dodging my question.

"She does. We eat all the time."

"Then, how was it she lost Richard?"

"Richard hocked our brass candlestick lamps from off the sideboard."

"Well, it was worth it, I'm sure, to your grandmother."

"Yes, she loved Richard. She cried when she found out that he really wasn't an art student."

"Your grandmother is a smart little blister of a woman. Life's burnt her all over. But she has you now, as I have Clancey, God forgive me for

lovin' him as I never did another, but I do. I
do, as your grandmother loves you."

"Clancey was disappointed that the two of
you didn't have a fight after all, Mrs. Bottle."

"Wasn't he, though? You noticed that, did
you?"

"Yes, he *drooped.*"

"You noticed that, too?"

"I thought he might talk then and tell
Chauncey to get out."

At that Mrs. Bottle turned to Clancey, which
is what I wanted her to do all along. "Why
didn't you, Clancey? Why didn't you tell
Chauncey to go?" she asked the little green
bird, who trod nervously back and forth on his
perch, faster and faster, until Mrs. Bottle told
him not to worry about it. "We'll talk about it
later," she said as Little Bottle came in.

"Well," he said, addressing himself to me, and
disregarding the one-sided dialogue that had
been going on through the years between his
mother and Clancey, "your Uncle Chauncey
got what he wanted and more."

"More, Mr. Bottle? What do you mean by
more? What else did he take beside his
clothes?"

"A pair of skates."

"But they're my skates."

"That's what I told him."

"Where was my grandmother all this time? Why didn't you tell her?"

"I did. I called, and screamed, and hollered, but she stayed in her kitchen and told me to be on my way."

"I don't know what to do now without my skates, or what I'll say to my grandfather when he finds out what happened to them. He'll call me a chump for sure, and I'll really be one this time."

"I tried my best to stop him," said Bottle, "but all the same he skated away."

"But Chauncey can't skate, Mr. Bottle. Mr. Bottle, are you kidding me? Is he, Mrs. Bottle?"

"He's a thorn of a boy, Little Bottle is," said Mrs. Bottle, as Little drew his hands from behind him, each grasping a skate, my skates.

"Wasn't he makin' off with them? Well, he was, the narrow-hearted thief, stealing a kid's playthings."

Clancey clapped his wings at that, and Mrs. Bottle told him that they would talk about it later, and Little didn't seem to care if they would or not, or could or not. I thought they did.

# 20

The next morning was so cold that a frost stole over the linoleum of our back kitchen and my grandmother had to wipe it dry. The multiple windows were icy, and you could not see out of them. It was like being in an igloo, I told my grandmother. "It is," she agreed. "Or maybe worse, for all we know," she added, drawing me out of the cold into the big warm kitchen, where we ate our eggs and bacon by the stove, whose grate she kept shaking, making the live red ashes fly.

"It's time you dropped your old overcoat with its little fur collar, like an old skin, and put on your new overcoat for good, like a new skin," she said.

I did as I was told and was glad of it. The streets were white. Twenty-fourth Street stretched farther than ever, and the rare people on it looked statuesque against the thinly laced whiteness on doorsteps and pavements.

On the corner of Twenty-fourth and Tasker,

outside the yellow-painted Acme grocery, lay a black horse with blue smoke coming out of his nostrils. When the pistol shot that killed him ran echoing through the canyons of brick houses, I was glad Horatio had not died like that, in the street in the shadow of wagon shafts. How I longed to run to my mother then and tell her all about it. Since I could not do that with my mission unaccomplished, I held in what I had just seen and heard, only to have it gush out of me when Sister Hildebrande asked us for compositions and I wrote about the horse. Sister's veil fell between the two of us when she bent over me to read what I wrote. She only murmured at what she read, but it was an encouraging murmur.

Such was not the case of Father Stienhagen, who at that moment came into the classroom, huffing and blowing, exhilarated by the bitter cold of that clear morning.

"Vhat are ve doing? Vhat are ve up to, this fine morning?" Father Stienhagen demanded of the class.

"Composition, Father."

Hildebrande stood rooted by my side, when I wished she would fly, do anything so as not to attract Stienhagen's attention to me and my compo.

But the dreadful priest, with his fixed smile, was drawn to me and my doings as surely as

172

night follows day, and he was on us and snarling over what I had written as if it was a letter from Luther.

"Vhat iss this?" he sputtered. "This iss no composition. This iss madness. This is file."

"There's nothing vile about it, Father," Sister Hildebrande told him, keeping her eyes averted from him and me too. "It's true he's made a mistake. I expected him to write about A Visit to Grandmother's Farm."

"Vell, vy didn't he?" the enraged priest cried out in the cold classroom. "All the others haf, I'm sure. Haf you?" he demanded of my classmates.

"Yes, Father," came the automatic response.

"Vy," Father Stienhagen shouted, waving my composition aloft, "haf you not done as the others?"

"Because I've never seen a farm, and I did see the horse," I replied.

"Show-off. After school. Ich habe genug. After school. Forever."

Alone in the classroom with Hildebrande, while the nun sat at her desk correcting the compositions, I wrote A Visit to Grandmother's Farm as she instructed me to do. Afterwards we exchanged compos.

"You can throw this away if you like," she said, handing me my original.

Of course I did no such a thing, but instead took it home and showed it to my grandmother, who lost no time listening to my complaints, but plumped herself down in her chair by the stove and read voraciously, rocking herself with abandon as she did so. Afterwards, saying nothing to me, she thrashed about in her enthusiasm preparing food enough for ten, and when Gramp came down she told him I was going to be a writer.

But she said nothing of the affair to my father, who was fretting in an egotistical way, and could see nothing beyond the fence of his own frustration since his loss of Cissie to Elf Shultz, both of them off to Minnesota, with the wind from North Dakota blowing down their young necks.

Such endeavor he found dispiriting, and he told my grandmother as much when she sat on the seat of the hat rack in the lower hall begging board from him while he climbed hastily into his overcoat. I watched and listened to them from above, leaning over the bannister in the upstairs hallway.

# 21

My father was sly. He knew how to get back at her when she asked for money. He knew how to exploit her old feelings for him, feelings she could never entirely discard, much as she seemed to want to, and especially so since they were foreign to what she had become. She had left Dad behind her, but he knew how to tow her back. He knew her weaknesses, and was expert in playing on them.

"I don't know that I can stay here any longer, Mom."

"Nobody said anything about you leaving, Jim."

"I don't know that I can pay my way in two places at once."

"It's not much I'm asking for, Jim."

"It is when you think of what I have to send elsewhere."

"I don't begrudge a penny there, Jim. Forget I asked you for money. I'll manage without it. There's my savings. That money's as much yours and your father's as it is mine. I'll dip into it. I don't plan to live forever."

"Besides," my father said, as if she had not even spoken, "the holidays are coming up."

"What have holidays to do with it, Jim?"

"The boy, I mean, will want to be home then."

"He won't!" My grandmother flared up. "He's as much as told me he won't. He shows no signs of dissatisfaction with his life here at all. I give him everything."

"I know you do, Mom, but he's pushing me behind your back."

"He's not."

"He is."

"Leave him then, and go home yourself. You have three others beside him. Here, there's only the three of us, counting his grandfather."

There was a chortle over my shoulder. It was Gramp. He'd been in the bathroom. I thought he had gone to work; so did my grandmother, obviously. I wondered what he would do, and how much he had heard of the dialogue below at the hat rack.

"You chump, you," he said to me, hating me for listening, I suppose. But wasn't he listening too? Neither of us was to blame. We hadn't planned to be up here. It was as if we were caught in a trap, all four of us.

"We'll leave tomorrow, Mom," my father said, causing a stifled expression to break from my grandmother. "You're right," he continued, "if I stay here, I should give you something."

"I didn't say that, Jim. I'm only asking if you've got anything to spare."

"Not and give up there, too, Mom. I just can't see my way. I don't know why I can't. Tell him to be ready."

Not even my grandmother's earrings moved when he left after threatening her with my removal. We waited upstairs for her to take refuge in the kitchen by the fire with her book, but she did not budge. It was when she looked up and saw us and said nothing that I think I began to love her. She went back to the kitchen without a word of complaint or blame, as if she were treading barefooted over thorns, because she did not care, because she did not feel anymore, numb as she must have been in everything but the decision she had just come to.

I knew, when I went down to her in the kitchen, and Gramp had left for work without a word to me, that she was going to kidnap me. That was her decision. She did not seem to care for her house anymore. She banked the fires, but left the rest, brass candlestick lamps, oil paintings, brass bed, rugs, books, her Doré

Bible. The stuff on our back sufficed.

"I'm glad you have your overcoat," she said, wrapping herself more tightly in the mink stole Uncle Tom had bought for her. We embarked on the ferry at the foot of Market Street for Atlantic City. "The sea," she informed me on the train, "gives me courage." She looked at it next morning as if it were hers.

This was the old Atlantic City, shuttered and wild in winter, and unbuttoned honky-tonk in summer. We were there in the shuttered wilderness. Our boardinghouse was Gothic Protestant, run by an ageless-looking female with a lipless face and calculating Yankee-blue eyes. A world of frost and boarded-up storefronts. My grandmother asked me if I remembered being born here. I said I did not, though I had been told I had.

When the sun was out she sat on a board in the sand and looked at the sea while I brought her things that reminded her of Galway. I placed them in her fine hands and she handled them as she might have had they been jewels. She had a thousand dollars she showed me, but since she wasn't Gramp, I never asked for a dime of it.

We masqueraded the funny, ugly place we had come to, so that it would have been any place, anywhere, in any country by the water.

178

Because of Gramp she called her sister in Westchester, instructing her to look in on him. Instead, the sister arrived the next day at our boardinghouse, and our lipless hostess with the calculating blue eyes brought her in, sure we owed her money.

The sister was a droopy widow who smoked cigarettes and carried her own cocktail mix about with her, stirring it with the tip of her little finger. She couldn't get over us being "down the shore" in winter.

"How'd you find me?" my grandmother asked her.

"A dignified woman and a little boy? You are not to be mistaken, Mary Ellen, for an *un*dignified woman."

"Well, we've got things to do, so you better get back home to Westchester," my grandmother told her, which she did, but not before getting drunk and blaming it on the sea air and me, saying I moved too much, and too fast, and made her head swim.

The next day being a Sunday, we quit the Gothic Protestant, after inquiring of the whereabouts of the nearest Roman Catholic church. Claiming ignorance of that sort of thing, the boardinghouse keeper closed her door on us, sure, I could see, that we were running away, running away from something else, whatever

179

that might be, probably the law. She hated Catholics, and she hated Jews, she hated blacks, and she didn't like Democrats. She thought the church we were looking for might be somewhere down there. She pointed us to a neighborhood where black and white had united because they couldn't do anything about it. Some of the houses looked as if they had been blown upside down by the wind and had been left to stay that way, their front doorstep where the chimney should have been. Last year's grass stood in dry yellow clumps in cluttered backyards. Thin cats dodged us. Dogs did too. There weren't many children, but when there were they appeared to be small grandmothers and grandfathers.

"This was probably where you were born," my grandmother told me. "Because your mother hadn't a penny, and — well, you know your father."

I saw Richard McQueegly before she did. He was standing on the boardwalk with his back to the sea, and with the heel of his left shoe hooked to the rail behind him. He wore no hat, and his hair was yellow as ever, and though he was without an overcoat he did have on a tie. One of his low-cut black shoes was missing a lace. It was hard to think of him getting down on his knees again to scrub a kitchen floor; I wondered if my grandmother wanted him to when she said, on catching sight of him, "There's Richard McQueegly, and, now that he's seen us, he's about to take off."

He didn't, though, but accepted my grandmother's invitation to join us at mass. Did he know of a church in the neighborhood? He led us to a worn wooden structure with a crooked wooden cross over its crooked door, and promised to have lunch with us following the service. He knew just the place, a fish restaurant, that was famous enough.

"I'm surprised you never heard of it."

He looked around, surprised himself at where he was, amongst the old, the sick, and the poor. A pimply boy priest told, in his seemingly endless homily, of how the world would be better with bigger families. "As if he knows anything about it, poor bugger," Richard whispered to me. During communion he took a coughing fit and fled.

"To think he missed a good meal," my grandmother said, afterwards. "Well, that's not all he's missed," she added. "He missed the boat."

Though poor and run-down, and hiding its head in the sand out of the wind, as it were, the ramshackle neighborhood where we heard mass appealed to us. Old grass wheeled in the hard gray sand and the sea talked to you all day long.

181

We found a room in a well-kept cottage owned and run by the widow of a clam-digger. We had breakfast with her, and sometimes supper, but that was about all, for the days were good and we spent all of them out of doors.

The widow wore the same taffeta dress the whole time we were there; it rustled and shrieked and made all sorts of noises and seemed to change color as well. "She brags so," my grandmother said of the widow, "and she has such a high opinion of herself that I think I'll sell her Brooklyn Bridge."

"Brooklyn Bridge? But Brooklyn Bridge isn't yours to sell."

"No, but my little house is," she said, pointing out a pink-and-green-painted dwelling that looked more fit for ants to live in than people.

"The sea's about to take it, and so's the sand, to say nothing of the wind."

It certainly looked crooked, and it was a good deal sunken.

"There used to be a cellar, but we lost it," she said. "Now there's nothing but downstairs, upstairs, and there soon won't be left that."

The floors buckled and the doors refused to close.

"Missus," she said to the clam-digger's widow that night after a supper of codfish soup with hardtack, "I'm going to give you the opportunity of your life. You know the little pink-and-green house?"

"I do. It's a pretty little house, though it needs propping up."

"It didn't when I was in it, and that was only today. It was as steady as the Rock of Gibraltar. I never felt so secure in my life. 'Stay here, and settle down for the rest of your days,' something told me. Only I can't. I need the money."

There was a ghastly shriek of taffeta as the widow pulled her chair close to my grandmother's.

"What're you asking, if you don't mind the inquiry? I'm in the way of bein' a real estate agent myself."

My grandmother moved her chair as far away from the clam-digger's widow as was possible, which wasn't even far, since the house was small and the rooms tiny.

"Why, what's got into you, Missus?" the clam-digger's widow asked. "You act like you was stung by a bee."

"I was, or thought I was," said my grandmother. " 'Stung,' is the word, Missus. If it had even crossed my mind that you were in real estate, I never would have brought the subject of my little house up. I'm keeping it."

"But why?"

"Because I would not trust myself to do

business with a real estate shark. I wouldn't have come in if I'd seen your shingle."

" 'Shingle?' Who has a shingle? My God, I'm a poor old clam-digger's widow, living alone by the sea, and you accuse me of I-don't-know-what."

"Well, I'm sorry," my grandmother said. "I'm mistaken. I thought you were interested."

"I am, but that doesn't make me out a shark."

"Five hundred dollars cash and not a penny less," said my grandmother.

"Done," said the clam-digger's widow.

Both appeared to feel they had gotten the better of the other. My grandmother was especially pleased with herself, confessing that she had not seen the property until this very day, but had bought it and forgotten about it, though never altogether, for a mere two hundred dollars from an indigent salesman, climbing steps as he traveled from door to door, a sickly man, who never wanted to see the little green-and-pink house again because of something bad that had happened to him in it, though he would not say what.

The little green-and-pink house on the beach, sea-worn and wind-battered, half sunk out of sight in the hungry sand, was a mystery to me, a sad, romantic place, but to my grandmother's practical mind it represented profit and nothing else.

We met Richard again, or else he was following us, one or the other, and the three of us started to go everywhere together, my grandmother paying the way. We would eat pickled pigs' feet on the beach while my grandmother stretched her stout legs in the sand and laughed at her foolishness.

Once her hair came down as she stood musing by the sea, and she let it blow around her shoulders, like a part of the white waves.

Lots of times the three of us walked our own way, or sat apart, and came back to one another refreshed and more anxious to talk together than ever.

She was free enough with her money with Richard, but she never gave anything like that to me, and she told me why. "I've never helped anyone by giving them money. On the contrary, I helped to ruin them. I wish you luck and the health to withstand poverty. I want to die believing in you. I know you'd leave me like a shot and go to your mother. That's why I've kidnapped you. It won't be for long, nor will I be. Here, give this five dollars to Richard when next you are alone with him."

After giving me the money she threw herself back on the sand and closed her eyes.

"You don't know it," she said, "but I'm home

185

again in Galway here. Primroses and skylarks. I met your grandfather in Liverpool, that greasy place. Do you know the lady on Bannister Street who sings so well? Sure you've heard her yourself. Sometimes, when the wind's my way, and she is at it, I tell meself I have never heard betther singin' nor so beautiful a voice. Yet it's only Bannister Street that hears her, and it's only one song that has stayed with her. 'I'll Take You Home Again, Kathleen.' Don't let it be that way with you, little missioner. Let the world be yer counthry."

I gave Richard the five dollars.

"I don't deserve it."

"Yes you do deserve it, Richard. My grandmother likes you. You give her pleasure. She — believes in you."

"She did," he replied, in his quick way, "but she doesn't anymore. Say," he asked, after a bit, "did you ever get the brass candlestick lamps I hocked on you? They've been on my mind."

"Yes, we got them back."

"I'm glad to hear that. They made the dining room."

"It was thoughtful of you to send us the pawn ticket, Richard."

He eyed me out of the corner of his little eyes, and scratched his brilliant yellow head, to make sure I wasn't putting him on, but he never asked me.

"It was, wasn't it?" he replied to that.

"Richard," I said, "have you ever been to jail?"

"Not often," was his light reply.

"Not often enough," my grandmother said, when I told her.

We came home with sand in our shoes. The last thing we saw was not the sea, nor the widow in her taffeta dress, but Richard McQueegly's bright head as he waved us good-bye. And it was good-bye.

# 22

She bullied her way through St. Ursula's school, where the vigor she had gained by the sea kept all at bay but Father Stienhagen, who was foolish enough to reproach her for my truancy.

"Business being business, Father, was I to let my bit of beach property get eaten away by high seas and shifting sands? I'll take your advice, Father, when it's helpful, practical, and profitable. But to suggest the boy kiss his inheritance good-bye for a mere few days of school is neither helpful, practical, nor profitable. I thought you were German, Father, but I find you are Latin. Not lazy, but lax. I'm richer since I last spoke to you, Father. That does not mean I'm rich. It means I'm no poorer. I have money in place of a weather-beaten, sinking house."

"I'm glad to hear it," said Father Stienhagen, thinking of a new chasuble, I guess, but he looked at me as if he'd like to swat me, which did not faze my grandmother a bit.

"Not everybody's going to like you," she told me, as she saw me to my class. The other nuns looked through me, but Sister Hildebrande looked at me.

"Well, Sister," my grandmother said, loud enough for all the tallow faces to hear, "he never looks at me the way he looks at you. He must like you. I have only just got done telling him that everybody doesn't like him. Do you, Sister?"

The note-taking little German faces were registering my grandmother's every word, and Hildebrande knew it. It was more to protect me than anything that she ignored my grandmother's question, and ordered me rather stiffly to my desk, which I was not to retain for long, though, happily, I did not know this at the time.

We were into arithmetic, a subject in which I was neither interested nor interesting, when Father Stienhagen came into the classroom and rubbed my slate clean, for he was about to promote me, and he could never have done so with evidence of my dismal math record before him in black and white.

"I'm putting you in the class ahead," he said. "It iss not adwanced enough for you here."

189

I looked at Hildebrande for what I felt was the last time.

My new teacher was a tall, bearded, bass-voiced nun, with hair on the backs of her hands, and she paralyzed me with fright. Hildebrande's drifting, dancing way was replaced by a marching man in a nun's habit, who smelled like a day laborer who never washed any more than his hands and face and neck.

There was nothing to do but run away.

When Franceline bent over me I nearly vomited, she stunk so, whereas Hildy smelled as I imagined the desert flowers she told me about did.

My grandmother was out of patience about the matter before I had finished my complaint. She saw Hildy as a softening influence on me best removed. A tougher teacher was more to her taste. Besides, she was preparing for Thanksgiving and ordered me out of her way whenever I brought the subject up.

The house was full again. Chauncey had returned, gun and all, and more crazy to do damage than ever. The male majority had a euphoric effect on my grandmother, not like the sea, but a drug, a drug to which she was openly addicted.

I had to leave.

Horatio would have, father or no father. Besides, Cissie had come back, with Elf after her, and had taken up again with my father. And though my grandmother knew all this well enough, she said nothing about it. She was like a pirate keeping her thieving ship on its course. I had no one to turn to. Even Hildy let me down, though not hard. "Do you ever pray?" Hildy asked me, the only person who ever had. I almost told her that the only time I came near to praying, outside of school, where they made you, was to think of Horatio, but I stopped myself just in time, though of course my mother would have understood.

One night I found Elf lying on the pavement outside Oyster's. I saw him from my grandmother's bedroom window. It wasn't late. He must only have been home an hour or so from his old job, which he had taken up again, having failed to find a footing out in Minnesota because of Cissie's restlessness.

I didn't recognize Elf so much as I did his tools, fallen out of his carpenter's box, and scattered across the ice-cold pavement. The light from Oyster's was dim enough, a dirty light, but it was enough to see Elf.

I put on my little overcoat, the one with the fur collar, in my excitement, skipping my "new skin," as my grandmother called the overcoat

191

she had bought for me, and ran across Twenty-fourth Street to Elf. As I fell down beside him on the pavement I lost all control of myself and I began to cry savagely. I suppose I should have taken Hildy's advice and prayed. Instead I cried like a baby. Then I remembered Shultzie wanting to get my mother's letter back to me from Hildy. Shultzie came to me as if he was there: "Get Elf up for me, little missioner. Don't let him lay there like a bum."

"Elf," I said, "Eif, Shultzie's here, he's come to take you back to Minnesota."

I hardly knew what I was saying, but whatever it was, it had a wonderful effect on Elf. There wasn't anything wrong with Elf but a broken heart. He wasn't even drunk. He was like a sailor in a foreign land, weakened with longing for his own kind. Anything was liable to tumble him over.

I got him up and carried his tools for him, but after that I did not know what else to do about him and I started to cry again. The lights of my grandmother's house looked as if they were going away from me, like a train pulling out of a station at night.

Then, for some reason or other, maybe because I felt people had failed me, I thought of Clancey, the dodgy little parrot. I thought at first that no one was home at the Bottles'.

192

"Come now. You can make it, Elf. Come now." I said. There was no light, but then there hardly ever was. It was the sort of house that is best entered by the back way. There are houses like that. Coal-black in the front, especially in winter, after night has fallen, as was the case now, but bright and friendly enough when you find the right way to go in.

"Why, what in the name of the nails of Christ are you carryin' in your pitiful, stumblin' way, little missioner?" Mrs. Bottle cried out when she saw us stumbling through her cabbage patch, forgetting, in her excitement, to tell Clancey, before she let us in, that they would talk about it later, what she always said to the little parrot, silent on his perch, when you came in on them unexpectedly.

"Little!" she hollered. "It's the missioner, and he's got the man from Minnesota with him."

After that, it was Minnesota this, and Minnesota that, so it was no wonder Clancey came under the spell of it, and burst out, to the astonishment of all of us, but Mrs. Bottle. *"Minnesota's the place!"*

"There," said Mrs. Bottle, "I always knew he had it in him."

"He's right, too," said Elf, standing up. "It's all wrong, me being here, while Anna and Peter and Father are out there in Minnesota."

*"Minnesota's the place!"* said Clancey, much to the relief of his mistress, who slapped herself and said she'd swear but she doubted he'd do it again, and so did I, but it was neat that he did.

Elf kissed me good-bye before he left. He smelled like wood shavings.

# 23

The subject of Cissie Networth — she was never to be called anything else in her short life — came up during Thanksgiving Day dinner, and Uncle Tom took it upon himself to appear to be more knowledgeable about her than all of us, which was probably true, though my father might have disputed it.

"Why," said Tom, "Cissie's gone back to operating on the telephone."

"She ought to be desthroyed," Chauncey said.

"I offered to marry her again," said Tom, paying no more attention to his brother than any of us did. "She said she'd take me, if I left her her freedom."

"Now there's a gem," said my grandmother, sucking a turkey bone.

"I said I'd make up my mind," said Tom, "and I have, and I will marry her, if she'll have me."

My grandfather put down his knife, always a sign of a declaration of war on his part.

"Well, I did, Jack," Uncle Tom said, defending himself stoutly, I thought. I felt on his side. Cissie needed somebody to take care of her. "You'd like her, Jack," Tom told my grandfather. "You all would." Here everybody put down his knife. I did too, because I liked the feel of the thing.

My father seemed puzzled. "I think you should show some consideration for me, Tom," he said. "Cissie and I are going together again."

Gramp looked fiercely around the floor for a place to spit, but didn't because it was Thanksgiving.

"If it wasn't for Thanksgiving," he told my father, "I'd get up from the table."

"Good for you, Jack," my grandmother laughingly congratulated him. "You're showing sense."

"You're damned," Gramp told her.

My grandmother took being damned lightly enough, which was more than Sister Hildebrande had done when I told her about it. Hildy had turned pale under her freckles.

"There's no such thing," she said. "If there is, it's none of our business."

"Like hell?"

"Where do you hear such talk?"

"Well, my grandmother said our baby brother would go to hell if he wasn't baptized."

196

"Your grandmother's a pirate."

She looked like a pirate today, in the black silk thing she had wound around her head to cook in. She sat amongst her drifting, dreamless men, and she loved them, but she looked down on them. I thought of my mother and left the table and went and wrapped myself in the green-and-red velvet folds of the parlor curtains, and was praying to the spirit of Horatio for courage, when my grandmother called me. Uncle Tom had brought eight bottles of wine and was telling everybody which color to drink with what, but nobody paid any attention to him.

After dinner the kitchen table was cleared for cards and I was sent out to call in Little Bottle. I took the back way out of the house instead of the front, thus arousing the interest of the company.

"Now what's he up to?" my father demanded of my grandmother, already settled in her chair by the kitchen stove with a book.

"Why, the quickest way to the Bottles' is out the back and up the alley," my grandmother informed him.

"Ah, he knows the ropes," cried Uncle Tom. "He'll be stealin' yer girls from you one of these days, Jim. Then where'll you be?"

The Bottles' kitchen was dark; so was the rest

of the downstairs. Clancey was on his perch by the side yard window. "Are you alone, Clancey?" I asked him. I put out my hand to him and he walked up my arm and nestled against my neck. "Clancey's cold," I said.

"Clancey?" Mrs. Bottle's voice came downstairs to us. "Are you talking to me?"

"It's me, Mrs. Bottle. I'm looking for Little. They want him for cards at my grandmother's."

"Little's over at Oyster's poisoning himself, leavin' me to do his piecework for him."

It was true. She sat in a tiny wallpapered room upstairs in the middle of a little bed surrounded by her son's piecework.

"It's me who does the work, and himself who gets the credit," she told me. "Go pull him out of Oyster's. If anybody c'n do it, it's you. I'll feel betther knowin' he's at your grandmother's playing cards, and not lushin' it down at Oyster's. Don't forget to put Clancey back on his perch on yer way out."

Little Bottle wasn't in the bar at Oyster's. He was in the back room and so was Cissie Networth, as everybody still called her. Sweeny made a dive for me as he had done before, but I evaded him.

"Here's my little son," Cissie said, when she saw me. "Come on over here and give your adopted mother a hug. All the same," she added, rocking me in her arms, "I'm marrying Tom McLaughlin. Tom'll give me a nice home in Foxchase, or somewhere, and my freedom as well."

"That," said Stephanie, "is quite an order. I'll believe it when I see it."

"Seein's believin'," everybody shouted.

"Happy Thanksgiving, sweetheart," Cissie whispered to me.

Then Stephanie stood up and sang "I'll Take You Home Again, Kathleen," and I stood listening to her. Afterwards Little Bottle took me by the hand and we left Oyster's.

"Now you mustn't listen to Cissie," Little Bottle told me as we crossed the dark, cold street. "Cissie talks. Cissie's soft. She should have stayed with Elf, but all the same she came back."

"Why did she?"

"Why, she said it was like bein' put out on an ocean not knowin' how to read a compass, Minnesota was. It scared her to go outside nights, and it scared her to think of what was outside when she was inside."

"What was it that was outside that she was afraid of?"

"Vastness," Little Bottle whispered, at the foot of my grandmother's steps and pointing up at the sky. "Vastness like that. Only here we got

199

houses, and out there there weren't nearly any." He gestured reverently at the multitude of brick houses around us. "Cissie didn't have nothin' but that," he said, pointing at the sky again, which was very black and made me appreciate my grandmother's house in a new way when we got inside.

My grandmother sat asleep in her rocker by the stove. The card players, hunched over their cards, scarcely noticed our entrance.

"You'll have to wait to get into the game now, Little Bottle," Chauncey told him irritably. "What took you so long?"

"Well," said Little Bottle, dancing around the table, and checking everybody's hand, "there were adieux to be said."

"How is Jenkins tonight?" Chauncey asked.

"I didn't notice," replied Bottle, bringing a chair in for himself from the dining room.

"Well," said Chauncey, "if they call me over for him tonight I'm not takin' this."

And here, to the consternation of all, Chauncey took his pistol out of his pocket and placed it beside him on the table.

"Tom," my father said, "will you take that thing away from him? It was you who got it back from the authorities for him. Why, I don't know. Unless you like to show you've got pull, Tom."

"I do," said Tom, "and I'm pullin' Cissie out from under you, me foine boyeen."

"Cissie's waiting for you, Tom," said Little.

"She ain't. She's waiting for me," said my father.

"Well, one thing," said Bottle, "she ain't waitin' for Elf."

"You say Jenkins is all right, Little?" Chauncey persisted.

"No, I said I didn't notice."

"I'm going over to see then," said Chauncey, and he stood up. "I'm worried about him. He could die, me not bein' there. Die with the delirium tremens. What a death. It's too horrible to contemplate."

"Now what in the name of God do you think Jenkins did when you were in Moymensing? Sit down," Tom told him.

"He took the pledge while I was in. And he visited me, which is more than I can say for some. And I won't sit down."

"Stand then, but button your fly," said Gramp.

Chauncey made as if to attend to himself, but stopped and silently apostrophized the ceiling instead, everybody watching him, which is what he most liked. The dead quiet woke my grandmother. "What are you doing standing, Chauncey? Sit down. Somebody take that pistol

201

away from him. It's all your fault he has it back, Tom."

"Well, give me the thing, Chauncey," said Tom. "It might as well be mine as yours, the blame they're putting on me because you have it."

"Take it," said Chauncey. "It's nothing to me. Nor is anything I own anything to me. What good's havin' anything if you're treated like a bum, anyway, a poor dispossessed, a leper, by your own? I'm leavin', Mary Ellen."

"Well, now," said Gramp, "it *is* Thanksgiving."

"I'll go with you, Tom."

"I must say," said my father, "that it's an interesting card game."

"Well, Jim," my grandmother laughed, "you know your Uncle Chauncey would rather misbehave than anything. He's always been that way. I remember —"

"You can't come with me, Chauncey," Tom told him, "Cissie's there. It'd be different if you could stand her, but you can't. Anyway, I'll be changing residences soon. Go find a room of your own and stop threatening your sister that you're leavin' her at your age, for God's sake."

"So I have no place to go. I'm to be thrown out into the street because of your whore."

"Come now," my grandmother quietly re-

202

marked. "You're not at Moymensing."

"Yes," said Tom, "and I'll knock you down, if you say it again."

"I don't blame you, Tom," said my father. "Shall we play?" he asked, as if to strangers he had met at an inn.

"Jim's right," said Little Bottle briskly, "play cards."

Little snatched up the deck and attempted an "accordion," but the cards seemed to have a mind of their own, and scattered across the table instead. I put my arms around him and held him, because I did not think he could sit up under the heavy bombardment of black looks from his feelow players, but would fall out of his chair to the floor in his embarrassment.

"That was some trick, Mr. Bottle," I said. It came out sarcastically, I guess, since my father laughed, but I didn't mean it that way, and my grandmother seemed to know I did not.

"Get Mr. Bottle a nice clean cup and saucer, and a nice cake plate besides, and we'll show him our mince pie," my grandmother told me. She handed me her book to put aside for her while she put on the coffee and fired the stove, then placed two pies in the oven and opened the side yard window a mite for air. When she closed the window you could begin to smell her pies.

"Sit down, Chauncey," she said, but he would not. He turned on his little feet in their high soft black leather shoes and left the kitchen — this time leaving his gun behind him.

"Hide that thing, Pop," my father said. "Throw it in the flour bin on the hutch behind you."

My grandfather took up Chauncey's pistol, turned in his chair without rising, and buried the thing in flour, all without making a sound.

"There, now, that's the end of that," said Tom. "None of you would have ever forgiven me if anything had happened with that thing tonight."

"Well, it's a good one, I must say," said my grandmother, her head thrown back in laughter. "Who would ever think to look into a flour bin for a gun? Not Chauncey. Chauncey doesn't know what a flour bin is."

"Ah yes I do," said Chauncey, before he was halfway back into the kitchen from the dark dining room, where he had been listening to us making fun of him, when all the time we thought he had gone to the rescue of Jenkins. He was raging, and said no more, but buried his hand in the flour and went out of the kitchen with what he had come back for, and left the house — with his gun.

204

"It's our own fault for playing with him," said Tom. "Chauncey can't be played with and never could. You remember, Mary Ellen —"

"Put out your pipe, Jack," my grandmother said, cutting open her pies, whose sweet aroma rid the place of all acrimony, the perfume of cooked raisins and mincemeat rose and filled the room like a sign of grace. Into the white coffee cups my grandmother poured the strong black coffee, and the white pitcher of cream and the sugar bowl were passed from hand to hand. "Let us remember the people who have nothing, and those who have everything but don't realize they have," my grandmother prayed.

I thought of my mother and my mission. I thought of Horatio and the roller skates Gramp had given me and I went to him and buried my face in his thick boyish head of hair. My father looked at me as if he thought I was going too far as usual. Little Bottle put his head down on the table and sobbed. "Come now, Bottle," Uncle Tom told him, "that's no way for an old soldier to act, for God's sake. Think of the future." At that the front doorbell rang and Tom said, with an uneasy laugh: "Speaking of the future, there it is now."

"Who in the name of God could that be?" my grandmother asked. "Don't tell me Chauncey locked himself out in his rage against us and has forgotten his key."

"Go answer the door for your grandmother," my father directed me.

Jenkins pushed me back into the vestibule when I opened the front door to him. "You certainly took your sweet time in answering," he told me, giving me another push, which I returned. "Push me, and I'll knock you down, you little troublemaker."

"You're the troublemaker," I said. "What is it you want? We don't like you here, you know."

"Why, of all the little uneducated little snot-noses. Go get your grandmother. Never mind. I'll go get her myself."

"You won't," I said. "She doesn't like you. Besides, we're having our pie and coffee, and it's quiet now without Chauncey."

Jenkins bent over and stuck his nose in my face. "Chauncey'll end your quiet for you for good and all, if you don't get your grandmother for me. Then where will you be, with your thick, fine drapes and all?" he asked, rubbing his hands in the curtains hanging in the parlor doorway. "Oh the airs of some people," he murmured to himself with great bitterness.

"The least you could do, Jenkins," my grandmother said, coming out in the hall to us, "was to have closed the front door. Come back into the kitchen, for God's sake."

"Thank you I will, Missus. I'm that stiff with the cold, Oyster's being the damp, drafty place it is."

"Here," my grandmother said to him, as he came into the kitchen, staring and sighing and rubbing his hands as if he'd never before experienced such a splendor of comfort, "here, take this cup of coffee. You make me cold just to look at you. What in the name of God are you prowlin' about for anyway?"

He sipped his coffee greedily without saying anything. He had sharp, black, unfeeling-looking eyes, like shoe buttons. All the same he was pitiful, even if he was mean and spiteful.

"I hate to say anything to spoil the peace and quiet of this house," he said.

"Well, then, don't," Gramp told him, without looking his way.

"Now, Jack, he has something to say," remonstrated my grandmother.

"I do and I don't," the impossible former schoolteacher explained himself, not explaining anything.

"Well, for God's sake, have a piece of my pie. You don't seem to have the energy to say anything through, man."

"Oh I couldn't eat pie, not *mince* pie, Ma'am. *Mince* pie'd run right through me."

Gramp, who loathed talk like that, about your insides, suddenly asked me if I still had my skates.

"Oh he does," cried Jenkins, lighting here, lighting there, like a moth, "I see him on them every day. Oh he's the very devil —"

My grandmother stepped aggressively up to him. "What's Chauncey up to over there? I assume he is over there? He can always be found at Oyster's after he has run away."

"Ah," Jenkins sang out. "So that's it. He's run away from you, is it? I thought it was something like that. He says none of you want him, and it's all Cissie Networth's fault."

Tom stood up; so did my father. "Now you stay right where you are, Jimmy," Uncle Tom told him. "It's time you grew up and recognized the fact that all the world is not your private playground." Uncle Tom could smile and at the same time not smile. That's what he did now, in his very one-sided exchange with Dad. Dad of course acted as if he was not quite sure what Uncle Tom was talking about. To make himself perfectly clear, Tom tapped the back of his hand on the front of my father's pants. "Cissie's mine, Jim," he said.

"She should never have come back," Little Bottle blubbered, raising his wet face to all of us. "She should have stayed where she was.

Vast though it was to her, she would have got used to it. She told me herself that she would have. It was the big sky out there that bothered her. The big sky and the few people."

"I bet she wishes she was back there tonight," Jenkins said in so low a voice that Tom asked him to repeat himself.

"You heard me well enough," Jenkins defiantly replied. "I said I bet she wishes she was back in Minnesota tonight."

"She doesn't at all," said Tom. "She came back for electric light and cars, and the solidity of houses made of brick. She wasn't meant to be a farmer's wife, for God's sake. She came back for the security and comfort I'll give her and that no one else will or can. I've had enough of your insinuations, Jenkins. Good-night. Good-night, Mary Ellen. The pie was so good. Everything was fine."

"Don't forget your wine, Tom," my grandmother told him.

"No," he said, "keep it for yourself. Good-night, Jack."

Gramp said nothing in the way of a reply, thinking more of his pipe, I guess, than he did of Tom. Before he left, Uncle Tom took Dad by the shoulders and turned him to himself. "Good-night, Jimmy." No one ever called Dad that, unless Tom did when he was little.

"Good-night, Tom."

That done, Tom turned brusquely on Jenkins. "Go on, go on!" he said to him. "It's Oyster's we're bound for, the two of us are, me for the last time, you not."

"If it's for Cissie you're crossing the street to Oyster's you better not."

"Why not?"

"Why she's gone's why not. And Chauncey after her with the same gun that nearly got me."

# 24

"Tom!" my grandmother called after her brother as he rushed out of the house, knocking Jenkins over in the bargain. "Wait for me. Let us go together. Don't go without me, Tom."

"Get your overcoat," she said to me, throwing her shawl over her head, a thing I had never seen her do before, not over her head. It made her look young and vigorous.

"The rest of you stay here," she said, needlessly, since Gramp and my father showed no signs of budging. Nor did Jenkins. "I don't mean you," she said to him.

"I don't think I can move for the moment, ma'am," Jenkins told her from the floor, where Tom had inadvertently put him.

"Stay there then, for all the good you'll be to anybody, or ever were."

"I'll have you know I taught school in Lancaster and was about to be made principal when —"

"God help us," my grandmother said, cutting him off.

She stepped by him with Little Bottle and me on our way to the front door.

The neighborhood was roused, as neighborhoods are, either by too great a stillness or a great noise. In the present instance there was no noise yet, but people were out and looked tense and expectant. There was a crowd across the street outside Oyster's saloon.

When Little Bottle emerged from the house in front of us his mother was waiting at the bottom of our steps to take him home and out of trouble's way. They turned down Bannister Street whispering to each other with their heads together, as children do, only their talk was not of mud pies or castles in Spain, you can be sure, but of horror bound to come. Besides, as he often told me, Little Bottle had been a good soldier, and was used to taking orders, as my grandmother seemed to have been born to give them.

She looked as she might have as a girl, wearing the shawl over her head and clutching it with her hands beneath her chin. When we joined the crowd outside Oyster's side entrance on Tasker Street no one recognized her, though it's true we kept apart out by the curb, where you could still smell the yeasty odor of beer from the saloon. Its liquor-soaked habitués reeled about the damp pavement trying to show concern despite their drunkenness, which disabled them. Uncle Tom moved amongst them like a man determined to make order out of disorder.

"They went through Ringold Street, and up Morris Street," Stephanie told Tom. Her big broad flat face bent over me. "You could catch up with them, little missioner, if you had your skates, couldn't you?"

"Whenever there's trouble," said my grandmother, snatching me out to the curb with her, and keeping her face averted from the others and her voice low, as she bent over me, "it's always this place. Now you know yourself that Cissie should never have come back. To think it was to a place like Oyster's that she came back to. I have half a mind to travel out to Minnesota one of these days, and take you with me, just to see what she left. Would you like that?"

I said I would, but she surprised me, as usual. It was as if the two of us were alone, and had nothing to do with those around us. Uncle Tom was too distracted to notice us. Trouble had separated Tom from us; it had separated all of us, my father, Gramp, instead of bringing us together, as it is supposed to do.

Every once in a while a trolley passed us going west, washing us down with its yellow lights. But it was the sky my grandmother attended to. She was all wrapped up in her own thoughts. "Is that what Cissie was afraid of out there, the sky, because it was so big? Why, it's big everywhere, only she never took the time to look up at it here, I guess."

"Surely somebody must have gone after them," Tom shouted.

"Sweeny did, Tom. Big Sweeny," Stephanie told him.

"Well, where is he?" Tom cried. "You people act as if we were in the Sahara Desert. They can't be farther away from us than calling distance." Here Tom commenced to call for Cissie and Chauncey at the top of his voice, which amused my grandmother. A trolley car passed us filled with people returning home from Thanksgiving Day dinners. They looked out the windows at us. I was sure they heard Uncle Tom calling Cissie, because they were all grins, too, like my grandmother. "Tom was always throwing his voice when we were little. He liked the sound of his own voice, still does."

"Cissie," Tom called, "Cissie."

"Listen to him, the fool. Well, he can't have her."

"He can't?"

"You know yourself, as well as I, that she belongs to Elf, don't you?"

"Oh yes."

"Sure you do," my grandmother said, lightly, approvingly, as the shots all of us were expecting rang out in the midnight air, Thanksgiving Day being just over.

# 25

"The shots couldn't have come from up Tasker Street. Cissie didn't go up Tasker Street. She went through Ringold Street, with Chauncey after her," said the man with his knees coming through his pants.

No one ran, some could barely walk. Larry Oyster alone stayed behind in his bar. The rest of us went first through Ringold Street, then out Morris Street. On Morris Street people were running from their houses, leaving their front doors open. Lights were on everywhere you looked.

There was a crowd around Cissie on the pavement in front of St. Ursula's when we got there. The lights of the church were lit, though not all, and the central doors were being pushed open.

"Chauncey will have gone," my grandmother told me, as Father Stienhagen appeared in the partially open doorway of the church and began giving last rites to Cissie even before he reached her. "Chauncey's hiding now," my grandmother said. "He'll be hiding where a cat could find him."

Someone came up behind us, murmuring into my grandmother's ear. It was Jenkins, bringing up the rear of the stragglers from Oyster's Bar.

"Chauncey's home, ma'am. He told me to come tell you, so you wouldn't worry for his safety. He's in his bed, sleeping like a child. Here's his gun. He told me to give it to you."

My grandmother took the gun and put it under her shawl. She told me later that it felt like a toy, only ice-cold.

"We thought," Jenkins whispered to her, though I heard every word he said, "that you ought to be home as well, ma'am, in case the crowd turns on your house. God knows what they would destroy, or steal, in their wrath against Chauncey."

"What has he done now?" my grandmother had the nerve to ask, when all around us people were talking about him, and cops asking where they were likely to find him.

"Why," said Jenkins, horrified at her air of insouciance, "he shot Cissie, ma'am, killed her, as he threatened to do."

"I don't know anything about that," my grandmother replied, brazening it out, her hands hidden beneath her shawl, the two of them bunched in fists under her chin. The gun was as plain as could be to me, at least the shape of it was, since she had slipped it into the deep pocket of her apron, which was so long that it touched the tops of her shoes.

Father Stienhagen offered to go with Cissie to the hospital in the ambulance, but Tom disputed that.

"I'm as good as married to her, was married to her, you might say, in the eyes of God, for God's sake," Tom told the priest, who had obviously left his ears at home in the rectory, for he looked at Tom with that smile that was no smile, and replied nothing.

"Sure he is. Sure you were, Tom," people were saying, but the tenders of the ambulance chose Father Stienhagen over Tom, who was left with his supporters, who turned out to be more of a nuisance than a help, to him, you could see.

The wooden-faced old nun who had signed me in at St. Ursula's shut and locked the church doors on us and turned out the light. There were only the street lamps now, and they were few and far between, and dim. Trolley cars went by infrequently. Overhead, the sky that Cissie had feared so out in Minnesota came down on us, enveloping the flèche of St. Ursula's in fog.

Stores that ordinarily would have cast some light were dark because of the holiday. It was only a matter of minutes before the pavements were white. The procession from Oyster's turned away from the church and went down Morris Street and through Ringold Street to the saloon, where Larry Oyster waited on his doorstep in his long white apron that reached to the tops of his polished black shoes. On his big arms were fastened deep-blue ladies' silk garters to keep his sleeves up and his white cuffs from getting dirty. His rings had diamonds in them, and so did his tiepin. A heavy gold watch chain crossed his gray, white-striped vest. His ambitions being political, he said at once to Uncle Tom, "I don't think there's anything we can do for him this time, Tommy." Uncle Tom did not seem to know who Larry was speaking about. "Or aren't you thinking about Chauncey, Tom?" Larry kindly asked him. "Oh yes," Tom replied in a breaking voice, "I'm thinking of him. Thanks for asking, Larry."

As Tom stood hesitating on the pavement outside the saloon, and all of us stood there, my grandmother on the edge of the crowd with me, Larry spoke up rather impatiently.

"Well, come on in, everybody."

219

As they hesitated, those who frequented the place, Larry wanted to know why.

"It don't seem right," the man with his knees coming through his pants spoke up. "Not without her, it don't. She was the youngest of the lot of us, and now we're not to see her again, ever again, as she was."

Larry lowered his meticulousy combed head for a respectful minute, thoughtfully. He reached for his apron and wiped his hands as he turned and went back into his saloon, leaving those who chose to do so to keep their vigil for Cissie outside the place rather than inside it.

Soon men who knew nothing of what had happened entered the bar and planted one foot on the rail and placed their orders as if everything was going as usual. But the peace and quiet, the business as usual, were deceptive, and no more meant to endure than the snow, which fell in little weightless pieces, but managed to cover, change, or disfigure everything it touched.

Even the "red devils," full of cops come to round up Chauncey, were changed. They looked bigger, for one thing. They looked so harmless in white, so innocent, that it was a surprise, as well as a reminder to all of us of what they really were, when Big Sweeny stepped out of one and pointed his long arm at my grandmother's house.

Cops mounted our front steps, a flash of light covered our house, flooding my grandmother's bedroom, I was sure, her parlor, her hard-fought-for things, the vestibule to the foot of the hat rack, in the downstairs hall, where I had seen her sit begging board from my father.

Others than those who knew about Cissie formed a curious crowd on the pavement across the street from my grandmother's house, the police blocking any closer acquaintance.

"Why, what did they do?" people asked, when my father and Gramp appeared in custody, in their hats and overcoats, and lastly Chauncey in his, and all three were taken off to the precinct for questioning.

"Holy cow!" Uncle Tom burst out at the sight before all of us. "They've taken everybody in the house they could find."

"I'm glad I gave them coffee and pie only a while ago," my grandmother told me, more amused than anything by the sight. "It will sustain them during the rigors of being questioned at the precinct."

Inside Oyster's men stood watching over the opaque decoration of the window on the Twenty-fourth Street side the goings and comings in number 1533, and talking about it.

The snow muffled all communication out-
doors, whitened shoulders, made people in the
distance look like exclamation points. All
the lights had been left burning in my grandmother's house by the cops. No wonder Uncle
Tom ran across Twenty-fourth Street and
howled when no one answered to him. He
thought he was locked out purposely, it
seemed, and looked as if he felt that nobody in
the world had any use for him now.

"Oh, Mary Ellen," he cried, throwing himself
on my grandmother when we crossed the street
to him. "I didn't know you for sure. What in
the name of God are you wearin', for God's
sake? So black and dark, I'd taken you for a
shawlie, and not yourself at all."

My grandmother threw off her shawl with a
proud laugh. "There," she said, tossing her
head, with the pirate band she had put on for
cooking, "is that better, Tomasheen?"

"You haven't called me by me old name in
years, Mary Ellen," Tom said. "Oh, Mary Ellen, you've heard Cissie's dead, haven't you?"

"She's not at all, Tom. Wait and see."

"But they treated her like dead, they carried
her off like dead, and Stienhagen went with her
as if to her grave."

"He's a fool," said my grandmother. "A senti-
mental fool. He liked it that way. It was divine

222

justice made to order."

"But he gave her the last rites."

"If it was up to Father Stienhagen, he'd give the last rites to every boy with a cut knee."

"Are you sure Cissie's all right, Mary Ellen? I'd send you on a trip home for a present, if I thought you were."

"Home, my God?" my grandmother burst out. "Where's that you mean to send me for a treat, Tom?"

"Why, Galway, Mary Ellen."

"Oh, Galway," replied my grandmother. "Would I know it if I saw it, Tom? Would any of us? What if our skylarks and primroses are gone, then what?"

"You're right, Mary Ellen, as usual."

Inside the house my grandmother put Chauncey's gun back into the flour bin, and when asked of its whereabouts she denied all knowledge of it. Dad and Gramp were driven home from the precinct in less than an hour, but Chauncey was detained despite all his swearing that he had spent Thanksgiving Day in bed because of a touch of the flu. "He asked us to ask his sister, Mary Ellen, if it wasn't true or not that he did," one cop told my grandmother, who looked down at her fine hands and said nothing.

"Gramp," I said, going to him in his back

room with its high-backed wooden bed, "what was it like in jail?" For he never would tell. "Gramp," I said, in the dark into his hairy ear, "I think you got a kick out of leaving Chauncey behind you in jail, did you?" But he still wouldn't tell.

My father gave me a wider berth than ever. I think his feelings had been hurt by just about everything, especially what Tom said to him about growing up.

Tom did not know what to make of my grandmother when she said, with more than the sound of relief in her voice, "Well, now, Cissie can go back to Elf."

"She can't," Tom burst out. "What are you afther saying, Mary Ellen? Are you trying to kill me now?"

"Either that, or she'll go into a convent. You'll never have her, Tom."

"A convent is it? Well, Mary Ellen, you don't know her."

"Nothing's going to be the same for that girl after being on that church pavement and being taken for dead. Everything's going to change for her. It may be the best thing that ever happened to her. She owes more than her life to Chauncey's poor marksmanship. She owes a new life to him."

"But not with me — or Jim?"

"You can forget Jim."

"Maybe I'll treat both of us to a trip home, Mary Ellen, and we'll take the boy here with us, primroses or no primroses. Why not? Why should things be the same anywhere, when we're not the same?"

"The best present I could get from you, Tom, would be for you not to use your political pull to get Chauncey out of jail."

"You can be heartless, Mary Ellen. You always could be. But I suppose you're right."

"Of course I'm right. Let him cool his heels."

# 26

The next morning the snow silenced everything outside and I felt I was alone in the house
even before I went downstairs. Cissie must have
died after all, and we were all in for it, all of us
to be ostracized by the neighbors and by the
parish of St. Ursula's. The Murderous
McLaughlins. I felt more concerned about
Gramp than anybody, really. Gramp wasn't at
all like the McLaughlin men, who were garroty
and garrulous. He wasn't at all gregarious. He
liked to be off alone by himself so much, like a
cat. I did not know what the Bottles would do
without us, especially Little Bottle, if we were
forced to move.

Of course Gramp often got up and left the
house in the morning and went to movies all
day long, beginning with *The Family*, on Market Street near City Hall, until it was time for
him to report for work. His bedroom door was
open, and there was a dent in his pillow, but
Grandpop wasn't in it. I looked out one of his

windows down the alley where I could see Mrs. Bottle shoveling a path through the snow around her cabbage patch. It looked to me as if she had put Clancey's perch in the other window so he could watch her work, for she was waving and talking to beat the band, and not to herself.

As I walked toward the stairs my heart missed a beat when I thought of Chauncey being sure to be in the lower hall looking up at me as he rolled on the balls of his little feet in their soft high black shoes. I didn't think I could go back to St. Ursula's now because of him. I knew I could not. Anyway, I didn't want to. The kids there would walk on me.

I was afraid to go out in the street. How would I ever get home again if I continued to feel like this? All those tallow faces, and me the only Irisher. Sister Hildebrande was in another country from me now at St. Ursula's. My new teacher was a horror. Not a day passed that she did not say she was going to skip me back a grade, but she didn't dare because of Stieny.

The two of them couldn't wait to tear my compositions apart, and me with them. "It's good for you," my grandmother said. "They'll make you tough. I hope not too tough," Stieny said my compo, "Out to Grandmother's Farm," was frightening. "This grandmother you write about is like no other in the class; she is a monster."

"She came out like that, Father. Anyway, I thought she was — funny."

" 'Funny?' You are the vun who iss 'funny.' "

There was nothing to do but go home. My father was never going to give up his mother. Besides, he liked the life too much down here to go home, where all was as bare as the inside of an American Indian's tent, except for our dining room stove. I missed that stove. I remembered my mother firing it, and the light it threw on the two of us, the morning I left for the Municipal Hospital, taking the knowledge along with me that I loved her better than anybody else in the world. A thrill went through me when I thought of arriving home in the snow. Then my grandmother called me from outside, and that was that.

She was shoveling snow off the pavement, and when I came to the parlor window she leaned on her shovel and looked up at me, her breath coming hard, I could see, and her rather thin lips bluer than usual, stretched across her false teeth, which looked greener than ever.

"She has no idea that her teeth are green, and false-looking as anything, especially this morning," I said to myself, as if I were the grown-up and she was the little boy.

It was a time before I noticed the sled tied to the silver-painted railing running up the side of the high brownstone steps of my grandmother's house, a brand-new sled. "Whose sled is it?" I asked my grandmother, after rushing to the front door. "Why is it tied to our railing? What's the tag on it say?"

"Look for yourself," my grandmother told me, and she returned to her shoveling, as I came down the steps in my shirtsleeves and read the ticket attached to the sled by a bright new piece of wire:

**This is the Property
of the Boy at 1533
South Twenty-fourth St.**

I looked up from the ticket at my grandmother. She was still shoveling, but when she saw me looking her way she stopped and said, "You know your foolish grandfather."

He was waiting for me around the corner. He hardly spoke the whole day, but watched me from the top of an embankment, tobacco smoke winging from his pipe, as I flew away from him down over the snow-covered gravel and across the buried railroad tracks, and back to him again.

"Your turn, Gramp."

The two of us went down together, through the flakes that had begun to fall again, calling sledders from all around, as well as those without sleds — kids in washtubs, or belly flopping on washboards, followed by their dogs, their Nellies, their Teds, till a red-bannered sky at the hushed end of the day said it was over and we trudged home between the lights of houses with suppers' smoke coming out of chimneys and night come on as we reached Twenty-third and Tasker, where Gramp dumped his pipe out in his hand and threw away the ashes as the light of his trolley approached in its journey north.

"Don't tell her," he said, what he always said, as he climbed aboard for work, meaning my grandmother.

"Well, my God," my grandmother said, when she saw me, "you made good use of it. Take off your wet things and sit you down by the stove and tell me of your day."

I did, but she fell asleep, or seemed to, but I don't think she did, really. I think the day I spent with Gramp made her sad, not jealous, but sad. She was resigned to her nature, which could never be his, could never lie in wait for me around the corner and take me away for a day's excursion which remains priceless.

To the little hedonist at the top of the embankment I owe a day's bliss. She was of a more soldierly nature and she knew it. A tear stole down her dark cheek, glistened as did the jet-black stones jiggling from her pierced earlobes.

She was relieved as I was when the doorbell rang.

"Who in the name of God can that be?" she asked, pleased all the same.

"Suppose Cissie died?" I said.

"Don't say such a thing, when you know it isn't true. It's too common for words, you saying such a thing. Sensational talk like that is so common. It comes from people whose lives are not only wanting in the necessities, sometimes, but, more important, it indicates a spiritual vacancy. Is this all the good you've gained from a day spent sledding with your foolish grandfather? Go answer the door."

# 27

Two of the strangest-looking people I ever saw stood at the front door, their dark clothes outlined by the night-sparkle of the white street behind them. One was dark, one was light, one was fat, one was lean, but both were women, and sisters, obviously, who had never done anything but they did it together. They stared at me together, they had agreed to come to the house together, and, now, much to my alarm, they prepared to leave together, having decided they'd been mistaken together.

"Oh, we've got the wrong house," said one, the fat one. "There's no *boy* in the house we want, Mae."

When they turned to go I almost reached out and grabbed them back, so anxious was I to hear their story. My grandmother felt the same.

"Come in, come in," she cried, pushing me aside, and reaching for the two women, who sighed relieved sighs at the sight of her, though I could see that they did not know one another to speak to.

"Go in and turn on the parlor lamps, all of them," my grandmother said to me in a low voice.

I did as she told me, while she herself switched on the light in the hall. Electricity wasn't all that new, but still not everybody had it.

"Give me your stuff, and let me hang it here. You must be bleeding from the cold, as my grandson was when he came home, after wearing his grandfather out sledding him the whole blessed day."

She drew a breath, waited, watched. She told me afterwards she knew they weren't Catholics, because there wasn't a forward hair to their bodies, and that it wouldn't surprise her if they didn't turn out to be Christian Scientists, or something dry like that.

"We've come to relieve you," said the thin one, in a pecking way, like a bird drinking.

"Let's make sure first, Mae, that she's the lady."

"Oh, she's his sister," said Mae. "There's no doubt in my mind."

"We're the Networth sisters, Cissie Networth's aunts, Mae and Tiny," said the fat one, Tiny, "and we came to relieve you of any worry you might feel about her."

233

"I wasn't worried," said my grandmother, steadfastly.

"No," said Mae, the birdy one, scrutinizing my grandmother in the light of the hallway, which was about the brightest in the house, if not in the neighborhood, "I can see you wouldn't be."

Did she think my grandmother was a pirate, too, I wondered, like Sister Hildebrande did?

"She's as clean as a whistle," said the fat one, "not a bullet touched her."

"Come into the parlor and sit down," my grandmother said, on her dignity, but not too sure of her moves, I could see. She was seldom enthusiastic about admitting anything. She still had not said she was Chauncey's sister, and it did not seem very likely to me that she would.

"We followed a crowd coming out of Oyster's across the street, and then heard about a girl who thought she was hurt," my grandmother told Cissie's aunts, getting around that one.

"It's her own fault for coming back from Minnesota," said Mae, the thin one.

"She likes company, and there was no company out there, so she came back," the fat one, the nice one, told us, but looking afraid her sister would switch her for it. "So many were saying she was dead. We hoped you wouldn't think she was."

234

My grandmother was quiet.

The fat one bunched up the clasp of her pocketbook and leaned over it and addressed my grandmother as if they were alone.

"All the same, she's drained. She's changed. The difference in her is dramatic. She's not the same. We both think so, don't we, Mae?"

"She'll be different when she comes out of the hospital," said Mae.

"Well, yes," the fat one said, "that's what we figure on."

"Well," my grandmother said, feeling she was on safe ground, "from all I hear she's a pretty girl."

"We've lost her," the fat one said, beginning to cry. She took a small handkerchief from her pocketbook and laid it on her lap, and continued to cry. Huge tears rolled down her face, and her nose ran too, but she did not use the handkerchief.

"We still don't know," said Mae, taking the handkerchief and handing it automatically to her big sister. "I mean, we're not sure," Mae explained to my grandmother.

"I wish you were right, Mae, but I'm afraid we are. Very sure," the fat one said, and she sobbed as she fixed the handkerchief on her lap again, without using it, and took up her pocketbook and leaned over it again as she addressed my grandmother with touching vehemence. "You know what she did this morning? She cut her hair. She snuck a pair of scissors and bobbed her hair to the nub. You say you heard she was pretty. Well, she isn't anymore. She doesn't want to be. She wants to go away somewhere, she says."

"If she died," Mae said, suddenly, "she'd still be ours, if you know what I mean. But, this way, even while she's talking to us, she's no longer there for us."

"You've died to her," said my grandmother.

"Why, yes, that's it exactly, Missus," the fat Miss Networth told my grandmother. "Has anything like that ever happened to you? You seem familiar with the circumstances."

"No one's ever wanted to leave me until now," my grandmother said, drawing me to her.

"She's killing us," Mae said. "We're all she has. Now to be told we don't exist for her is too hard to bear. I'll tell you, Missus, I wish your brother had killed her."

"Mae doesn't mean that. But you know your-self, Missus," the fat one said, "that to lose someone you want is terrible. To be spurned, rejected, cast out. What's worse?"

"She was handed to us as a baby, now we don't exist for her," Mae said, and she put her big hands on her face so you couldn't see a drop of it. "People are rotten to one another," she said in a muffled voice.

"She'll probably go into a convent," my grandmother ventured.

At that Mae's hands dropped in her lap as if they were iron and she smiled. "In that case," she said, "we would stop seeing her."

The idea of Cissie going into a convent pleased them. They stepped briskly out into the hall and took down their coats from the hat rack themselves and put them on. They had come to relieve us, but we had relieved them. Tiny, the fat one, was all smiles. Mae felt the velvet of our parlor curtains when she thought nobody would catch her at it, but I did, since my eyes were on a level with her great big hands.

Cops came to the door while they were there, thrilling the two of them, you could see. Mae forgot about our curtains and began to peck in the direction of one police officer and then the other. The cops were rather like the Networth sisters, at least outwardly. One was stout, the other lean, one was dark, the other light, though not white-haired, like Tiny, but blond. They said they were searching for a gun. My grandmother looked blank, of course, but not so Mae and Tiny.

"We're never done asking ourselves about it,"

said Tiny, sparkling under the allure of males in uniform. "After all, where there are bullets, there's got to be a gun."

"Bullets?" the slower of the two cops asked.

"We heard the old nun went around collecting them off the church steps. Souvenirs, I guess," said Tiny, getting frisky. "It's a wonder," she added, with a smile at my grandmother, who made sure not to return it, "that one didn't get the priest."

"Served him right if one did, the way he was so generous with his last rites with our niece, when there was nothing the matter with her," said Mae, speaking bitterly, which seemed to be the only way she knew how to speak.

"Say," the fat blond cop said, "she cut off all her hair at St. Agnes's. You know that? They say she was pretty before, too. Why she do it? She tell you?"

"She tells us everything, n'always did, didn't she, Mae?"

"Yes," Mae said, "she was a sweet kid. But she's gonna be a nun now, so that's the end of her."

"You his sister?" the dump fat cop with the blond hair rudely inquired of my grandmother. "He says he has a sister."

"We have a sister in Westchester," said my grandmother.

"You think she'd know anything about a weapon?"

"I haven't talked to her."

"Was she here for Thanksgiving?"

"Not that I know of."

Tiny Networth obviously would have liked to have left my grandmother's house with the police officers, but her sister Mae detained her, waiting until the "red devil" had pulled away from the front of the house before she spoke what was on her mind.

"Elf's married again," she said, looking down her long nose at my grandmother to see how she would take it.

"The Shultzes," said my grandmother, as she always did when that family was brought up, "are an outstanding family."

"Well, he's married again, anyway," Mae hammered away, bitterly, "and his heart is mended."

"Which is more than you can say for ours, Mae," her more jovial sister commented ruefully. "Cissie's torn up a lot of ground in her short passage on God's earth. I don't think she's done, neither. No I don't. Tell us, Missus," she said, giving her full attention to my grandmother, "do you think Cissie will stop tearing up hearts, once she puts herself away? I don't. It's just not her nature to let people alone. Look how she's made herself look like something the cat dragged in at St. Agnes's."

"I wonder why she chose the church steps?" my grandmother asked, not expecting an answer, apparently, and not getting one, for that matter. "I suppose," she quietly added, "she just couldn't go farther."

"Oh that. We don't know anything about that," said Mae.

She looked at my grandmother, and she looked as if she was suffering.

"I'm only glad I didn't see her there," she said, hoarsely. "It was bad enough the way she got herself to look this morning at St. Agnes's."

"Yes," said Tiny, "we never want to see her again, if she's going to look like that."

"All the same," said Mae, "it's hard. We would rather have her running around than this."

"Yet, you know something, Mae," said Tiny, forgetting us, obviously, "she seemed at times to be all right inside herself. In the depths of her being she might have been at ease."

"Oh," said my grandmother, with rare enthusiasm, but forthright as ever, "she's given up the world."

"Or been scared out of it!" Mae burst out.

We watched them go down the steps to the pavement and walk slowly through the snow sparkling under the street lamps. Above the houses stars looked sowed like golden seed about to blossom in precious fruit.

After the Networth sisters turned down Bannister Street no one else came by. There was noise from Oyster's, but no cars were out. I was thinking of my mother, and whether my father had gone home, scared, too, like Cissie, at the way things were turning out, when my grandmother asked me did I think it was too late to go to St. Agnes's hospital.

I fell asleep on the trolley car and hated to wake up, but all the same I felt the trip was worth it when I saw Cissie, especially since she reached for me when the two of us came up alongside her.

"She's excited," said the sister who had brought us to her. "You'd think she'd been shot at, the way she carries on. A miss is as good as a mile."

"What's it like out, little missioner?" Cissie asked me, and I told her.

"There's nothing wrong with me," she told my grandmother, but she really would rather have talked to me, so I told her I'd been sledding all day.

"That's nice," Cissie said, looking apologetically at my grandmother for talking to me, I guess. "You know," she said, because I could see she couldn't help it, talking to me, I mean,

"Elf and me were great sledders." She laughed, then cried, and touched her hair as if she missed what she had cut off this morning. "I used to belly flop on Elf," she said, "and, you know, it was just the softest thing. I was never afraid. I felt no harm could come to me when I was with Elf."

The sister came up on us, her white starched apron shining almost like the snow outside. It was time for us to leave. "Don't go," Cissie cried, taking gentle hold of me. "Stay and tell me what else you did. Elf and me used to sled down an embankment across the railroad tracks. It's probably all houses today."

"No it isn't, Cissie. That's where we were sledding today. Kids with their dogs, and all. Afterwards we walked home and the sky was red."

"It's black now," Cissie said, shivering and looking at the windows facing Broad Street.

"Now, there, you've had a good visit," the sister told the three of us. "And don't tell me you're afraid anymore, either, Cissie Networth," she added. "I heard you laughing just now. A laugh is the best remedy in the world. If you can laugh, you can forget your fears as well."

"No," Cissie said, brightly enough. "I'll never forget my fears. I'm going to have them till I die."

"I've never heard anyone so young talk to the extent you do, Cissie Networth, about death," said the sister, giving her a sedative in a glass of water. "There," she said, "drink that down."

She did, greedily, forgetting even to say good-bye to us, so great was her desire now to escape consciousness.

At the door of the ward my grandmother handed me her rosary beads and told me to run back with them to Cissie. "Tell her they're yours," she said, typically.

Cissie, already groggy, pushed me away, saying she meant never to take anything from anybody again. When I persisted, she struck me with her flailing arm, not meaning to, I'm sure, but it hurt all the same.

"Now, there," my grandmother said, outside on Broad Street, "my heart's broke," and she cried.

Cissie died the next day, and my father went home, packed and went home, without a word to me, but I could not follow him, even though my mission was over. I could not leave my grandmother, not now while her heart was breaking and breaking. I seemed to hear it, even though it made no sound, and feel it, though I would have been hard put to tell where. All I know was that after Cissie refused her rosaries her heart began to break, and it continued to break when Cissie died, because my grandmother could not get used to it, that she really had, that she was too young, that she wanted to go sledding again with Elf, even though he was married and they couldn't, of course.

I couldn't leave her with her heart breaking on me all day long and all night too.

Nothing would do but she must find primroses in the dead of winter for Cissie's wake and tracked me with her all over town to florist after florist and was on her way out of town to a great hothouse when she found a canny little black gardener turned shopkeeper on South Street and he gave her her primroses and her heart broke again, for they brought back Galway to her and skylarks overhead, so that she was almost loath to part with them, and when she did — again her heart broke.

The Shultzes came east for the funeral, and Shultzie lost no time before he leaned against our front doorbell.

"Wow! What a family. That uncle. Let me see his room again."

I did.

"Where're the bloodstains, the target he shot at?"

"There never were bloodstains, Shultzie."

"There weren't?"

"No, that was all your imagination."

"Well, anyway, Minnesota's mine. We own to as far as I can see, nearly. I'll tell you one thing, I'm not going to school anymore. I can't go to school, I'm a farmer now."

"Gee, Shultzie —"

"Come on out."

# 28

My grandmother must have heard us, for after Shultzie left, she thrashed around as if she had something urgent on her mind. She did. "You must always be ready to go. Make that your creed. To be able to pick up and go and be at home anywhere, though I hope not in jail, though many a great man has found himself in jail. Try not to be afraid of anything except ties. We'll talk about it tonight by the stove."

But we didn't. She nodded and dropped her book and asked time and again who was at the door when there was nobody. I went to look all the same. It was so quiet out, it was like "stille Nacht, heilige Nacht," when the Shultzes sang it around their kitchen table. It was as though a wreath had been laid on the neighborhood.

"I think I'll take my sled out for a bit," I told her, coming back into the kitchen. "Maybe I can get Mr. Bottle to come out."

"God help us" was all she said.

Little Bottle had got himself a steady job.

Clancey was moved into the parlor window, where Mrs. Bottle sat most of the day now, anxiously waiting her son's return from his employment, of which she was touchingly proud.

All three were in their parlor, sitting in the dark light of a kerosene stove, and they were glad enough that I had come by.

"How about a sled ride, Mr. Bottle?"

He was out in a jiffy, wearing a stocking for a cap, and we pulled one another up and down Bannister Street. "Come see my grandmother, Mr. Bottle. She's afraid every minute that I'm leaving her, now that my father's gone."

We found her asleep by the cold stove, her book lying open on the bricks at her feet.

"Why," she said to me, "I thought you'd gone for good."

Little fired the stove for her and tended the furnace as well. She had water on for tea when he came back upstairs from the cellar into the kitchen.

"There's a pie at the top of the cupboard, Little. Reach for it, won't you? We're low on pie. Remind me to tell you to get us some green apples tomorrow," she said to me, "and I'll make us some pies."

But she didn't. Instead, she gave me a nickel and told me to go out and call Reiner. "I don't

trust Fishman. Fishman would put me to bed."
Reiner, though he lived away up on Girard
Avenue, came down right away in his Ford.
"I'm afraid of Fishman," she told him. "Fish-
man would put me to bed."

"A good rest wouldn't hurt anybody, after
what you've been through."

He meant Chauncey.

"Besides," he added, seeing she was not going
to say anything about that, "your stairs are a
haul and a climb. Why not put your bed down
in the parlor?"

"My brass bed?" It was a question of taste
with her, of appearances, not health. "Why, it
would look awful. I'm not sick, am I, Doctor?"

"Your heart's a little funny. What heart isn't?
All the same, I'd keep in touch with Fishman."

Outside, Reiner offered to drive me home, even
though I had my schoolbooks with me. "Come,
I'll spin you home. You can come back yourself
by trolley." He looked up at my grandmother's
house. "She'll never know the difference."

"Tell me, Doctor Reiner, did my mother have
any more babies since I've been down here?"

"No she did not. There are enough of you as
it is. You sure you won't come along?"

"Would you drive me to school, Doctor
Reiner?"

"Sure, hop in."

He liked to drive. In those days driving a car was an adventure. We had no snow chains, so it was a "spin," I guess.

"Now I want to see you home soon," Reiner told me kindly, as he let me out of his machine in front of St. Ursula's. "After all, your father's home now. Isn't that what you came down here for?"

"Yes, but —"

"You're going to have a long, interesting life," he said, taking my face in his soft, strong hands. "Don't you want to start living it now? You mustn't stall."

"Stall, Doctor Reiner?"

"Stall, yes. Here, let me show you." He started up the Ford, went a bit along the curb, then faltered. The motor spurted, failed. "There, you see, I've stopped dead," Reiner instructed me. "You won't do that, will you? Promise."

"Oh no, Doctor Reiner," I shouted, since the whole thing was funny to me, "I'll keep going, no matter what. I promise."

I couldn't tell him about Horatio, but I thought of him, his spirit, all the same.

"Good-bye, Doctor Reiner. Thanks for the ride. It was swell."

Except for the side entrance, all the rest of St. Ursula's was closed and barred to me. The hum of teaching filled the cold halls, all the classroom doors were closed. Through the hum a nun's voice would rise like the voice of a hunter urging on his dogs to greater endeavor, or a class would shout responses with thrilling enthusiasm.

Not for the first time did I feel cut off from that sort of group effort, sure in my heart that it was not my way now to learn things, nor ever would be. Besides, there was the great thing of discipline, brilliantly and assiduously observed at St. Ursula's. It would have been silly for me to have burst into class with the excuse that my grandmother was unwell and that I had spent a good part of the morning getting a doctor for her. I would have been laughed at. Where was my father, to do that sort of thing? Just like the Murderous McLaughlins to do everything backwards.

So, instead, I knocked on the principal's office door, expecting my old adversary, the wooden-faced old nun, to tell me to come in, and not Hildy, sweet Hildy, whose freckles had all now faded for good.

"Well," she said, from behind the old wooden-faced nun's great desk, "what are you up to? Come in, come in. I won't bite you."

"Oh, Hildy," I cried, jumping protocol in my relief at the pretty-faced sight of her, and feeling alone with her at St. Ursula's, deliciously alone.

It was worth being late. I dropped my books on the floor and rushed to her. "My grandmother's dying, Hildy. She's afraid. She's different. Oh, Hildy, she's not a pirate anymore."

The great little nun put her arms around me and held me, reassuring me that death wasn't so bad, and that, anyway, it wasn't our business, which was to live and be brave when we have to.

"Hildy, what are you doing in here? Did you do something wrong? Are they punishing you?"

"They may be," she laughed. "I'm principal now, but it won't be for long."

There was a peremptory knock on the door. Hildy said, "Come in." In attempting to do so, the caller fell over my books, not altogether to the floor, but close enough to it to make him furious. Hildy stood up at her desk. Well, I thought, now that she's principal, he can't yell at her the way he used to do, but all the same he did.

"Father Stienhagen," said Hildy, "I'm so sorry. I'm forever leaving books in the wrong place. It's an old habit of mine. Are you hurt? Here, sit down. You can go now," she said to me, hoping I would escape the pastor's wrath, but no such luck.

"Vhat in the name of Gott iss wrong mit this dumkopf now?"

"I'm late, Father Stienhagen. My grandmother's sick. I had to call the doctor for her."

"That vas no reason to vait until he had attended to her so that he could drive you to school, vas it? I saw you getting out of his car. You probably vaited all morning for him."

"I didn't, really," I said, edging toward the office door.

He let me go.

"Vell, Sister Hildebrande, you'll soon be quit of us at last." I heard him say as I was about to close the door. "They tell me you haf a brilliant mind, but I confess I haf yet to see evidence of it. 'If she iss zo brilliant, let her be principal,' I said. But I do not find you much of a principal. Less than average, I should say. Perhaps somvhere else you vill shine. I haf been told you vill by those who should know."

"If you'll excuse me, Father, I must run with this permission to enter class for that late boy who was just here."

"Dumkopf. Now somebody will tell me he is brilliant someday. A murderous McLaughlin. Vell, I von't belief it. You, maybe; him, neffer."

Hildy came running up the hall after me with the necessary slip of paper, and my books.

"Oh, Hildy, where are they sending you?"

"School," she replied, ecstatic. "Back to learn things."

"School? And you're glad? Oh, I know, they're punishing you, and you're sad, really, but you're hiding it."

"No, I'm glad and I want you to be glad for me, little missioner."

"Don't you call me that comical name, Sister."

"Why not? It's as good as another. Besides, it suits you. I'll remember you by it. Will you remember me?"

"I'll remember you used to have freckles, Hildy, and now you don't have them anymore."

I don't think Sister Hildebrande liked me saying that, or if she did, she did not think she should show it. Her brown eyes looked bright, tear-lit, but that's silly, nuns don't cry.

# 29

Uncle Tom was at my grandmother's when I got
back from school. He looked morose and use-
less to himself. He sighed, and sighed and gave
me a half dollar, then forgot himself and
gave me another. My grandmother witnessed
the transaction and smiled. It was her only
smile that I saw that day. She sat by the stove
and rocked, but otherwise she did not stir.
Both she and Tom appeared to be hampered in
their conversation by Mrs. Bottle, who had
been sent by Little to see that we did not want,
but she overdid everything. She made the kitchen too hot, and the dust fly, and caused us to
pay more heed to the time than we wanted
to, or saw fit, for she insisted she must be sure to
be home for Little when he arrived from his
job, of which she was excessively proud, according to Uncle Tom.

"What's he do?" he asked airily, though he
knew well enough that Little Bottle was a
tailor.

Mrs. Bottle did not leave without promising to be back later on in the evening.

"Don't trouble yourself," Tom told her, wanting to be rid of her, "there's nothing you can do that I can't do as well. Now go home and have yourself a good night's sleep. I'm sure you deserve it."

He wound up being very angry with poor Mrs. Bottle, who you could see was wondering what in the world she had done to annoy him. However, the thought of Little Bottle coming and going just like everybody else in the world, and like everybody should, revived her good feelings, which were never far from her anyway, and she said good-night, promising not to return until morning.

"Well, Mary Ellen," said Tom, opening one of the bottles of wine he had brought for Thanksgiving, and which were lined up on the hutch, glowing night and day, even in the midnight dark, I was sure. I got us fancy glasses from the china closet in the dining room and washed and dried them until they sparkled, because, ordinarily, my grandmother would have told me to do it, but tonight she seemed to me to be beyond remembering things like that, unlike Uncle Tom, who was all for straightening things out, and getting back to normal. When he held up his glass and toasted the future, my grandmother

255

shuddered, but sipped her wine without further comment.

"There's nothing wrong with you, Mary Ellen, that a little trip home wouldn't cure," Tom told her.

"Home, Tom? No, this is home. What about Jack?"

"Of course it's home," said Tom. "And I mean you to come back to Jack. But, Mary Ellen, there's just so much a body can take. That's what is wrong with you. Here, have another sip of burgundy."

She did not cover her glass with the palm of her hand as she might have done at other times, but watched the bright liquid flow until it could go no more, then drank it.

"Run get me a blanket from my bed and put it over me," she said to me. "I'll sleep this night by the stove."

"But the stove's bound to go out, Mary Ellen," Tom told her, much concerned, "and you'll get no rest."

"Mrs. Bottle will be in early and will see to the stove. She's a good soul."

"Mary Ellen," Tom persisted, when I came down with the blanket from her bed and put it around her, "I hate to hear you so resigned."

"Unlace me shoes," she said to me, her English changing and reverting to a brogue, as it sometimes did, though not often.

"Mary Ellen," Tom said, "it's not our fault, about Cissie."

"Be that as it may, Tom, it happened."

"Yes, but there's no reason to dwell on it."

"No, but there's no escaping it, either."

"Let me take you away. Galway's not so far. Within a week of today you'd find yerself back in old places, masthered by the memory of old times."

"We'll talk about it, Tom."

He stood before her, overcome by remorse, by all that he had done, and all that he had failed to do. "I've failed you dreadfully, Mary Ellen," he admitted, looking as if he could not bear to hear the words, let alone say them. "Help me undo what I've done a little. Help me, Mary Ellen. On my knees, I beg you."

He made an awful noise getting down on them, but he meant it, I guess. He looked sincere enough, but that didn't mean he wouldn't do everything all over again. Too, it was hard, impossible, really, for Uncle Tom to look repentent with that mouthful of gold always grinning at you, no matter how he felt, really.

The next day Little Bottle and Jenkins dismantled her brass bed and carried it downstairs and set it up before the parlor windows. It was my heart that began to break now, especially when I saw how she had been waiting all day for me to come in from school. I don't know why she waited, really, and obviously so hard, because I was no sooner in the house than she fell asleep.

At night I would get up and say, "I'm going home, Horatio," waking her, but not meaning to.

"Is that you up?" she would ask.

The next day I would be back in school, or running for Fishman, and he would come and sit in his hat and overcoat, dropping stuff all around him, pills, stethoscope, everything, and scarcely bothering to pick some of the things up, the way he had done when tending to Shultzie.

"Why don't you go down the shore?" Fishman told my grandmother, in his erratic way, letting fly letters out of his pocket, a lot he cared. "You told me you had a little property down there. I'm sure you like the sea. Sure you do. I'd go with you, if I didn't have to support six children and a constantly pregnant wife. All this trouble's why you took to bed. Not that I believe half of it. The Irish are a tough race. They can't help it if they're crazy. They need the sea, they're seafaring people, they need its calming effect. You know who's boss when you

258

look at the sea. Who told you to bring your bed downstairs? There's nothing wrong with you that a little trip won't cure. And don't call Reiner. All Doctor Reiner cares about are flowers and cars."

That night my grandmother told Uncle Tom that we would go with him to find their old Galway. Instead of being elated, Tom looked as if he was wondering what he had let himself in for. "I knew you'd see my way, Mary Ellen," he told her in a dismal tone of voice that made my grandmother laugh at him derisively. When the doorbell rang they looked rather relieved, as if they secretly hoped that it would be something that would make our projected trip impossible.

"Who in the name of God do you suppose it could be, Mary Ellen? It can only be about Chauncey, a sinking feeling tells me."

"Shall I answer?" I asked, the only time I got the distinct impression that my grandmother would rather not have had me there, not at the moment, anyway.

"There for a minute I was half counting on the trip," she admitted. "Now it's all over, like so many other things I counted on. Yes, answer it," she told me.

"No don't!" cried Tom. "I mean," he explained himself, "don't be in such a hurry."

I sat down, swallowing my curiosity.

We probably would not have answered it had it not rung again — and again and again.

"It couldn't be the Bottles, they come in and out the back kitchen," said my grandmother. I knew somehow she was going to take her annoyance with the way things were turning out on me and she did. "What are you sitting there for, like it was music to you, when you know the house has been ripped wide open to all comers, and we're as common as dirt to a neighborhood now that used to respect us and acknowledge us as decent people, but now we've fallen, and everything has fallen on us. Go answer the door, but hold your head up."

I held my head up, but with no success, for it was the sister from Westchester, who never liked me, and blamed having to wait in the cold on the front steps all on me.

"It's you, is it? Did it take you so long because you knew it was me, and hid out in the hopes I'd go away?"

"No I didn't know it was you. How could I, when I was in the kitchen?"

"No fresh talk, please, or you'll have me head swimmin' even before I get in there," she said, plowing by me like a peddler, with a great rag bag that sounded like it was glass she was selling.

As soon as she got into the kitchen she began

giving me orders. "Go into the back kitchen and run me some cold water. Your water's colder out there, Mary Ellen."

When I came back with her cold water she was crying, so I guessed they had told her of the trip. "Running away," she said. "That's what it amounts to. Leaving him." She was worse after she had mixed herself a drink with the ingredients she always carried about with her in her sack. "We would never have left home, if it hadn't been for you, Mary Ellen. We'd all be there still, if it hadn't been for your ambitions you used to call dreams. I say drat your dreams. Look where they've brought us."

"We thought you might come along with us," my grandmother told her, making Uncle Tom writhe.

"How long do you intend to stay?"

"We'll be two weeks away, if that, counting everything," said Tom.

There was a terrible jostle of bottles as she drew her sack protectively to her, thinking of it first, her supply, of its running low, or running out, its loss or breakage, or evaporation even, and of herself only afterward, the idea of travel being dreadful to her.

"I don't see why you're goin'," she said. "Two weeks. It hardly seems worth it."

"We'll only take the clothes on our backs,

nearly," Tom told her, warming up to the trip himself after going through an obvious period of coolness about it. "We travel light, Lillie," he added, with a golden grin at her and her sack. "Not like you."

"Well, I thought I'd stay the night commiserating," said Lillie, "but I see I've run into high fliers pushed by their dreams again. You never cared who you broke, or who you hurt, Mary Ellen. You haven't changed."

"I hoped I had — for the better," my grandmother dryly replied.

"Even now that strive of yours is with you, your old strive, Mary Ellen. Don't you think it's time you gave in, and gave up? I do. Chauncey would not be in this counthry if it hadn't been for you and your drivin' dreams, to say nothing of being in jail."

"You're perfectly right, Lillie," said my grandmother. "It's all my fault."

"It's just as well, Lillie," said Tom, stepping between the two women. "You stay home and do what suits you."

"I'll worry," said Lillie.

"Well, you always did, and it suits you," said Tom, whose good humor had been restored by Lillie. Even my grandmother was smiling, despite the mean things her sister said about her. They really liked one another a lot, the

262

McLaughlins did, even though nearly every-body else called them the Murderous McLaughlins. A lot they cared.

"I followed you once, to this counthry," said Lillie. "Don't expect me to go trailin' afther you again, if anything happens. Be a good boy, and get me some more cold wather from the back kitchen," she told me, adding, even before I closed the door out there on them, that I made her head swim. "He moves too much, and too often," she said. "I could never put up with him for any length of time, and, oh Jesus, certainly not on a rockin' boat crossin' the Atlantic in the icy turbulence of winther. He's not like Jim at all. Now Jim's solid. He must take afther his mother, though I have never met her and don't want to, not if she was to make my head swim, too."

After she mixed herself another drink with the cold water I brought her from the back kitchen and the concoctions she had herself brought from Westchester, she eyed me mis-chievously, though this was not easy for her to do, since the downward set of her face, sagged and puffy, was best fitted to express lugubrious-ness.

"And you heard everything I said, didn't you?" she asked me.

"Yes I did," I replied.

"What do you think of it?" she asked.

As I hesitated, looking to my grandmother for permission to speak up and defend my mother, she addressed me again, teasing me.

"Come on," she said, "I know you have a temper, redhead."

"If I do," I said, "I'm not proud of it. Only stupid people are proud of their tempers. Besides, it's not my mother, or me, that makes your head swim —"

"All right now," said Uncle Tom, and he was right to squash me.

I had not looked at her during my angry tirade against her, but at my grandmother, who had lowered her head, to give me mine, as it were. When Tom spoke, and I did look at old Aunt Lillie from Westchester, she looked stunned, mortified, she looked hurt beyond anything at what I had said, and I hadn't half said all I had in mind, either.

"No drinker likes to be moved from his habitual source," Tom said of her, after she left, but she had cast a pall over our departure just the same, bringing Chauncey close as she had, when he was close enough as it was.

Flocks of gulls met us as we embarked on a dirty Irish freighter in Brooklyn and followed us for miles out of the Narrows, shrieking and swooping down close to the deck, so that we had to duck our heads, they were so numerous and winter-hungry.

Pursued by thoughts of what Chauncey had done, where Chauncey was, what Chauncey would do without them, my grandmother and Uncle Tom were as dominated by their brother as if he had them chained to him, and they could hear, as well as nearly feel, his every cry, heartfelt enough, since he had always depended on them, and always expected to. Even I felt we were running away from Chauncey, from all my grandmother and Uncle Tom had helped him to do, in a way, and the shrieking gulls, following us for miles, seemed to tell us we were.

"It does no good, Tom," my grandmother said. "I might as well have stayed where I was. There's nothing worse than a traveler who keeps looking backwards, and that's what we're doing."

"I'm not, Mary Ellen. Don't say such a thing. You're not either."

But on the train to New York he had remained away from us as much as he could, and he seemed to hate it that he must be with us during the cab ride to the Brooklyn docks, where we had arrived in falling snow that hid the skyline of New York, but threw my grandmother back all the same to when she entered the country with Chauncey on her back, for they had left Lillian behind, then as now, with a mother and father they were not to see again, except now they might, but only in their graves, if we happened to find them.

The only other passengers on the freighter looked as driven and haunted as we felt, a dentist and his wife, going back to Limerick, whence they had come these many years, to live on the fortune amassed in Boston from pulling teeth.

Mrs. O'Roarke cried all the time, saying she was really very happy. "I am, really, very happy, and — grateful."

We took our meals with the officers of the ship, all Irishmen, who looked on us, my grandmother said, as if we were Zulus. Almost at every meal the captain said, "So you are all going to make your homes in Ireland, aye?" It did no good to tell him we were returning to the States practically on the next boat. "Well, I wonder how you'll do?" he would say, regarding us in a sea-blinded-looking way. The other officers never said a word, but ate like police dogs. The cargo was American canned goods of all sorts, and that was what we were served, morning, noon, and night.

Mrs. O'Roarke used to point to the sea, when the dentist wasn't around, and say to my grandmother, "See that, I'd like to throw myself into it."

O'Roarke's beard and moustache met and formed a cruller of hair, disgusting to think of, but worse to see, especially at meals, where, when he looked my way I expected him to say, "Open, please."

Mrs. O'Roarke wore a watch on her dress.

"Without them, I'd go crazy," my grandmother said, speaking of our fellow passengers.

All the same Chauncey was seldom out of her mind. "And there's no running away from it, much as we may try," she said to me, meaning, I took it, what had happened to Cissie Networth because of him, and Tom, and Dad, too, I guess, or maybe even all the McLaughlins.

I wandered over the greasy deck, staring at the sea, and wondering, sometimes, if we were sailing over sunken cities. The taciturnity of the crew struck me like a slap in the face, but the captain took me up on the bridge with him. By this time I was wary of the gulls that had swarmed the freighter in Brooklyn, following us as they had for miles past the fog-obscured Statue of Liberty out of the Narrows, so I asked the captain about them.

"We meet birds, but not many. It depends on where we are. There are some that wander far from land, but not many. They are like people in that," he told me, looking at me with his milk-blue eyes that made me ponder how he could see through them, they looked so opaque. "I wouldn't settle for Ireland, if I were you, though," he whispered.

There was a shower bath in the cabin I shared with Uncle Tom, a first for both of us, my grandmother refused to use hers. "I miss my tub," she said, looking backwards, as we all did.

But I liked being on a boat, and when the rest were seasick, or hung over, for my Uncle Tom and O'Roarke did nothing but drink all day and much of the night in the salon, I would huddle by the warm stacks on deck out of the wind and write letters to my mother that never got sent, and imagine her answering me with letters I never got, congratulating me on the success of my mission, since she had Dad back again, though not me. One thing, as Shultzie liked to say, I sure was paying for it, crossing the Atlantic in the dead of winter, having given up the world for life in a cloud, because that's what we sailed through, and met in Galway, sunlessness and wet.

At mealtimes Mrs. O'Roarke pushed plates of food from her, while O'Roarke looked to me as if he would get up any minute and knock her off her chair.

My grandmother claimed that the O'Roarkes were childless, though they omitted to say as much. "You don't have to ask, for fear it will be a matter of stillborn babies or worse," my grandmother said. "It's plain the woman's never had a happy day with that man, and dreads where he'll take her now, and what he will do with her when he gets her there."

They were like two knives in the same holder, my grandmother said.

When questioned by his sister about his drinking buddy on board, Uncle Tom replied that O'Roarke talked of nothing but sports and Boston politics, though preferring silence to either, and oblivion in drink above all. "I think he's murdered someone," said Tom, "or the two of them have, or have helped, or been connected with a crime they are fleeing from, but are reminded of, every time they look into each other's eyes, which is seldom enough, God knows, even when they're alone, or especially then, for he swears he does not touch her."

"They're enough like us to make me try and talk to her," said my grandmother, and she tried, but it did no good. Mrs. O'Roarke ran about the deck as if she meant to work up enough momentum to cast herself into the dark green oily-looking waves we were slicing. "The motion of the boat is not enough for her; what she really wants is for it to go *down*," my grandmother said. "She seems to know, as well as I do, that this is no voyage, but only a way of keeping ourselves in motion, for fear of what we will think about if we stay still. At night I wonder what my last thoughts would be, if we capsized, and joined the multitude who have drowned before us."

I listened, in awe of her, to such talk, seeing pictures, but feeling little, really, certainly not fright. I don't think she did either. It was as if she were singing, but in a dirgelike way, keening, perhaps, and she never looked better. Her face streaming wet, not with tears, but with the sea, our mother; kissed wet, the two of us were, by her, my grandmother said.

Against this world of sky and water, of cloud and wind, of the whistling, and the wet slap of waves on deck, our problems melted, only to rise before us with the land, as though Cissie Networth was a growing thing now, reinvigorated by death, blooming before us after her stay in the earth as plants do. The rose, the tulip, the jacinth.

"I think she gave us up with ease. I think she died happy," my grandmother would say of Cissie, adding that if she were told to count loved ones, Cissie would be first, me next. "Cissie Networth taught me how to face dying, and you have taught me how to live with hope again."

At our landing Mrs. O'Roarke refused to leave the gangplank, holding on to what ever came to hand. In his anger and perplexity with her, O'Roarke saw fit to tear off the watch she always wore on the fronts of her dresses and toss it away into the water of Cork Harbor, as if to say that she would have no more need of knowing the time now.

"You sonofabitch!" O'Roarke said to her in front of us.

It seemed very cruel, and determined our attitude about everything all the time we were in Galway, searching for houses, schools, searching for graves.

It was cold and damp and close without any wind, and Uncle Tom made things all the more close by never letting us alone except at bedtime, and then only reluctantly.

Galway Bay was hidden by fog for me the whole time I was there, and nature made Uncle Tom restless, he was forever suggesting that we go somewhere else.

"If only he'd go without us, but no," said my grandmother. "Since he touched foot in Galway he seems to be afraid to go anywhere without me for fear he won't find his way back again, and that we'll be separated for good."

271

We asked a bus driver to take us to Drone, in Galway, and the man, a young fellow, a regular know-it-all, said he had never heard of Drone, and that as far as he was concerned, it did not exist. There was only one other passenger on the bus besides ourselves, a clean old lady with a live hen in a basket. Tom was in tears, but my grandmother withdrew into herself, letting him fight stupidity and bigotry for what it was worth, for the driver said he was sick and tired of people coming back to the country wanting it to be the same as when they left it; that as far as he knew may have been a hundred years ago.

"No, I was born there, we both were, me and me sister Mary Ellen," said poor Tom, adding, pitifully, that "it was no hundred years ago, neither."

At this the old woman came forward with her hen in a basket.

"There was a Drone near Athenry," she said, "but it faded as people like yourselves left. It's nothing but stones today. There it is now," she said, pointing out of the windows of the bus at a pile of stones, where our driver was happy to let us off.

Graves there were, and a few houses as well, but they were not the right ones, the ones Uncle Tom and my grandmother remembered. The old buildings were all fallen down. Even the trees were new. Except for the flow of hills in the distance nothing was the same, my grandmother said. But I could see she liked being here all the same, for her eyes never stopped taking in the land. Elation took the place of disappointment. The dead were dismissed, though not forgotten, for they were everywhere underground.

"You are in an old country," she told me. "Look," she said, picking up a stone from the ground and holding it for me to see in her fine, freckled hands, "not a wrinkle. That's time's work."

# 30

Then Uncle Tom remembered the fields of
Athenry and nothing would do but that we
must go there, but it was misted over when
we did, and the animals were all in shelter
from the cold. It did no good for my grandmother to tell Tom we were in December.
He wanted summer now that we were
here. He wanted youth and the way things used
to be. He wanted a schoolhouse that was no
longer standing, and graves he had not seen in
the first place.

So we went back to West Galway again, as if
we were being chased, it's true, but we were
consoled by people who came up to us, wanting to talk, not by people wanting to know
where we had come from, though that was part
of it, but people who mostly wanted to talk.

The preliminaries of conversation were ignored, and we were into a subject before we
knew it. This happened to us on a road outside
Oughterard, which we found to be a dead end,

and made Uncle Tom ask why it had been built in the first place, leading, as it seemed to us, to nowhere.

We had come so far on foot for nothing, we thought, since the route did not lead to the lake as we had hoped it would, and were in the process of turning desolately back to town when a nimble-footed man appeared and made a beeline for us. This sort of thing had happened to us before and was nearly always a pleasant relief from our worries of where to stay and where to go, to say nothing of wondering why we were here in the first place.

The day was warm but you knew the man coming towards us would have worn the same amount of clothes had the temperature been low. Aside from heavy pants and tweed coat and vest and solid boots that had not known a shine on them since their acquisition, this man wore a hat, not a cap. It was a yellow hat, and it had a brim, the front part of which was worn turned up, as if its wearer meant not to miss any passing thing. You knew he wore it summer and winter, needing it in the morning dampness, and supporting it no matter the heat of the height of day.

"Irish men seem to pay a great deal of attention to their hats, if not much to anything else they wear," my grandmother murmured, not meaning to be heard by the man in the yellow hat, but she was all the same.

He took the thing off his head and began talking about it as if we had all known one another for years. It wasn't particularly exceptional except for its color, at least its owner seemed to think so, for he ceased talking about it in the middle of a sentence and fixed us with a look serious enough to suggest matters of far greater importance than his hat. Fearing a sermon, perhaps, Uncle Tom interrupted the man in what he was about to say and complained of the road being a cul-de-sac. More pleased than not by this interference, obviously, the man in the yellow hat let Tom fume against propertied people who got roads built to their front doors for the asking, while the poor have to make do getting home as best they can. All the time during Uncle Tom's tirade the man in the yellow hat also paid attention to the road, but not, as it turned out, for the same reason as Tom was doing. He was a farmer, of course, not a scholar, so he wasn't about to browbeat Tom with special knowledge, and yet he looked as if he knew a thing or two.

"The politician's hand is everywhere seen here," said Tom. "It's the same the world over. Somebody builds a house and wonders out loud in front of the right people how in the world is he going to get into it and out of it, there being no road to speak of, not for carriages, anyway, and horses, and God knows what all. How is he going to get the piano he bought into the house if there's no road? He gets his road all right," cried Tom, very much excited at the whole idea, and bored to death by his surroundings, which he nearly always was out of doors, his main concern being how to get back inside again.

"He gets his road and who pays for it?" asked Tom, mainly addressing the man in the yellow felt hat, but not forgetting my grandmother, or me either. He was drinking a lot and the slightest thing made him hit the ceiling. He was flying now, having the time of his life. The only thing was, nobody cared about what he had to say. I know I didn't, and I was sure my grandmother didn't. We were both waiting to know what the man in the yellow hat had to say for himself.

After Tom cursed the politicians of Oughterard, as if he knew them, he went on to list the names of the people who would finally end up paying for the road, a road they themselves never use.

"Johnny and Minnie Finch will pay, that's who, and have paid for this road," said Tom, making up names, since he did not know a soul in Oughterard, to say nothing of the whole of Ireland. "Little Minnie and Johnny, slaving all their lives, slipping on the sinking stones to their door. They have no road. No, I'll bet they don't. And they don't use this one that they've given their hard-earned pennies to build to the lousy politicians. Why, it's the same the whole world over. An old story. Why am I troubling you with it?"

No one said anything to this, and Tom was silent, but not for long.

"How are you, anyway?" he said to the man in the yellow hat, as if they had only just met.

"Why," replied the man, thinking nothing unusual of the proceedings, apparently, wrapped up as he most certainly still was in his own thoughts, whatever they were, and what *he* had to say, whatever that would be.

"I'm consumed with a sense of me own importance," he cried, in a most gratifying manner. My grandmother smiled appreciatively. We were deep in a thing without knowing what that thing would turn out to be. Even Uncle Tom was impressed. But not enough to keep him still.

"Why, what in the name of God would cause you to be in such a state as that?" he asked the man, who replied by walking up and down on the road, pointing to it at random, as if he saw things there that we did not. Yet when he did speak, it was of something that happened so long ago that I wondered how it could worry him still. My grandmother and Uncle Tom soon caught the man's mood and also looked concerned. I couldn't make them out. He was only a man we had met on the road, a man in a yellow hat, not our brother. The sight of the three of them made me more homesick than ever. I felt for the cards in my pocket that I meant to send home, and was composing what I would write on them in my mind, when I was pulled up by my grandmother, who warned me to pay attention to what the man we had just met in the yellow hat was saying, and I tried, but I longed for home and present things, not a tale of suffering of long ago, of famine and strife, of burnings and evictions, of wearying marches and dragging feet, of mothers left behind with their babies at their milkless breasts, of fallen beasts, of beatings, of the grim trudge of countless feet, for they kept coming, and they kept dying. I did not want to hear that. Yet I was listening despite myself. I was part of it too, this wake on the side of the road that had seen so much misery and was so silent now, as silent as the dead of '46 and '47, the years of the famine, of the great hunger. For, no matter what I would do with my yearnings for Ingersoll Street and my quiet home there, my grandmother and Uncle Tom saw to it that I counted these great masses of starving, marching people as my people too, as much as they were theirs, or the man's in the yellow hat.

"There's no more sadder road," he said, "than this road outside Oughterard, where they fell in 'forty-six and 'forty-seven; no sadder road in all Ireland."

At this a car drove up without quite stopping and received all of the attention of the man in the yellow hat.

"Hello, Jimmy," cried the man at the wheel, staring in great surprise and appreciation, too, to say nothing of curiosity, that Jimmy should be so engaged on the road outside Oughterard. The woman seated alongside the driver gave us a severe going over, and said hello to Jimmy with her lips only, it seemed. At any rate we did not hear her, for the car crept by, and Jimmy, the man in the yellow hat, ran after it, after saying good-bye and God bless to us. We heard him talking to the occupants of the little car, which of course had pulled up for him at the side of the road, as we returned to Oughterard.

He talked about us, saying how we had come down the road by mistake, thinking it would lead us to the shore of Lake Corrib. We heard him tell how we were from America, when we'd come, even how long we meant to stay, though we were no more sure of that than he was. To hear him go on you would have thought he knew all about us, down to how much money we were carrying between us. We were a story, as interesting to the man and woman in the car as we had been to the man in the yellow hat.

"Why," said my grandmother, "I don't remember saying a word to him, or hardly. How in the world do you think he found out so much about us, Tom?"

Tom laughed. "He collected us as he talked," he said. "Collected the way we looked, his idea of what we were worth, about when we arrived, and about when we'll leave. The story of the road outside Oughterard's an oft-told tale with all of them, he could tell it in his sleep. It meant no more to him than it did to this boy here."

# 31

We rode the Connemara railway train from
Galway City to Clifden. My grandmother wore
her shawl like other women, over her head, so
that we did not stand out, but could observe
without feeling that we were being observed,
my grandmother said. She hoped I would remember everything. I said I would try, but it
was hard to pretend to feel as she did, when I
did not.

As soon as we left Tom behind in
Oughterard, promising to meet him in Dublin
at the Shellbourne Hotel, the sun came out, as
if the land had been hiding what it was from us
until then. Clifden was high and full of the
smell of the sea. Its houses all ran together and
each was painted a different color. We took a
room in a little yellow house, whose owner
warned us she had only one door key, which
she hid under the doormat outside on the
pavement, for everybody to see, and she advised us to do the same with it, which we did,

but my grandmother carried her money with her everywhere all the same.

Our landlady served us mountains of potatoes, and asked had we run away from America, and my grandmother said we had, to enliven things, for the sun did not stay long, but played hide-and-seek with the clouds, the wind, and the rain, forcing us to remain indoors reading more than we liked. The man of the house mended my shoes, charging next to nothing for it. When my grandmother demanded to know why he did not put out a shingle, he said he had enough work as it was, and would not be bothered by a steady flow, or trade. He had been born in New York City at Bellevue Hospital, where his mother had died giving birth to him.

"I'm a Yank, born though not raised there," he would say.

We were glad when Sunday came and we would have something to do by going to mass. Country people came from all around in carts pulled by donkeys and ponies, but most walked as we did, though from further away than the town of Clifden. They spoke their own language, which put me in mind of Shultzie and his family, and the songs they used to sing in German around the supper table on Ringold Street before they moved out to Minnesota.

The church was respectable enough in size and shape to fit any big city, my grandmother said, after we had settled ourselves in a pew with others, for the place was soon crowded, though you would not have known it from the quiet.

As soon as the preacher stopped opening and closing books, and stood in one place to sermonize, the babies in the congregation grew bored with having nothing of interest to watch, and so started up in their mothers' arms, gibbering in their restless way whenever there was a second's silence, which occurred often enough until the preacher got going. Then, even the babies settled down, snoring fitfully, some of them, but most dozing quietly as the sermon of violence and retribution unfolded. As it did, sunlight poured through the windows and people looked its way as if they were as sorry to miss the feel of it as I was.

I wasn't sure what the priest was talking about, but he held me, too, as much as the sunshine did, and soon even more. I did not know what rape was, or even chastity, but they were the main words of the sermon, and I would have to look them up on the sly sometime when I got home, if I ever did. One thing was clear in the sermon, and that was that a twelve-year-old Italian girl, poor and illiterate, had "refused," said the priest, "to be raped," and so her assailant had stabbed her to death. Her name was Maria Caracci and she had been made a saint in Rome, where her mother was met by the cries of thousands of people when she went there to receive the honors due her daughter.

"La Mamma! La Mamma!" the priest chanted, imitating the crowd he was later to tell us he had neither seen nor heard, and at the same time awakening all the sleeping babies, and startling the others into bawling.

"I would not have known of any of this," said the priest, "had not a kindly teacher slipped me the daily papers. I was a seminary student at the time, locked and barred in seclusion from the world."

I saw him as a young man, sorry that he had buried himself, waiting impatiently for news of the outside world he had left, and maybe now regretting that he had with all his heart. He looked at us for a long time at the end of his sermon without saying anything. He stood letting the story of Maria Caracci sink into us, and it did, I guess, though my grandmother never mentioned it, nor did I till now. I was wildly seduced by the way the priest cried, suddenly, "La Mamma!" imitating the Italians who had come from all over Italy, he said, to praise the mother of Maria Caracci. I myself wanted to say La Mamma! as I came out of the church at Clifden, but the sunlight seemed to have made an end of the priest's tale. Other stories called us, old stones, old houses with their rooftops gone. Still and all, I managed to chant, "La Mamma," over to myself in the crowd. It gave me singular pleasure. I was wondering if I ever was to bring honor to my mother as Maria Caracci had brought to hers, when my grandmother beckoned to me from the top of a wagon to come join her. I did so, but with Maria Caracci still on my mind. Tears came to my eyes. For the first time I saw her dead, a twelve-year-old girl, who had missed the fun and excitement of learning how to read, who had died because of a held-back kiss. Only Aunt Frances could explain why to me, but Aunt Frances was far away on Ingersoll Street, not just uptown, but across the Atlantic Ocean.

When the going grew steep we stepped down from the cart with the driver to give his donkey a rest. The donkey did not seem to have experienced joy in his life and looked old and hopeless in contrast to the grazing cows we passed who eyed us as if they thought we had a nerve — creaking by on a day so fine that they had been let out of their stables, as if spring had come and summer flies were not far away, when in reality we were still only in December, which made me think of Ingersoll Street again, and my mother going out to buy us Christmas presents, and of Aunt Frances, who held me against her, as my grandmother never did.

When the sea came into view my grandmother gave orders to stop by the side of the road, where she sat down on the stones and looked out over the land and the water.

"It's a great place, Connemara, but I don't think you'd be comin' here to live now, would you – or back – as the case may be?" said the driver, who stood in awe of my grandmother, I felt. When she failed to answer him he went on anyway. "There's no money to be made, or saved here," he went on, in his sing-song way. "Ireland's emptying out," he said. "Look at yerself," he went on, determined to rouse her. "You left, didn't you? Now yer back. But whether to look down on us or to envy us, God alone knows. Or is it that you mean to stay, honest?"

"I don't feel I ever left" was my grandmother's reply, finally, given ever so soberly, without once taking her eyes off the great view before us – the stones and water, the humps of hills like velvet dromedaries in the misted distance.

"Is it to America you tried givin' yerself?" the driver asked.

My grandmother shook her head yes. What was sure and solid about her seemed to melt in sadness. The sun went out. She stood up. "We must be getting home," she said, meaning Twenty-fourth Street and my grandfather, I thought, but not so the driver, who caught fire at her words and sang back to her that she was home, to her obvious appreciation. She looked at him in such a way as made me feel that he had said the right thing, that he had said what she expected him to say, and above all, needed him to say.

For seconds they stood like lovers, touching though apart. An air of intimacy enclosed them. He was, in his way, a handsome man, soft-spoken, and gentle in his movements. She was not nearly so soldierly and severe as she usually was.

She was a woman who was rarely spoken to as the driver had just done — telling her what she had done and could not do. She was unused to being spoken to like that. Yet she seemed to me to like it, to have waited for it, to even want more. With her it was always strive and effort — total scorn for dreamless stay-at-homes. Her brag was that she had made the Atlantic crossing practically on her own, with

288

her younger brothers in tow, her mother and father left behind. Now, to be told she could not give herself to America, her adopted land, did not seem to anger and hurt her, but rather to please her in a way that only a painful truth can.

"What's your donkey's name?" I asked the driver.

"God knows," he answered, looking at my grandmother like a man in love, even a young man. "God knows if he ever had a name," he said, putting his hand on my shoulder, as if to tell me not to take it to heart. That was Irish.

# 32

In Dublin Uncle Tom burst into tears at the foot of the statue of Daniel O'Connell, while my grandmother told me how O'Connell had helped liberate Ireland from under the yoke of British imperialism, but had died a broken man for all that, his nerve having failed him, as it does nearly all men in the end, she said.

"Why, Mary Ellen," said Tom, wiping his eyes with a great white handkerchief that contrasted notably with the gold of his teeth, which gleamed, reflecting the intermittent sunlight, like a monument themselves, "do you realize, girl, that the last time we were in the counthry, that it was still not free, and that today it is. Old Ireland's on its own, Mary Ellen. Did you think you would ever live to see the day?"

Much moved, my grandmother replied that she did not. "I never thought we would get together," she said. "I didn't think we had it in us. We are so divided in our natures."

It was more than if we had left a wreath at the base of the monument. We left a part of ourselves there. But late that night, at the hotel, after a lot to drink, Uncle Tom called for Chauncey in his sleep, and for Cissie Networth, to come to him. He apologized to me the next morning, since I was his bed companion, but ruefully reminded me at the same time that I would do likewise when I was his age.

My grandmother, who slept in the room next to us, looked at Tom across the breakfast table as if she could see through him, but when she spoke she appealed not to the romanticist in him, the man who fantasized Cissie Networth as a spirit now, and his brother Chauncey as a prisoner whose innocence was apparent to all but his judges, but as the immigrant Tom was: in love with property more than anything else, as most immigrants are, for property is a sign to them that they belong, that the tear they feel in themselves between their native and adopted lands does not matter after all, except in the dark, where they will always be Irish.

The dining room at the Shellbourne was higher than any room I had ever been in, and its wide windows and heavy curtains, the view of St. Stephen's Green across the street, made me feel I was in a palace. I was greatly in awe of it, but felt we had as much a right being there as did anybody else. I wondered that my grandmother was able to speak to the waiter as she did, as if she feared we had to have more than ourselves to be waited on with respect. She spoke of Uncle Tom's limousines as if they were the most important things in his life. Nor did she forget to mention her house on Twenty-fourth Street. That Grandpop was left out in her inventory saddened me, though it plainly impressed our waiter. Had we talked of going home to people, and not things, he would hardly have listened. But the litany of possessions made him drop spoons. It was as though we had given him a car and a house instead of merely bragging about them in front of him.

"Is everything all right, Mr. McLaughlin?" he wanted to know.

Uncle Tom said it was with an air that implied he had known better, and the waiter was his for life.

The task of facing going home was another thing. "Why we haven't seen nothing of what we came to see," Tom cried out in the dining room, causing the waiter to look at us over his shoulder as if he was wondering how proper-tied a man as Mr. McLaughlin, with all those gold teeth, his money in his mouth, as it were, could, at the same time, sound so troubled.

"I hope everything's all right, Mr. McLaughlin?"

"It's not," Tom told him, man to man. "Me sister here is bent on dragging us home."

"Why should she do that?" the waiter demanded, not daring to look at my grandmother, or not bothering. "Why, you've only got here, for God's sake. To think you would go before spring, to say nothing of summer, is hard for a man to bear, Mr. McLaughlin. Especially a Kerry man."

I looked at my grandmother to see what her reaction to this declaration of love would be, but to judge from the expression on her face, and what followed, you would have thought the waiter had been quoting no more to us than the time of the trains out of Dublin.

"So you're a Kerry man, are you?" said Uncle Tom.

"I am," the waiter stalwartly replied, at the same time throwing his napkin to hell. "I take it as a personal affront, Mr. McLaughlin, if you'll pardon me, you leaving the country without so much as a glance around, you might say."

"Of course I'll pardon you," said Tom, much taken with the fellow, you could see. "My sister will pardon you too," he added. Then, for good measure, he added me: "And the boy will pardon you. We all pardon you. After all, we're all Irishmen here, say what you will."

"My God, that's true," said the waiter, going pale. "They can't take that away from us, Mr. McLaughlin."

"They better not," said Tom, looking at the walls for enemies, and the window curtains for protruding gun muzzles.

"We leave from Cork Harbor," said my grandmother, as if none of the above had been said, at least not by those present, and if it had, it hardly mattered.

"A fine harbor," said the waiter, retrieving his napkin as well as his role in life. "There's no better harbor in all Ireland. Except, of course, that the harbor should not have been in Cork at all, but in Cove. Everybody knows that," he cried, looking as if he was going to do away with the napkin again as well as his job, both having a habit of coming and going in his life, apparently, at least in his imagination, and until he reached home at night and faced the wife and kids.

"Cove's the place," said Tom. "Why, when we were coming into the counthry I thought we'd stop at Cove. I said as much, didn't I, Mary Ellen? Instead, we went on up the River Lee to Cork."

"Not that I'm knocking Cork," said the waiter.

"I'm not neither," Tom said.

"But, as you said so yourself," said the waiter, "the port should have been at Cove."

"Sure it should," said Tom. "It's the trouble with the counthry entirely. Nothing's where it should be. O'Connell shouldn't be in Dublin, he should be in Cork, standing there as a reminder of past, present, and future, of all the counthry's been through, and what it might have to go through yet."

"Yes," said the waiter, "but they wouldn't like that in Dublin. They're used to O'Connell in Dublin. They think of him as a Dubliner."

"Too bad about them," said Uncle Tom. "I'm from Galway, and I wouldn't mind. I don't see why they should."

"Why, I do," said the waiter. "I think we have as much right to O'Connell as the rest of you. Come to think of it, Kerry's the dead center heart of the country. I don't know where Dublin's getting off having O'Connell in the first place. He's out of place entirely in that mishmash of people, most of them foreign secretaries, with no sense of the history of the country, as why should they have? They have no dead who died for Ireland."

"I can see him in Cork," said Uncle Tom.

"I can see him in Kerry," the waiter said, aiming his napkin across the room, but restraining himself with an effort, as he thought of his job, no doubt, and the fact that he probably would never see us again, for my grandmother rose, like the leader she was. "And I," she said, "can see us missing the boat if we don't get started."

"Why," said Uncle Tom, likewise rising, "when I think of how we came in. We came in like we were sneaking in. Why? We were under emotional strain, and there was no one to meet us. Not a soul. It's a wonder we didn't turn around and go back. That's not the fault of Ireland, mind."

"I should think not," said the waiter. "You should have told us you were coming. You can always get a thousand Irishmen out, so long as there's no sign of profit in it for them, and no cost to anybody but themselves."

"There should have been something," said Tom. "There should have been O'Connell. It would have made all the difference. As the Statue of Liberty made to us. You've heard of the Statue of Liberty?"

"Yes I have. It's a kind of Act of Contrition you have to make before entering the country," said the man from Kerry.

"Not at all," said Tom. "It's a statue."

"Of the Blessed Mother?"

"Well, in a way. Except that she carries a torch."

"Night and day?"

"All the time. She's what you see first thing, and she represents liberty. Everything that O'Connell should do in Cork, and can't do, since it would be pointless, anyway, in Dublin."

"I can't see O'Connell carrying a torch," said the waiter.

"He wouldn't have to carry anything," said Tom, "he'd just be himself."

"Well," said the waiter, "I see what you mean, but we'd never agree, we'd all be at one another's throats about it. I say let people come into the country as best they can, let them find their comfort, too, where they can. God knows we're not keepin' anybody out who wants to come in. The Statue of Liberty doesn't appeal to me at all. There's lots don't deserve liberty, but watching. There's lots don't want it, but look to being taken care of. Liberty's all right in its way, and if you can afford it, but it's not for everybody. Why, God help us, there must have been lots entering your country who fell down at the sight of it, sick and weary, as many of them must have been, children, too, or those with child, they didn't want liberty, they wanted to be taken care of."

"Yes, yes," said Tom, something in the man's speech touching him, "it was a terrible crossing for some, a terrible tug between the old and the new, many a broken heart was never to mend. But all that's over and forgotten with us. We're happy there."

"I'm glad to hear it," the waiter said, with strange quietness.

"Yes," said Tom, "we have all we want — more than we ever had here. Why, we had nothing here — to speak of."

Suddenly he jerked himself up and stuck out his chest. "Four cars. Limousines, too. How's that for a poor boy who knew no more of the world that the fields of Athenry?"

Upstairs we packed our belongings in silence. I always took care of my own things, packing and unpacking when it was required, and seldom bothering my grandmother and Uncle Tom, who were anyway so preoccupied with their visit that they scarcely had a word for one another, to say nothing of me. I was along as an appendage, hardly more, and I don't think I would have been missed if I had not been there at all. Indeed, I used to feel sometimes that I was traveling with two strangers, who were as considerate of me as their emotional state allowed them to be, which even so was not very much. This did not go unnoticed. I was often taken aside by strangers in

Ireland and given a hug or kiss out of sight of my grandmother, who, though she loved me, seemed to be incapable of such shows of affection, Irish though she was, and they were, yet different in this: that they saw something in me that was missing. A hug or a kiss meant a continent to me then, or half a hot buttered scone slipped into my hand when no one was looking.

There was no one out and no one up when I came downstairs at the Shellbourne with my bag but the waiter from Kerry. He was alone in the dining room and about some business of his own. He was a huge man, with a handsome, straight nose, but he moved amongst the many chairs and tables with the skill and grace of a great footballer grown a bit rusty in the hinges, though, as I say, he was about some business of his own, not having to do with his job at all, which was all right, since there was no one in the dining room now that wanted serving anyway.

He was all in a sweat when I reached him, as well he might have been, for he was kicking his napkin, tied into a ball, under the rungs of chairs, scoring goal after goal in a soccer game he was playing all by himself. He wasn't quiet either, but cheered himself on, and cursed his opponent for all he was worth. "It's Cork I've been playing against," he said, when he saw me.

"I hope you won," I said.

"I did," he told me, brightening at my interest. Then he looked crestfallen and confessed that he always did win against Cork, being a Kerry man himself. "I see you're all packed and ready to leave us," he said, sitting down on a chair and drawing me to him. He smelled of onions, but that was all right. I liked everything about him. "What do you think of us?" he asked me, wiping the perspiration from his face with the "ball," which he had untied into a napkin again. "Do you think you'll ever come back? Would you like to live here?" He did not mean me to answer his questions. That was nice too. All the time he talked he was "collecting me," as Uncle Tom would have said. Suddenly he asked about my mother in such a way that I saw her, and it took my breath away. My grandmother never mentioned her, and Uncle Tom did not seem to know who she was.

"Well," said the waiter from Kerry, "you'll have a lot to tell her about us when you meet."

It was the best thing he could have said because it was true.

"You know what," he said, shyly, "I'd like to give you something from the kitchen, a present that no one will be the wiser about but the two of us. Something that will bring us together again when you go home to the New World, and you're remembering this and that, and

300

maybe me. What'll it be? Say. The kitchen now, it's a great place out there. You've never in your life seen such things. The cook's in a rage all the time, as we would be, too, if we had his responsibilities. But we don't, do we? So what will it be? You can have anything you want, honest. Ice cream?

"Yes, ice cream."

"Chocolate sauce?"

"All right — thank you."

I could hardly wait for the waiter to get back, I missed him so when he went away. I was already telling my mother about him in my imagination when he came back with my ice cream sundae, though he would not have called it that.

"There now," he said, when I had finished, "there's a bon voyage for you."

"Well," said my grandmother when she and Tom came down, "you might have told us where you were. What are you in here bothering the waiter for? He has enough to do, I'm sure."

"Oh, it's all wasted on him," said Uncle Tom. "The whole trip. We might as well have brought along a chimpanzee."

# 33

Of course we went through customs coming home and we loved it. It was the high point of our trip. We none of us had ever seen New York Harbor before, and that day the winter sun was bright and in process of setting when we docked. Our pier wasn't grand, like the piers where the great white liners tied up, Uncle Tom said, but it was a revelation to us.

We came home on the same Irish freighter that had sneaked us out of Brooklyn under cover of fog, and now brought us back to face skyscrapers brazened by the blaze of the sky in the west. Going over we had only to put up with the O'Roarkes, but coming home we had eleven of their kind, only worse. Five of them fainted saying good-bye to relatives in Cork harbor, but that night every one of them danced in the salon to a tinny phonograph.

I think the bartender had been doing something else on the ship on our way over, because he had not been visible then; now he was, though barely. The hard-boiled mob from South Boston cheered him and made much of him generally, but he himself never said a word except to me. "What'll it be?" he would ask me when we were alone together in the salon. "Name your poison."

"Nothing, thank you."

"Stay that way if you know what's good for you."

There was a stewardess who did the meals, such as they were. Boiled potatoes and canned sardines, canned peas, canned peaches, and as much tea as you could drink. Indeed, the only words I ever heard from her, both crossing over and returning home, were "Let me heat up your tea for you."

She was an overbearing woman, tall as a mast, my grandmother said. Uncle Tom was sure she beat up the Jamaican cabin boy. The Jamaican sat in the open kitchen door in the evening making up his face with the aid of a hand mirror, which he allowed me to hold for him. He wiped himself clean before retiring and told me he only did it to keep in practice.

"In practice for what?"

"Why, for the life."

"The life where?"

"Why, for wherever she be. God knows she ain' heah, be she?"

303

"No she be n't," I would reply, trying to talk like him.

He did not seem to have anything but summer clothes, grassy shoes, and the night of a storm he appeared in the salon in his bare feet, makeup streaming down his face, begging to kneel on the floor with the toughs. One of them was named Magda and she wore iron-looking jewels. Magda said: "Damme if I haven't forgotten the Hail Mary."

The next day the sea undulated sedately, like a thousand green glass bellies, and there was no white water. Our captain, who seemed to have expected just such a day, did not even trouble to mention the storm of the previous night to my grandmother, who was the only grown-up passenger present at meals.

Green green green. Everything was green. My grandmother said it was worth the trip to see it. Even the sky looked green. The grass has come up from the bottom of the sea thousands of feet below us.

The rest of the crossing was smooth, with bright, cold days and starry nights, when my grandmother would stand on deck looking at where she came from and making me face that way as well, since she planted me in front of her and placed her black-gloved hands on my shoulders.

Our captain, miserable with his other passengers, treated us as old friends. He took us on the bridge at night and whispered to me of fish that die in a day ("But their days are longer than our years. Now how do you like that?"), while my grandmother had the ways of navigation explained to her by another officer in answer to her intelligent questions. No one spoke above a murmur on the bridge, and all our faces were lighted obliquely or from below. The opacity of the captain's eyes went unseen up here, where soft bells rang, and radium-tinted needles on black-faced clocks told those who could read them where we were and where we were going.

The roughnecks in the salon beneath us might as well have been dancing on the ocean's floor for all we could hear them in this little dark church, where the instruments and those who could read them were all that counted.

My grandmother, generous as always where she thought I was learning something to my advantage, bid a silent good-night to her instructor and retired to her cabin, leaving me with the captain.

"I see you didn't settle for Ireland," he said to me, as soon as she was gone. "Why?" he asked me, in a musical whisper, making meaningful conversation out of nothing, which is Irish.

"Didn't you like us? Or are you saving us up to tell on us to your mother? Sure you are," he said, as if I were asleep in his arms. "She must be waiting anxiously for you, to hear all you have to say," he said, taking my hand and leading me off the bridge and out into the night. "There," he said, pointing. "It won't be long now. You'll look back on us someday. Mind you're nice to us, hear?"

In those days people traveled much more ostentatiously than we do today. Trunks full of clothes were taken abroad as a matter of course. Our fellow passengers' masses of luggage shamed my Uncle Tom into lying to the customs man in New York harbor that we had lost most of ours on a stormy crossing out of Rossaveal to the Aran Islands, which of course was untrue.

"Damn the Aran Islands. I hope I never see them again, and if I do it will be too soon," Tom told the customs man, a lanky, lazy fellow, who was looking to see the amount of bribes he could amass by the end of the day from the incoming voyagers, and took everybody for a liar, a thief, a smuggler, or all three. He half closed his heavy-lidded eyes on looking at you, as if he meant to keep his version of you, no matter what you really were like.

"Well, let's see what you got here, anyway,"

he laconically addressed poor Uncle Tom, who was sick at the prospect of opening his suitcase on his dirty drawers, and had forgotten all about his Irish whiskey, which was all the customs man saw. "Now you can't bring that in," he told Uncle Tom, smiling a knowing smile, which Tom tried to return along with a ten-dollar bill.

"Jesus! Not in front of everybody. Are you crazy? D'ya wanna get me canned?"

But as Tom was attempting to pocket the bill, the customs man grabbed it from him. "Give it here," he said, "but not like yer givin' me the moon, hear? You people from freighters are all alike. Cheap."

"I don't see how you can say that," said Uncle Tom. "We were booked on the Bremen but had to take this scow because of a telegram telling us of trouble at home."

"Won't let you alone, huh?" said the hateful customs man. "Can't even do a bit of travelin' in peace at your ages, huh? How 'bout you?" he said to me. "You got anything t'declare?"

"Of course he has not," my grandmother spoke up. "Examine our bags and let us go. We don't have all day, as you seem to."

"Now, lady —"

"Don't you 'lady' me," my grandmother cried. "I'd as soon report you as not, taking bribes because of a poor bottle of whiskey. There was really no need to go through our things at all. You have only to look at us to see we are decent citizens who have always paid our way."

"How do I know what you are?"

"You have only to look at us, as I say, and not with an eye to what you can get out of us dishonestly, either, detaining us while you feather your own nest."

"I'll keep you as long as I want," said the customs man.

"Just you try — Tom, button up your suitcase — just you try, is all I can say. A lout like you. You're a disgrace to the counthry."

"I'll have you know I'm as good —!"

"You're not!" my grandmother cut him off. "If I thought that, I'd slit my throat tonight. Now, mark our things and let us go. This is not my first time coming into the counthry, you know. No, and I've known worse than you. But I was young then, and took your kind as the way of the world. Well, I'm not about to do that today. Mark us up, I say, or to the nearest policeman I go. I'll spend the night in court, and gladly, against you, you bribing thief with your hangdog manner, and the insinuating way you look, as if you know a thing or two that we do not. You're a bum!"

Our fellow passengers, giving themselves airs

with their customs men, viewed us from over their possessions without making a murmur in our favor. When my grandmother turned from our customs man to them, they looked away, as if they considered her a scandal.

"Phew, Mary Ellen," my Uncle Tom exclaimed, "where in the name of God did all that come from? I didn't know you had it in you anymore, girl."

"I didn't meself, Tom," my grandmother replied, being just as McLaughlin as she pleased, I thought.

They at least had the decency to wait until we were well outside the customs warehouse before they laughed outright together.

"You'll never let the girl you were go, will you, Mary Ellen?" Tom told her, glowing with pride in her. "Why, for all the years that have flown in between, and all the things, good and bad, we've been through together, New York might have been Boston, and the two of us as we were, when we first entered the counthry. Nobody could have stopped you then, that day. Oh Jesus, that day, Mary Ellen. Will you ever forget it? I won't."

My grandmother said nothing to all this, but advised me to look at New York, the greatest city in the world, on our way to Pennsylvania Station in a taxi.

# 34

Now Uncle Tom was home and settled in my father's old room; he talked of our trip as if it had been a success. Gramp, intuiting the truth, waited with patience unusual to him for Tom to reach the end of his narrative, which was not long, since there was so little to tell. He shared none of Tom's memories of Galway, knowing less about it than I did. Born and raised in Liverpool, during his parents' wait to ship out, he finally did so himself, leaving his people behind forever.

"When I think how we could have done the trip long ago, I wonder, Jack, and so would you, it was that easy; no way like it was when we came over and landed in Boston sick and tired, lonely and lost, poor as mice, if not poorer, but with stars in our eyes, for all that."

Invariably Tom would talk of times past, way past, when he meant to describe the trip we had just taken, and my grandfather quickly noticed as much.

"Which trip are you talking about?" he asked Tom, getting his own eggs and toast, for my grandmother sat by the fire in the stove, doing nothing, not even reading.

"Why, I'm talking about this trip, the trip we just made, with the boy and all."

"Kidnappers, the lot of you," my grandfather blurted out.

"I don't know how you can say that, Jack, when the boy will remember it for the rest of his life."

"What's there to remember in searching old houses and graves in the dead of winter under cover of close skies?"

"Oh, there was still lots left to see, old friends to talk over old times with," Tom lied, looking vacantly at the floor, his mouth hanging open. "I'd do it all over again."

"Well, you won't have to, if it's runnin' away again you mean, for they've locked up your brother and thrown away the key, leaving him to rave till the end of his days that he didn't do what he did do, nor cause what he did cause, but was asleep here the whole time after Thanksgiving Day dinner."

"I'm as to blame as he is," Tom said, his head hanging lower than ever. "I'd do his time for him, if they'd let me."

"Toime hasn't anything to do with it. He

311

might as well forget toime, since he's in for all toime," said my grandfather, who reserved his brogue for such occasions as this, when he meant to show his forthright Irishness, in spite of other times when he chose to designate himself as English, born and bred there, and without any knowledge whatsoever of the Other Place.

He cleared his things from the table himself, looking all the while at my grandmother in her rocker by the stove.

"Leave them, Jack," she said, of the dirty dishes, "Little Bottle's mother will be in later to do them. Drat her."

He did them all the same, and I dried.

"I don't see how you can say we ran away from Chauncey, Jack, when the two of us have looked afther him like a baby all of his life, you might say," Uncle Tom complained.

Gramp said nothing to this but went out into the hall, where I followed him, and he got into his overcoat and put on his derby and wrapped his scarf around him.

"Tell them," he said, giving me a nickel in an absentminded way, "that someone was here saying Chauncey can have visitors, and if they'll go see him, or not."

"I can't," my grandmother said when I told her.

"I couldn't," Tom sobbed.

Gramp was out of the house and halfway down Tasker Street for his trolley when I caught up with him.

"She says she can't, and Uncle Tom says he couldn't," I reported to him.

"We'll go see him ourselves," he said, climbing aboard a streetcar. "But don't tell her," he warned me as usual, meaning my grandmother, just before the motorman shut his doors between the two of us.

# 35

Gramp was as good as his word about going to
see Chauncey in prison, though I never
dreamed he would take me along, but he did.
He leaned over my bed early one morning and
told me to meet him around the corner after
breakfast. "Don't forget your schoolbooks." He
loved to fool my grandmother, and she loved
fooling him. "If you're ever to write the story of
the Murderin' McLaughlins you ought to see
where one of them spends more of his toime
than he should." It would not have been to my
grandfather's taste had we waltzed in and out of
Moymensing without a by-your-leave. Aunt
Lillie was right about it being more like an
Egyptian tomb than Egyptian tombs are to
themselves, not that she'd know. It seemed
to be more guarded than it was inhabited.
"There's more cops than robbers," Grandpop
said.

A red-faced man with rose-colored hair told
him right off that I could not go in. "Anyway,"

he said, "for all I know he might be in solitary and wouldn't even be allowed to see his old mother. We'll be glad to be rid of him."

"Don't say that," said Gramp.

"Why not?" the man with the rose-colored hair asked. "Don't you want him neither?"

"This boy," said Gramp, unwilling to answer that out of the kindness of his heart, "means more to him than most."

"I'll see what I can do. You didn't say you'd be two. He'll be surprised, I'll tell you that. He wasn't any too keen to see *you*, you know."

"He owes me money. There's no reason for his dislike of me than that," explained my admirable grandfather.

The day was wet and the building was damp. It seemed to be all cellar. The sweaty walls were painted green, the benches used and infirm, and everywhere there hung remonstrative instructions printed in colored crayon by first-graders, if that. Little broken families clung together like shipwrecks on oily planks in a fog at sea.

When Chauncey appeared behind a screen there was a general chorus of greetings from the visitors, as if they had all come to see him. It was soon apparent we alone were his visitors, and that the others were there to see his comrades in detention, who trooped into the

315

screened room behind him, Chauncey having obviously pushed himself ahead of them in his excitement, childish as ever, even touchingly so.

His face fell when he saw it was only us. He would have wept hard tears had he known his sister and brother refused to come near him. He was cocky enough.

"I'll soon be out, Jack," he said to my grandfather, who controlled his joy at this news as best he could.

I was ignored by the prisoner until my "wiggling" got on his nerves. "I don't know why you brought him. It's not as if he's the sun to me. What's he still doing down there anyway, now that Jim's gone?"

Scornful laughter rose from couples chattering at one another through the mesh of wire. I wondered if many visitors wanted the man they were visiting home again soon any more than we did Chauncey. He looked thin again, not fat and springy as if he'd spurt grease if you pricked him. It was an extraordinary fact that this was the first time I had seen him without a necktie when up and about, for he prided himself on his appearance as bartenders do.

"You can tell your grandmother that she can expect me soon. Tom's used his pull, which is plenty, to get me out. They have nothing on me but that I'm supposed to have fired a gun. No one was hurt, or scratched, no one maimed. A girl died, they tell me. What of that? Girls die every day. What would I have been doing running through the streets Thanksgiving Day on a full stomach? It's preposterous. No gun's turned up, and no gun's ever going to turn up; not if I know me sister it ain't. She wouldn't let them have it for the world."

It seemed an understood thing that I would relate our jailhouse visit to my grandmother. When I did she backed away to the hutch, her hands sifting the flour in the bin for the gun she had put there.

"Here it is," she said, showing it to me. "What in the name of God am I to do with it? Go get your Uncle Tom. He's upstairs."

When I called Tom he came rushing downstairs, but on seeing the gun, all whitened with flour in his sister's hands, he gave her one of his long, circumspect looks and turned his back on her.

"Surely we have better things to do than involve ourselves with something that is none of our business, Mary Ellen."

"Jenkins gave it to me. Jenkins knows I have it. Jenkins must be bought, Tom."

"Or ignored, Mary Ellen. Who would take his word against ours? A poor alcoholic."

All the same there was a gun floating

amongst us, and I could not forget the sight of my grandmother's whitened hands. Our house was less than ordinary when I looked up at it coming from St. Ursula's. In her efforts to hide the gun my grandmother tore the rooms apart, then claimed to have forgotten where she put it. Even Gramp joined in the search for it, but without letting on. Uncle Tom went down the cellar for the first time. And all the time it was back in the flour bin.

# 36

Uncle Tom had no business in the cellar. No wonder my grandmother laughed at him going down there. She was the stoker who kept us warm, since she had taken up her chores again, under the instigation of Doctor Fishman, and fired the Bottles as well as the furnace just as she had done before we went away.

"The trip did you worlds of good," Fishman told her. "For one thing it got you away from that crazy bartender brother. I wish I had gone with you, and will next time. I don't know what holds me here where all is tame. Certainly not my family. I'm a particular admirer of the French painter Gauguin, because, for one thing, he abandoned his family. That's right. Quit his job in the bank and left his wife and kids to shift for themselves and took off for Tahiti to paint pictures."

My grandmother stirred herself with interest at what the eccentric little doctor was saying. She was all sympathy. She liked men. She

319

especially liked men who talked to her as Doctor Fishman did. He aroused something in her that her life left dormant for the most part, a sense of adventure, perhaps, and all she would have done if only.

"I suppose," she said, not too sure of herself, since she considered Fishman vastly educated, whereas learning in her own case was mostly a yearning. "I suppose you'd say," she continued, with a look at me for courage, "that this painter had a vocation."

Doctor Fishman, unused to so intent a listener, obviously, fell all over himself, literally, with my grandmother. Things flew left and right from him as he hastened to agree with her, his bag, his pills, his hat, even his overcoat, which he tore off in the excitement and thrill of having somebody he could proselytize.

"Of course he had a vocation," he cried. "That's just the point. You hit the nail on the head. That's what made him different. That's what made him great. That's what made him, in the eyes of ordinary men and women of his time — of his time, mind you — a scandal."

"God bless us," said my grandmother, with a commanding look to me to listen and learn, to learn and remember. She settled herself more comfortably in her chair. She was enjoying herself.

"But, remember, my dear woman," Fishman went on, handing me his overcoat, whose pockets bulged with books and newspapers, "remember that a vocation is like a plant that must be sunned and watered, taken care of, catered to, waited on, or else it will die. How many are the talents, do you think, that, unlike Gauguin, whose first name, by the by, was Paul, the same as mine —"

"Paul's a nice name," my grandmother said, feelingly.

I sat listening. This was a new side of Doctor Fishman, but not a surprise, since he was the sort of man who seems to get away with saying anything. His talk made me feel I had wheels under me, and that all I needed was a shove and I'd go far. Since he seemed to have the answer to wanderlust I wondered what kept him home instead of shooting up natives with serums in faraway places. He told us.

"If it weren't for that forever pregnant wife of mine, I'd show the world, I would."

"I'm sure you would, Doctor Fishman," my grandmother retorted, egging him on, I felt, for with that he went crazy.

"Where's my coat?" he shouted at me, and when I gave it to him and he had put it on, he said, shaking his black bag at us, "I'll show her. One more kid, and I'll leave. What's she think I am, a stud? No more, hear?" he shouted at my grandmother.

"I'm sure six is enough," she told him.

"Six?" Doctor Fishman shouted again. "Six is ancient history. It's seven. And it wouldn't surprise me if number eight isn't already in the oven."

Suddenly he saw my grandmother's brass bed standing before the parlor windows.

"What's that doing here, anyway? Get it upstairs where it belongs. You're not sick. Not now, anyway. You were just all dragged down by that brother of yours."

"Doctor," said my grandmother, laughing at him affectionately, "you're a tonic."

"It's only common sense," said Fishman, and he was gone.

"All the same," my grandmother said of him, amused and bemused at the same time, "he has spirit. He's Jewish. He loves fine things, and learning, and listening to the call in him of distant places. He's Jewish."

She put her hand out and rested it on her Doré Bible and wondered aloud who the painter was who had left home to follow his star.

"I have half a mind to take us to the new museum they have built on the parkway to see what they have in the way of this Gawgan," she said, for that's the spelling she gave the guard when we arrived at the museum the next day.

"Never heard of him," said the guard, looking at my grandmother as if he was wondering if she was somebody. Apparently he concluded she was, since he winked us to follow him to a closed door under the grand staircase.

"There's a lady here who wants to know about Gawgan," he told the person who opened the door to us, showing that behind her was an office, and that she it was who was in charge.

She regarded us with a faint shade of annoyance at first, so that I could feel my grandmother begin to withdraw from her, the new museum, all desire to search out what she had come for. At such times as this, when, so to speak, she had not the courage to leave Galway and come to America for the first time with her two brothers in tow, some miracle thing seemed to rise in my grandmother like a wet whip and sting her on to action.

"It's this boy here, Missus, who will give me no peace until he sees the work of the painter Gawgan. But the guard tells us that you have nothing. We're only taking up your time. God knows you'll have enough to do to fill this place. It's as empty as heaven."

"That's only the first impression. You must come again. Gradually you will warm to it, and it will warm to you."

I thought that was an awful long speech from one who seemed to be afraid of us at first. But, when she dismissed the guard with a nod, I was happy to see she even meant to say more.

"It's true we have no Gauguin at the museum as yet," she confided in my grandmother, who clucked her tongue sympathetically, and a bit pityingly too, as if the painter in question meant the world to her, and much that was now wrong would be set right when the new museum added some work of his to its collection. Gradually the museum worker let her attention fall on me, silencing my grandmother, whose generosity regarding others, the possibility, even the necessity, of their advancement in the world, always in evidence, especially as far as I was concerned, was never more so than now.

The first thing I noted when a book was placed in my hands and I opened it as I thought was expected of me was that my grandmother had misspelled Paul Gauguin's name and I was glad that only the guard had heard her.

"We would never have heard of him, he would not have amounted to anything worth mentioning, had he not left home," my grandmother said on our departure from the museum, sowing seeds which sprouted in me in the dark. The harvest was not what she probably expected. It told me to quit her. It forced me up in the middle of the night to dialogue furiously with Horatio.

I waited for my grandfather to come in from work, and for Uncle Tom to sing himself to sleep. Gramp came in and Tom grew quiet. He seldom sang after calling out, as he sometimes did, "Is that you, Jack" It had a lonely ring to it. Tonight, instead of saying, "Is that you, Jack?" Tom asked wistfully, "Is that you, Chauncey?" Gramp finished in the bathroom. I heard his bedroom door close. Tom stirred when I opened my door, but he let me go. They all did at first.

I was crossing the Washington Avenue railroad tracks when Tom drove up. Had my grandmother been with him he would never have parked on the railroad tracks. Even in those days people knew enough not to do that. And there were seven, eight, maybe ten railroad tracks on Washington Avenue, since it was a wide thoroughfare, wide as could be, it seemed to me.

"Get in," he said, grinning at me humorlessly, his gold teeth reflecting the light of a street lamp. "I have a funeral in the morning and the car is needed. The driver is scheduled to pick it up at seven. So hop in."

"No."

"You want me pinched for kidnapping you?"

"I don't care."

"Come now, be a good boy."

"No."

"I cannot lay hands on you, your grandmother would not approve."

He did not seem to hear the heavy jangle of an approaching train, but I did. The chug of the locomotive, the drumming of the hollow boxcars meant nothing to him. He was deaf to all but his entreaties to me. He glared up the tracks at the locomotive's headlight as if it was no more to him than a lightning bug.

I went back with him out of pity, because I was sorry for him, because he begged me, because he humbled himself for my grandmother's sake, and because I did not want him to get run over by a train.

We drove back down Twenty-fourth Street past cowering row houses. I slept at first, but he woke me up with his gab.

"You must not listen to your grandfather. He's got the map of Ireland written all over him despite his straight nose. Why, we've all got straight noses, but that doesn't make us out English. He knows nothing of geography except what's shown to him in the movies. Tom Mix In Cement and the rest of it. You must not listen to him when he downs our trip abroad. He's not very bright. He's not very intelligent. It's the McLaughlins that count in your blood, me lad, not poor Jack's Limerick glue. Sure they were all from Limerick. I tell you he's Irish. Don't let him get away with putting on the dog about being English to you. His brogue's that thick sometimes you could cut it like butter. Whatever you do never ask him to spell, because he can't. Be that as it may, he dotes on you. He can't see himself goin' and comin' without you here. None of us can. So stay. I'll drive you home when summer comes. 'When summer's in the meadow,' " he added, choking with grief.

They were up when Tom brought me back. They must have heard us coming down Twenty-fourth Street, since they were at the door, both in their nightclothes. In order to escape from being cast in a pitiful light they acted as though getting me back was all Tom's doing, which it was, of course, but it was what they wanted him to do, at least my grandmother did, not that you would have thought so to see her. As I came up the steps carrying my bag containing my shirts and ties and a change of pants, my grandmother turned her back on me and retreated into the vestibule, where she stood behind the door, thinking of the neighbors, I guess, her hand on the doorknob, waiting until I passed her, before she locked up.

"You'll never guess where I picked him up.

He was crossing Washington Avenue with all the speed of a nine-day marathon runner when I discovered him. He was out of breath when he spoke to me, not that he said anything that made any sense to me, or to himself neither, I'm sure. I'm sure he would have fallen had he continued on alone any further. Then the niggers would have jumped him at South Street and robbed him of his poor suitcase."

As my grandmother and Gramp regarded me as if they were ashamed of the whole thing, it was Uncle Tom who spoke again.

"Well, he came willing enough."

Had I been alone with her my grandmother would doubtless have said that my stay with her would not be long. She would have joked about pushing up daisies at Holy Cross. As it was she seemed to be unable to speak. I could see that it was only after making a grand effort that she thought of something. Not to say, but to do. She led me into the kitchen and gave me a glass of milk and a piece of her raisin pie. The three of them stood and watched me eat it.

"There now," said Tom, after I had finished, "it's time for bed again. Without no shenanigans this time, please."

Uncle Tom sang when he got in bed, lying on his back as I had seen him do on our trip to

Ireland, his tenorish voice filling the silence as well as a need. My grandmother was probably lying on her back, as well, humming along with him. Grandpop would not be singing, but he would not have objected to their doing so.

Why were they so sad? Why were they so funny and at the same time sad? Would I be that way when I grew up? Was I that way already? It seemed to be something my mother and father, especially my father, fought against. Should I? Should I keep things separate and apart, the funny from the sad, as Father Stienhagen so fiercely intoned that I should, and as my little German schoolfellows at St. Ursula's seemed to do? Where had the game of Horatio come from? From my mother. But what made me play it with such a vengeance in every crisis? What made me listen with a mixture of shame and pity to my Uncle Tom singing "Danny Boy"? What made me cry at nothing, and play the stone while others wept?

Why were we sorry for ourselves, but sorrier for others? That was Irish. That is why Tom cried when he promised to drive me home "when summer's in the meadow," and why we were all thoughtful now listening to him sing it. Because he was really singing of the future without Chauncey, his responsibility, his little brother, his wayward little brother. Though when we met we might joke about it like everything else, in the dark we were Irish.

# 37

Little Bottle wasn't waiting for me after school now because of his job, but he made up for it on Saturday, his day off, when he took me shopping on the Lane. Merchandise was already on display for Christmas and Little could not resist purchasing a necktie for himself.

"I didn't know you wore ties, Mr. Bottle."

"I do when the occasion calls for it. Now let's go home to dear old Bannister Street and see what Mom has in the way of tea and cakes." He took my hand and led me down the Lane past shops whose lights had come on, making everything festive but me.

"Soon," said Little Bottle, "you won't be able to walk on the Lane hardly, what with Christmas trees and shoppers. It's a jolly time if you have a job and money in your pants pockets to jingle, as I have."

Since I said nothing to this, Little gave my hand he held in his a gentle shake.

"You mean you don't think so?"

331

"Not always. Not now. I'd rather be home now, Mr. Bottle."

"Don't say that. You'll have your years at home."

His neighbors did not want to stand talking in the cold, but he stopped them anyhow, wanting to show what a success he had made of himself.

"Why, Little, you look like you've been shopping."

"I have been," he told them, showing his new tie.

"It's a beauty, Little. You'll look dreadful smart in it. Make sure you don't give it away to anybody for Christmas."

"I won't," said Bottle, and we went to his own house, which was closed and cozy as a baked potato in its skin.

"We'll talk about it later, Clancey," Mrs. Bottle said as usual to her parrot as we came in on them out of the cold. Then she lit into me. "Clancey's taken to you to that pitch that I believe he would go into decline at your departure, to say nothing of Little." Since I did not know whether to agree or disagree with her, not knowing what she was driving at, she put me straight. "It's all over the neighborhood how you've turned out to be the murderous kind."

"I don't see how you can say that, Mrs. Bottle."

"Why, just the thought of you leaving her cuts your grandmother in two."

"I don't mean to go just yet."

"You don't, doncha? What was it you were doin' the other night without a good-bye to any of us?"

"It seemed the only way."

"If it hadn't been for your Uncle Tom McLaughlin you'd have been home by now."

"I wish I was."

"And leave your grandmother cut in two?"

"I have a right to go. If Mr. Bottle was far away from you, wouldn't you want him back?"

"Not if he was needed elsewhere." A lie. Because as soon as Little showed her his new tie she made fists. "Who is she, Little? Out with it. Her name?"

"Why, yourself," Little told her, and he threw the tie he had just bought on the Lane around his neck and grinned at her like a fool.

It was all right for her to keep Little at home, but not all right for me to go home to my mother.

"You have years ahead of you to go home, little missioner," she told me. "So stay where you're needed. It won't be forever."

"That's what I tell him," said Little, slopping down his tea.

# 38

Sister Hildebrande hid her day of departure from St. Ursula's from us, but the little krauts, some of them older than their years, found her out and decked her desk and office in unashamed display of their affection for her, which was more than my nature allowed me to do. They were so gemütlich, and I was cold, even though I was brimming over with scalding hot tears as I watched them.

"Don't be a spoilsport," Sister scolded me. "Think of how all this has been so strange to them, the language, the streets; many of them are from the countryside, as I am, and not used to the cramp of buildings, and the noise of traffic."

"There are lots of things that are new to me, too, Sister," I said.

"Yes? Like what?"

"Well, like this very minute."

"Yes, that's true. What do you intend doing about it?"

"Why, nothing, Sister."

My heart felt cold against her, for I felt Hildy was like my father now, and afraid I'd go too far. So I slipped away, hoping I would be noticed, but I wasn't. No more than other boys who had quit the party. They were herded together in an unheated vestibule sharing a single Camel cigarette among five of them.

"Leavin' the party? Goin' to visit your jail-bird uncle?" the wit of the gathering, a sharp-faced shrimp with long yellow front teeth, asked me.

"Don't you wish you had an uncle like him?" I said, feeling stupid and put-upon, which the boy suspected I did easily enough, as they all did, since they laughed at me scornfully.

"If you feel that way, why come to school at all?" another asked.

"Because I have to," I replied. "I'd rather be anyplace else than with dopes like you. Especially you," I said, grabbing the one who thought he was so funny.

"I didn't say anything," he cried. "What's wrong with callin' your uncle a jailbird when he is one?"

"Because you meant to be nasty," I said, raising my knee and kicking him in the groin as I had seen older boys do to one another.

The others did not answer his call for help

and I saw why. Sister Hildebrande had come searching us out. "What are you boys doing out here, when the party's inside? Come in until you're excused. It's still school hours, you know." She led us back to the party, where I was more miserable than ever. All because I had not gone home to Ingersoll Street, I told myself, and I determined to leave again that very night.

The thought of flight consumed whatever consideration I had for Sister Hildebrande, who had always been so good to me. Anyway, her back was to me, which I took as a direct insult. Hurt, I wanted to hurt everybody.

I was through the halls and down the stairs and on my way out of the hateful school building for the last time, I hoped, when I heard her light footsteps behind me. Instead of admonishing me for running away from her party for the second time, Hildy caught hold of my hair and gave it a playful tug. Suddenly I felt her hand soften and spread over the top of my head and rest there.

She left me without saying good-bye, but it was.

Little Bottle was waiting for me at the schoolyard gate the way he used to. I supposed he had slipped and started drinking seriously again and had lost his job but I was wrong. He was wearing his new tie. I wondered what the occasion was that called for sartorial display and Little Bottle soon told me.

"Why, your grandmother got your Uncle Tom and me to move her bed upstairs again. That's occasion enough to wear a tie, don't you think? I do. I took off early from work for it. We're all very set up at the change in her. She's taken a new lease on life since you put off going north."

"She has, Mr. Bottle?"

I felt my head for Hildy's blessing to see if it was still there.

"Why, now, what's come over you, little missioner?" Little Bottle asked me. "I should think you'd be happy."

"I am, I am, I guess, Mr. Bottle," I said. "Only I do want to go home someday, you know. I think I deserve it, now that I got my father away from the McLaughlins, don't you?"

"Sure I do. Of course I do. You know I do. Only —"

"Only what? Suppose you were still overseas and the AEF wouldn't let you go home? Then what?"

"Why, I'd go AWOL's what."

"AWOL? I don't understand."

"No, and it's just as well you don't for the

present. It won't be for long, staying, I mean. So try."

I felt my head for the feel of her, but it hurt now, there was nothing now. I wished I could have said good-bye to her like all the other boys, but I couldn't because I could not have borne the hurt of it, good-byes being the stinging things they are.

"You'll see," said Bottle. "Someday you'll look back on us and you'll be glad you stayed."

# 39

When I got home my grandmother was sitting by the kitchen stove with a cat she said had trailed her home from the Lane. Gramp said he never heard of taking a full-grown cat in before, but from the first he began to pay attention to everything it did, and Uncle Tom named him Rinaldo after one of his Havana cigars.

No one expected him to stay, least of all my grandmother, who was always calling him back into the house on the sly, after she had made a great show in front of everybody of putting him out for good.

"I wouldn't want to take someone's old red cat away from them," she said, but when a one-eyed woman came to the house inquiring after a red cat she denied we had one, though Grandpop did not.

"We have a cat," Gramp informed the one-eyed woman. "Why not take our cat? Go find the cat," he said to me.

"It's not ours to give," I let him know.

"I thought so," was Gramp's reply. "Then it's this poor woman's cat."

My grandmother laughed falsely. "My husband would give you the shirt off his back, Missus. It's a wonder we have a stick left in the house, and we wouldn't have, if it was up to him. He's a regular little Franciscan and only married me out of pity."

"You're damned," Grandpop told her, much to the confusion of our visitor, but it had no more effect on my grandmother than it ever did. She guided the woman to the front door telling her she had the distinct feeling that her cat was in good hands.

"Well, if you see 'im, n'you want 'im, then keep 'im. Don' bother me with 'im. I never had no luck with reds."

Gramp could not get over her.

"Well," he remarked, "there goes a savage."

It was hard to believe sometimes that Grandpop had crossed the Atlantic, he still seemed such a part of older things, of ways not yet mechanized. He was made of gentler stuff than the McLaughlins. Perhaps just the grown-up in him had shipped, regretfully, leaving the boy in him behind in Liverpool: writing him still, sending him telegrams, waiting for him to show up again someday.

Soon Rinaldo was knitting us together in a

way that nothing else that I was aware of had ever done before.

"What are you doing up?" Gramp would say to him when he came home from work in the middle of the night.

"Is it the cat, Jack?" Tom would call out from his room.

"Yes," Gramp would say of Rinaldo, "he never sleeps. He has the insomnia and refuses to take pills for it."

"Well, I don't want you scratching at my door, hear?" Uncle Tom would say, coming out of his room.

"No, and I don't want you bothering me," Gramp would tell the cat.

My grandmother said it amazed her how Rinaldo had settled down to a life indoors for the most part, spurning the world outside as if he felt it was not good enough for him now.

"God knows where he's been, but he's retired now," Gramp would say.

"Well, I don't want him to retire to my room," Uncle Tom would put in.

But they were no sooner quiet, Gramp having gone to bed after coming in from work, than Uncle Tom would be up asking about Rinaldo.

"Do you have him, Jack?"

"No I don't. I thought he was with you."

If Rinaldo was with me I would refrain from confessing so.

My grandmother acted above all these maneuvers. She did not seem to care where Rinaldo slept. Then one night when Rinaldo was with me my bedroom door was stealthily opened from the outside. Rinaldo sprang up out of my bed when he heard it, and so did I, but only after I felt sure that all was quiet again in the house. When it sounded to me as if everybody had gone back to sleep I made the round of the rooms, silent but for the snores of their occupants.

Gramp snored as if he liked it, Tom as if he felt it gave him away, but my grandmother's snore was frank and stately. When I opened her door Rinaldo leapt lightly from her bed trailing her rosary beads from the corners of his mouth like a catch of seaweed.

"I have no idea how he got into my room in the first place," my grandmother told me next morning, but I knew better. She was as bad as Gramp and Uncle Tom, the way she wanted to have Rinaldo with her at night.

"He's a regular star," Tom said.

"I don't know what you mean by that, Tom," was my grandmother's reply to that sort of praise of Rinaldo from her brother. "He's an ordinary enough cat. He'll wander away as he wandered in and none of us will know the difference."

"He might have been ordinary enough when he came in, but he's changed, Mary Ellen. He came down the stairs only just now saying his beads."

"Now, Tom, what's a cat know?"

"We're all crazy about him, Mary Ellen. It's the very devil how he's taken over."

"Well, then, it's time he went."

"You would never have taken him in at all had Chauncey been here, Mary Ellen. Chauncey being death on cats, as you know."

"I did, but I forgot," my grandmother said.

"Poor Chauncey," said Tom.

"Poor us who have to put up with him. And poor me that has to put with the two of you. Don't set me raging over a cat, Tom."

"Why, Mary Ellen, it's no great matter to me, whether you have a cat or no. I'm only afther sayin' that Chauncey never could abide by them."

Instead of sitting reading their newspapers as they used to do before meals Uncle Tom and Gramp looked this way and that now for Rinaldo, and wondered aloud why he was not always on hand.

"He's a cat with a cat's ways, for God's sake," my grandmother burst out. "A tomcat, too, not

343

a pussycat, as both of you seem to believe he is."

Nobody said anything to this, and the meal that followed was eaten in silence. Afterwards I trailed Gramp to the hat rack in the hall and watched him put on his overcoat and tie his scarf. It was a wonder to me how he managed to keep his derby from the wind. Today it blew off his head and bumped down the front steps when he closed the door behind us. He put it back on without cursing the weather, which was not like him. Also, instead of continuing on down Tasker Street to Twenty-third Street to catch his trolley for work he drew me into the narrow alley running behind my grandmother's house, looking all the while up at the wooden fences to each side of us.

"Is it Rinaldo you're looking for, Gramp?" I was bold enough to inquire, to which he replied that I was a chump. "If it is," I said, "he's probably down at the Bottles."

"The Bottles! What in the name of God would a cat in his roight mind want with the Bottles?"

"It's not the Bottles so much, Gramp, as their parrot."

We turned down the alley running parallel to Tasker Street, where I pushed open the Bottles' back gate into their cabbage patch.

"There he is!" Grandpop shouted, making a dive for Rinaldo.

"Don't scare him, Gramp. He might run away and never come back."

"Why, where would he go?"

"Wherever he came from, Gramp."

Grandpop took out his pocket watch and regarded me over its immaculate white face and Roman numerals.

"Well," he said, "he's only a cat. You'll have me late for me work, making so much of him as you do."

# 40

Little Bottle came around to Twenty-fourth Street to see me that night after his work, but it was for more than just to take a walk under the partially clouded moon, which made me more homesick than ever, the way it looked as if it was being chased through the sky, and made to go every which way but where it wanted to go.

"Mom sent me with a message for you," Little said right off.

"She did, Mr. Bottle? What message?"

"It's to be clearly understood that your cat stays out of our backyard. It's upsettin' Clancey."

"I'll see what I can do, Mr. Bottle. But, to tell the truth, I don't see how you can keep a cat in if it wants out, do you?"

"No I don't. I don't know anything about cats. Or birds. That's Mother's territory. She says Rinaldo and Clancey have struck up a friendship that bodes no good for Clancey, who's lonely, I guess."

"Lonely, Mr. Bottle?"

"You know yourself that Bannister Street, with its brick sidewalks and marble steps, is no natural habitat for a parrot. Cooped up as he is with Mother all day, Clancey must get the smothers, remembering Ecuador, when the sun pierces the forest glades like swords of gold, and his own kind on every other bough of every tree. Clancey must miss that. We know he misses it. That's why his fascination for Rinaldo."

"Rinaldo doesn't fly."

"No, nor does Clancey. But he seems to think he could now. So that if Rinaldo made a dive for him, he could escape him, only he couldn't. He's thrown back to times past, like all of us from time to time."

My times past were not so long ago as Little Bottle's, but he was right, I was thrown back to them, as he was to his, I could see, for he lifted his heels smartly, as though he would have the sound of his footsteps resound through the streets — as he sang:

*The first marine went over the top*
*Parlez-vous? (Come now, sing along with me)*
*The second marine went over the top*
*Parlez-vous? (Sing out, little missioner)*
*The third marine went over the top*

*To circumcize the kaiser's cock*
*Inkey dinkey parlez-vous (Don't, whatever*
*you do, sing that for your grandmother's*
*benefit.)*

That night Gramp swore to my Uncle Tom that Rinaldo had a green look to him. Tom said he noticed it too. I heard them talking in the upstairs hall outside my room. It was a wonder the way Rinaldo had taken the place of all their other interests. You could hear Grandpop, even before he came upstairs to go to bed, asking for him. I did not know what they would do without Rinaldo now, they had become so attached to him.

"He must have eaten something," said Uncle Tom.

"Oh, he did, he did. And didn't I see him at it?"

"Why, what was it, Jack?"

"Parrot."

"You saw him?"

"I seen him, and there was nothing to do but let him have his way. I wouldn't have gone near him for the loife of me."

Early-morning drinkers eyed me over Oyster's opaque windows on my way to school next morning and I wondered why. Kids at school acted funny too. Or funnier. I saw why when I

348

got home, where Mrs. Bottle sat facing my grandmother in the parlor. Her eyes widened pathetically when she saw me, though her manner, so volatile at other times, remained constrained. I think my grandmother terrified her. Her dark face was impassive, but there was something threatening about her all the same.

"Where's Rinaldo?" I sang out, the last thing I should have done as far as my grandmother was concerned, obviously, but just what Mrs. Bottle was waiting for.

"Rinaldo? Is that the cat?" she shot at my grandmother.

"There's a stray called Rinaldo that spent a night huddled against the front door" was my grandmother's disconcerting answer to that.

"A red cat?" Mrs. Bottle wanted to know, in an alerted kind of way.

"Red or white, it was too early to see. I was concerned that the milk wasn't frozen and wanted to get it into the house as quickly as possible. Strays abound, you know."

Just when I thought my grandmother had settled her hash for her and she was about to leave, Mrs. Bottle lashed into me:

"What in the name of the blessed rolls of the Last Supper has gotten into you? Don't tell me you got the tongue-ties or the bewitchments?

349

Aincha gonna ask for Clancey? Or do you know?"

"I think I know, Mrs. Bottle."

"You should. The whole neighborhood's up in arms about it, though your grandmother here denies even having a cat."

"What kind of cat, Mrs. Bottles?"

"A red cat. The reddest cat I ever seen. There's a gray blotch of what's left of its left eye, and the right is little better. It's a squint-eyed cat. I wouldn't trust it in broad daylight. A filthy, low sort of animal, built close to the ground, with more paw to him than leg. As like to crawl as walk, and related to the cobra, though hairy. Spit soars from him at the sight of Clancey, the devil."

Mrs. Bottle, despite her diminutive size and humble appearance, was a formidable speaker, but what she said about Rinaldo was bunk.

"Saying he's ugly and fierce, when he's beautiful and gentle," I said to my grandmother, after Mrs. Bottle had left us.

"That's all very well," she told me, "but how keep a cat indoors if it wants out?"

"We won't have to. I don't believe Mrs. Bottle."

"How's that?"

"She's not sad enough."

"Yes, she was much more concerned about

350

Rinaldo than she was over the loss of Clancey. I think you're right."

"She doesn't want anybody but herself to have anything, that Mrs. Bottle."

# 41

The next day being a Saturday I called on the Bottles unexpectedly, sure I would find Clancey. But I was wrong. The parrot was nowhere in sight. I still did not think Mrs. Bottle looked sad enough, to say nothing of Little.

They sighed enough, maybe too much, and they made commiserating eyes at one another, but I could not help feeling they were holding back more than tears.

I refused a cup of tea. Mrs. Bottle said she would have one anyway, and so she did, and so did Little. There was a noise from a cake tin in the corner of the kitchen dresser, which I took for a mouse, but the Bottles did not seem to hear it. When I looked at them in a questioning way they rattled their cups and saucers and passed Fig Newtons to one another, so I went myself to see what was up with the mouse in the cake tin.

It was a pretty little cake tin, with perforations on each end in the shape of butterflies, and the door opened in the middle, like a stage curtain. I was about to open it when Mrs. Bottle handed me a Fig Newton.

"There's no more cake in the house but this," she told me. "So don't bother my cake tin. I've just washed and aired it and I don't want anybody messing it up again. I think you ought to be home. Little, see him home. His grandmother will bleed if she thinks he's done the midnight flit again. Sit down," she told me, "I never did see a boy the likes of yerself in such a hurry t'grow up n'die."

"But there's something in there, Mrs. Bottle."

"Something in where? Now what are you talking about? Little, see him home."

"Something moving in the cake tin."

"There ain't. And who should know better if there ain't or not? Whose cake tin is it?"

"Your cake tin, Mrs. Bottle. Still —"

"Still what? Still water runs deep. See him out, Little."

At that point the cake tin began to move toward us, though ever so slightly, and I reached for its doors and parted them. There lay Clancy, like an actor at the end of a play, only I thought he was really dead.

"He'll be all right," Mrs. Bottle assured me. "I wanted to teach you a lesson," she confessed. "I thought that if I hid Clancey away for a day or two that you'd get rid of Rinaldo, but I was wrong. I didn't count on love."

"Love, Mrs. Bottle? I don't see how you can talk of love, after stuffing Clancey away in a cake tin like that, as if he were no better than a stale muffin."

"I didn't count on the love your grandmother bore for Rinaldo," Mrs. Bottle explained. "I forgot, in my own love, that others love too."

"Forgive us, little missioner, won't you, like a good boy," Little begged me.

I said I'd try.

"There's nothing we won't do when we love, nothing's too dirty," Mrs. Bottle told me.

"Minnesota's the place," said Clancey, making us all laugh, but remember too.

When I told my grandmother she became merry about the whole thing. Touching me lightly on the shoulder she pointed out the back kitchen window at Rinaldo seated on the fence enjoying the sudden snowflakes framing him like a halo.

"Where's my sled?" I cried, excited beyond anything. To think I hadn't noticed it had begun to snow. Drat those Bottles, as my grandmother would have said.

"There's not enough snow to sled yet," she told me.

"No, but I'll have it ready for when there is. In an hour?"

"In an hour? Anything's liable to happen to us in an hour. Your sled is in the cellar. While you're down there put a shovel of coal in the furnace. Blessed be to God for a warm house."

She was firing the kitchen stove when I came upstairs carrying the sled Grandpop had given me.

"I don't think I have ever seen anything more beautiful than Rinaldo out there," she said.

He was still on the fence, playing tightrope artist, blinking at the falling flakes.

"Oh," said my grandmother, in admiration, "there's nothing new to Rinaldo, nothing new under the sun, he's seen it all."

"I wonder if he feels glad and sad at the same time, now that it's snowing?" I asked. "I wonder if he's glad it's snowing, but sad when he remembers things that happened when it snowed in the past?"

"Oh yes," said my grandmother, "ain't he like all of us? Things both heavy and light have happened to him as to us all. His kitten days were happy days, I'm sure. Then he reached a time in his life when nobody wanted him."

"All that's over now," I said.

"Why, sure it is," said my grandmother.

She was full of a sense of activity, as she

355

was when I first came down to South Twenty-fourth Street to get my father to come home.

"It's the snow," she said. "It fills me with foreboding, yet at the same time I'm ever so aware of the good things I have by the grace of God. Still," she said, her breath visible to me in the bright, cold back kitchen, "there's something in me that tells me to take all I love to my bosom and hold them as if I would never let them go."

I moved away from her, afraid lest she meant what she said, and wasn't just talking, and would end up by smothering me to death. It was just as well for him that Rinaldo was outside.

She saw me move away and she laughed at me in her derisive way. Then her eyes rested on Rinaldo, whom she seemed to have in a way that she had never had, never loved, anyone else. Nor did she call him in, but let him remain where he was, though I felt that if he had called her she would have gone out to him through the falling snow.

"It's a good day for soup," she said, practical as ever, no matter what. "There's a leftover ham bone, too — but a dearth of vegetables. So come with me while I shop for them on the Lane."

"Can I bring my sled? Shall we leave

Rinaldo where he is?"

She said nothing to me except to shake her head in acquiescence to all I asked, her real interest being spent on Rinaldo, he was that beautiful to her that day. Off we went, making tracks through the snow. We stopped in Bannister Street and looked up the alley at Rinaldo. When he saw us he came down from the fence.

"It's more for the snow than for us he came down, he likes the feel of it," my grandmother said.

"Let's take him with us on the Lane," I suggested.

"I'm afraid he'd stay," my grandmother said. "The Lane's where he came from — I think." But since I picked him up and he did not seem to mind: "Come, get on the sled, the two of you, and I'll pull you, though Reiner would have conniption fits if he saw me. Now," she said, as if I ever thought she would remember it, "this is a sight betther than sledding up and down a railroad embankment with your foolish grandfather."

She did not wait for an answer, but took Rinaldo from me in exchange for her vegetables, which I carried home, instead of him, pulling my sled behind us.

"Drat that Mrs. Bottle and her Clancey," my grandmother burst out as we passed the

Bottles' house on our way home through Bannister Street. "Lying is nothing compared to what she would not do for that bird. Your grandfather is as bad about Rinaldo. At least Chauncey isn't here to torture us with his fear of cats."

But he was.

# 42

We heard his high-pitched voice as we came into the house and hung our coats on the hat rack. He was standing in the middle of the parlor floor regaling his brother, Tom, and my grandfather with stories of a job he once held bartending in a mining town upstate. No mention of jail, or prisoners. It was all mining town. It was as if he had come off the job today, when in fact he had just been released from prison.

"They're black, poor basthards, most of the time, and when they do wash their faces, they're usually too blind with drink, or exhaustion, to see themselves. It's a mean, rotten existence. They're more like moles than men. I was glad to have done with them. Ah, there you are, Mary Ellen," he cried, spinning around on his little fat feet in their high soft black leather shoes as we came into the parlor.

"Well, Chauncey, I hope you are all right."

"Oh I am, I am, Mary Ellen. I'm fit as a

fiddle and have already seen to it that I have me old job tending bar across the street at Oyster's. So you don't have to worry about me being on your hands. I'll be more out of the house than in, and will soon find a place of me own. So don't count on my always being here, Mary Ellen. Nor you neither, Jack," he added, addressing my grandfather, who humpfed.

The ringing of the front doorbell gave Chauncey the opportunity to speak to me in his old rude way:

"Will you go on answer the doorbell, for God's sake. What else are you good for? Is me sister Lillie to stand out there till she dies of old age and cold before you get a move on?"

Lillie was as bad:

"Gaping at me from the parlor window. Why didn't the tinkers get you while you were in Ireland? They knew a bad package when they saw one, bad cess to them."

She went directly to Chauncey and embraced him, but it was to me she spoke, catching my eye over the ex-prisoner's broad shoulder:

"Go get me a glass of cold wather from the back kitchen tap. Let it run first."

When I gave her the glass of water the company settled back to observe Lillie prepare her drink, but there was no preparation. Simplified by time and usage the preliminaries

360

were over before we knew it, and Lillie was smacking her lips and belching into her sack for a cigarette.

"Well, Lillie," my grandmother began good-humoredly, "you know more of Chauncey's movements than we do. He only just got in."

"Who else had he to tell or talk to but me?" Lillie bitterly responded to my grandmother. "The rest of you were scathered over the wather, leavin' us behind, the youngest."

"Ah, yes," said Chauncey, urbanely, "how was the famous trip to Ireland? You never said, Tom."

"I didn't?" Tom asked, nonplused.

"Of course you didn't. How could you?" Chauncey persisted in putting his brother on the spot. "This is the first time we've seen one another, Tom, since —"

*Since he went to jail,* but he could not bring himself to say so, nor did Tom want him to, obviously.

"The trip went well enough," Tom answered, adding that it had been taken more for my benefit than anything else: "We did it more for the boy's sake here, you might say, than anything else."

"The boy's sake?" cried Lillie, shaking her empty glass at me for a refill. "What in the name of God had the boy to do with it? You

361

ran away, is why you went. Ran away from trouble and affliction. Well, it's over now, praise be to God, and the less said about it the betther. Will you take this glass and go get me some wather from the back kitchen," she said to me, raising her voice. "I'm afther askin' you a dozen times."

"You haven't," I replied to her, to a congratulatory grunt from my grandfather. "You asked me once."

"Once too often, Lillie," laughed Tom, intercepting the glass his sister was handing to me, and slipping it into the pocket of his jacket. "There now," he said, raising his arms in the air, "no glass, no drink."

"I left a brother, and have come home to a Houdini," muttered Chauncey.

"Well," said my grandfather, too long quiet, so that you knew something was working in him readying itself for distribution amongst us, "he got you out of Moymensing, didn't he? That was no mean trick to accomplish, considering your unfitness to circulate in decent society."

At that Chauncey turned on his little fat feet in their high soft leather shoes and faced the other McLaughlins, begging in a helpless way from one to the other of them, then stopping, crestfallen and defeated, at Lillie, who could give him nothing, especially not shelter, which is what he now wanted, having been insulted to the point where he felt he could not possibly dwell under the same roof with my grandfather.

"Mary Ellen," he said, beginning with the head of the family, "I'm not wanted here." Since my grandmother said nothing to this, Chauncey next addressed Tom. "Tom," he said, "I'll go with you."

"Go where with me? I live here, for God's sake," said Tom.

It was then Chauncey's eyes rested hopelessly on his sister from Westchester, to whom of course he had nothing to say, knowing she had nothing to give.

My grandmother, her good humor gone with the unexpected but inevitable advent of Chauncey, prepared her vegetables which we had bought in such a spirit of fun, and tossed them in the pot with the ham bone. Since no one joined us in the kitchen, and Chauncey was back on the subject of miners, which was his way of telling he had been underground at Moymensing, cut off, desperate lest he die without a familiar face to see him off, we were left to ourselves, hoarding the fun we had only just enjoyed out in the open air under close skies, surrounded by whiteness, where even the tarred streets and bricked and cemented sidewalks sparkled pristinely, where all seemed pure and sure and reliable, where dodges were forgotten and all was straight dealing.

"Come, everybody, to the table," she called out through the dining room to the company assembled in the parlor. "Come, Jack, you'll be late for work."

My grandmother's reference to a job, not Gramp's necessarily, though he was respected for having one, no matter what it was, had its usual sanctifying effect, and the McLaughlins trooped after him into the kitchen, where the pea soup waited for them on the stove, ready to disappoint the life out of you, my grandmother said. But when she stirred the fire under it and set it boiling afresh, stirring it the while, she admitted it was enough to make your mouth water, just the smell of it, and she was right.

"Why, Mary Ellen, you're not eating yourself," Tom said.

"No I'm not. I'm not hungry. I'll have something afther. In the quiet."

The effort of trying to keep so wayward a clan as the McLaughlins in order showed on her. She tied the black silk scarf around her head, complaining of a headache, and took her chair by the stove.

"Well," said Tom, "we're all together anyway." Since there was no response to this, peacemaking being foreign to the McLaughlins, Tom added, characteristically, the devil in him, "All but the cat."

"What cat are you talking about, Tom?" Chauncey asked. "Don't tell me you have a cat in the house, Mary Ellen. If you have, I can't stay."

"Then go!" my grandmother stormed, as if she had been gearing herself for just such an encounter. "Of course we have a cat," she went on. "What business is it of yours, if we have or not? Where is he, anyway?" she wondered aloud, as if her quarrel with Chauncey meant nothing to her, really, in comparison to what she felt about Rinaldo.

"Chauncey," said Lillie, "look at it this way. What's a cat?"

"Exactly, Lillie. You're right. I'm a grown man now, no matther how like a boyeen I'm treated by me own. I have no fear of cats anymore, only a devil-hatred of them. I'd sooner fly at one than have one fly at me. With me, as far as cats are concerned, it's kill or be killed."

When Rinaldo, startling the others, but leaving those of us who loved him unperturbed, appeared as if out of nowhere, as if he could pass through walls and walk on water, and leapt soundlessly on the kitchen sink and drank the drops from the cold faucet, Chauncey, obviously overcome by a great fear, as well as a vicious need to obtain his own way, swerved in his chair at the table and fell with all the might and weight of his torso on the counter of the hutch, where he rummaged frantically in the flour bin for his gun, which in his childish expectations he seemed to have been certain he would find there, and he was right. It was. When it did not fire, he cursed it, then threw it, and we laughed at him, not thinking it would hit Rinaldo, but it did, and he fell before my grandmother reached him.

Chauncey stood shaking his flour-whitened hands at us as if that was all that was the matter, and looking at the doorway into the dining room, the only way of escape where he would not have to pass my grandmother and Rinaldo.

"Wash your hands at the kitchen sink, for God's sake, Chauncey," Tom told him. "Don't go trailing that stuff through the house. Have you no sense of decency, or of the trouble you cause those who must clean up afther you, if we are not to live like the scum of the earth."

"I'm scum. You're right, Tom. I'm no good," Chauncey slobbered, it being the sort of mea culpa he fattened on.

"Enough of that," said my grandmother. She

got up from the floor and took the gun out of the kitchen sink, where it had fallen after striking Rinaldo fatally on the side of his head, and dropped it into her apron pocket. "Come here to the sink and wash yourself off before you go upstairs," she told Chauncey, but it was Rinaldo she was looking at with a hurt frown on her face.

"Go cleanse yourself, Chauncey," said Lillie. "Make yourself decent. Remember what you were, as we all do, and try to do betther with the help of God. Here, you," she said to me, "take this cup and go run me some nice cold wather from the tap in the back kitchen."

I did as I was told, and after giving Aunt Lillie her cold water I joined my grandfather in the hall by the hat rack where he had gone to get into his things for work without even a glance at Rinaldo that I was aware of. Gramp seemed to be afraid of Rinaldo now, and of all the McLaughlins, maybe even of the house itself, maybe even of me.

"I love you, Gramp. Don't be afraid of me. I'd do anything for you, nearly."

He looked at me from Liverpool: a boy again aghast at what he had become. In my imagination he died as a man and was resurrected as the boy he used to be. Total purity poured from his eyes. He was an angel, so lost to me.

I flung my arms around his waist, embarrassing him, I guess, because instead of putting his derby on his own head, he put it on mine, while my wet face beseeched him to come back to me as he was, though it appeared to be a fact that he could not, that he was lost to me, as well as to the McLaughlins, especially Chauncey, who had caused him to die to us and to return to what he had been in Liverpool: an unmarked boy, yet to be raked by fortune's comb. He was serene enough. He hardly seemed to notice Chauncey pass us on his way upstairs to his room. I felt sorry that he would have to live in the same house with that sonofabitch.

# 43

The greatest thing my grandmother ever did was to bring us Rinaldo wrapped in the shawl she had worn in Connemara. "Give your grandfather his hat back and stop playing the fool," she told me. She did not stop as she passed us on the way up to her room except to say that. It meant a lot to me that she did not go out and call the SPCA.

Uncle Tom passed us on his way up to his room blowing his nose. Then came Aunt Lillie homeward bound for Westchester. "It's only a cat," said Lillie. "All this fuss. I've a mind to call the SPCA meself if Mary Ellen won't. What in the name of God does she intend doing with it?"

Lillie stared up the stairs as if she heard things. If she did it was only Uncle Tom singing sad Irish songs because he was sad too and Irish. He had a nice voice; there was something irresistible about Uncle Tom's singing. It cast a spell, as it did on Lillie now.

"When summer's in the meadow," she sang along with him. Then she stopped singing and stood at the foot of the staircase firmly gripping her sack of bottles and cigarettes, all she needed on her little trips from here to home in Westchester again. "Aye, it's a strange house," she said, while Uncle Tom went on singing and singing, as if his heart were breaking, "stranger than ever tonight, and should by all rights have a crepe on the door now, but what would people think of that? Strange, dark woman, Mary Ellen. Too dark to be Irish, and not dark enough to be Italian, though that is just what our mother called her: the Italian. She's no different now than she was then. But Chauncey's a bum. I don't care what you say, that was a dirty trick, taking a thing like that from her. I wish I could go up to her, I do indeed. I would if I thought I'd be welcome. You go up to her, Jack," Lillie said, turning on my grandfather, who looked to me as if he had turned to stone, a little stone angel. Everybody knew he never went into my grandmother's bedroom. "You go up," she said to me. "Let me out first before you do."

Lillie was joined in her departure from the house by my grandfather. Neither of them looked back at me standing hesitating at the foot of the stairs as they left.

When I went upstairs I found Uncle Tom out in the hall at Chauncey's bedroom door begging the former prisoner to let him in.

"Put poison under the door," Chauncey was telling Tom.

"I would if I had some," said Tom.

At that there was a great noise as Chauncey got out of his bed as if against doctor's orders and expected those who loved him to drop everything they were doing and rush to put him back into bed again. He opened his door.

"You have your nerve, saying a thing like that to me, Tom," Chauncey told him in a grieved voice, and he got into his clothes and left the house for the saloon across the street, what he always did in a crisis. He had scarcely closed the front door behind him than he opened it again and was back in the house at the foot of the stairs.

"I want that cat out before I get back," he shouted. "You hear me, I hope, Mary Ellen," and out he went again into Twenty-fourth Street, grunting compliments to himself, as if to say, "There, that will show her who is dealing from a full deck of that house of hers."

In the silence my Uncle Tom wondered aloud if Lillie had cleaned up the supper dishes or not before she left for Westchester. "I think I'll go down and have a look-see," he said, casting a mournful look through the bannister rails at my grandmother's closed bedroom door as he descended the stairs. "What's she going to do with the cat? What's she going to do with Rinaldo? She can't keep him in her room indefinitely," he said to me, not expecting an answer. I heard him running water and rattling dishes inexpertly in the kitchen as I left the house and went around to Bannister Street to see if the Bottles could be any help to me with my grandmother.

# 44

"Now what ails you, little missioner? Nothing seems to content you," Mrs. Bottle told me right off, without me even opening my mouth. "Ain't you satisfied that Rinaldo didn't harm Clancey after all? I should think you should be. Have a Fig Newton and pack up your troubles in your old kit bag."

"Don't try runnin' out on your grandmother neither," Little advised me.

"That's right," his mother seconded him. "We'll tell you when you c'n go home."

"My sled's outside," I said, not knowing what else to say.

"Are your horses tied up?" Little asked, laughing at his own joke.

They looked so happy and cozy in their minuscule kitchen, with Clancey posed against their yellow table lamp like a bird against the moon, that I lacked the heart to solicit their help with my grandmother, or for anything else, for that matter, so I decided to leave them.

Being sad myself I could not understand how anybody could be happy, the Bottles especially, since they were so poor, with no room in their house you could stretch out in without bumping into something and breaking it. They beamed and nodded at me, and Clancey sidled up and down Mrs. Bottle's arm, while their shadows gobbled up one another on the walls, and even the ceiling, where they hung suspended for seconds like announcing angels.

I was outside, passing dark row houses, when Little Bottle came running after me. "Mom sent me," he said. "Mom feels you're up to somethin', but I don't. Still and all, now that I'm here I'll see you home. Get on your sled."

"Thank you, Mr. Bottle. I really don't need anybody to see me home anymore."

"You don't, huh?"

"No, I don't. I've grown up more than you think."

"That's true," Little Bottle said, agreeing with me, the nicest thing he could have done, considering the way I felt. "And that's why," he added, drawing something from his jacket pocket, "I'm giving you this."

"Why, what is it, Mr. Bottle?"

"It's near enough to Christmas to be a Christmas present, ain't it?"

"But it's the tie you bought for yourself. You

can't give it away. You promised you wouldn't."

"Well, I have. I'm giving it to somebody who appreciates nice things, fine things. Somebody who likes dressing up."

"I do, Mr. Bottle?"

"Sure you do. You know you do. Now you wear it in good health."

"Merry Christmas, Mr. Bottle."

"Merry Christmas yourself. What's on your mind?" he demanded, roughly for him, as we came to my grandmother's house, which was dark, though it wasn't all that late yet. It was the snow. The snow made everything to do with people, and people themselves, dark, it being so white itself. "Are you sneakin' north again, honest?"

"No, it's not that, Mr. Bottle."

"Then what is it? Is it your Uncle Chauncey, up to his old tricks already, and hardly a day home?"

Little indicated Chauncey crossing Twenty-fourth Street just then from Oyster's saloon supported by his brother, Tom.

"Is this the cause of why you're so down in the mouth, little missioner? Not home a day and already up to his old tricks, huh?"

"Now what is he afther telling you?" Chauncey boomed as he came on us, much fortified by drink, and ready to take on the world, provided the world amounted to no more than Little Bottle and me.

"How are you, Chauncey?" Little asked. "You're a sight for sore eyes. How'd they treat you in Moymensing?"

"What's that to you, how they treated me, and where they treated me? I'll pay you not to repeat rumors that have little or no basis in fact, you little tailor, you."

"Then I'm mistaken," said Little. "You weren't in jail at all. Wherever you were you look all the better for it, Chauncey."

"I should," said Chauncey. "I've gained the experience of a lifetime, and mean to put it all down in a book someday, and don't you worry, I will. It's a gift, of course, and I have it. You don't think I mean to tend bar the rest of me life, do you? Not a chance. No, I'll put it all down on paper, and would begin tomorrow if only I had the place, to say nothing of the time. This house now," he said, making as if he would embrace my grandmother's property and toss it out of his way — "this house is no place for work. This house is infested. Have you got rid of that cat yet, Mary Ellen?" he roared up my grandmother's dark bedroom windows. "Are you parading around with a cat in your arms? I ain't comin' in if you are. I'll go stay with me sister Lillie in Westchester. I'll show you. I'll never come back."

Uncle Tom, showing his gold teeth in a savage snarl, hissed at Chauncey to come into the house with him.

"I won't. Not so long as the cat's in there, contaminating and poisoning the very air I'm supposed to breathe. Why, I'd rather be back in — the mining town, and will go back, if the cat's not removed."

He went into my grandmother's house all the same, and the neighbors withdrew from their doorways and windows, where they had been watching us. All was quiet except for the murmured gibberish from the knot of drunks on Oyster's wedge-shaped front step, and they were soon called back into the saloon by their thirst. Little went home. I was left facing the house I now hated. The only reason I went inside was because of my roller skates and my grandmother, but mostly my grandmother, I think. When I did so I was met by nearly all I owned to wear in the world tumbling down the stairs: shirts, pants, ties, the old overcoat with the torn fur collar, my "old skin," my grandmother called it, and my traveling bag.

Uncle Tom was outraged.

"That's no way to treat the boy's belongings, Chauncey," Tom was saying to his brother, who had slammed his bedroom door and locked it, after giving my things the toss. "Throwing the boy's clothes like that. What has he ever done to you, for God's sake? Here," Tom said to me, "he has cast your duds out of his room in a rage, bag and baggage. Just as well. You won't have reason to go back in for them. Take them. There now, you can put them by you as you sleep on the couch in the parlor."

I packed my two ties and the tie Little Bottle had given to me for Christmas, and my shirts and extra pair of pants in the bag and put it on the seat of the hat rack, Uncle Tom watching me all the while.

"Now go up to her," he directed me after I had finished packing, "go upstairs to your grandmother. You're the only one of us she will listen to now. She doesn't think anything of the rest of us in her heart. Go on now, go up to her."

"Suppose her door's locked?"

"It won't be. Even if it is, you can ask to see her. She can't refuse you."

"I don't want to."

"Why not, for God's sake?"

"She might feel she has to give up Rinaldo if I go up. It would be like taking all she feels she has in the world away from her."

"I don't see how you can say that when she still has you."

378

"She doesn't really have me anymore."

"No, I suppose not. Well, do what your conscience tells you," he said, and with that he went upstairs to his room and closed the door.

# 45

I should have known she would not be up in her bedroom. I wasn't surprised, only hurt that she had not taken me with her. Intermittent light from Twenty-fourth Street rippled across the papered ceiling of the dark room. She had gone. She had left us. She had left *me*.

Lucky for me Uncle Tom was asleep and snoring when I passed his door on my way back downstairs. I felt he did not deserve to know what had happened, to say nothing of Chauncey. I saw her in taxis. I saw her on trains. I saw her at the SPCA, the shawl she had worn in Connemara rolled in her arms as she knocked with her elbows for them to let her in.

I certainly did not see her in the kitchen, but that is where she was, in her chair by the stove, the grate bright and red enough for me to make her out easily. Her shawl was around her shoulders now, and when I felt for Chauncey's gun, after sitting down at her knees on the stool, it was no longer in her apron pocket. She had burned that too.

She had burned Rinaldo, but she appeared to lack the heart to let him go. She took the lid nearest us off the stove, sending our shadows hurtling about the kitchen like an army of black invaders, and stared into the fire with an expression of such longing that I had never seen on her face before, or on any face. Such a look must sailors' widows cast across the sea, expecting no return, yet looking, fine-combing the horizon with their stares, till a part of them goes seaward to stay, making a bridge of hearts between themselves and someplace on the ocean's slippery floor.

Yet unlike sea widows who may have had a lifetime with their loved ones, my grandmother had spent hardly any time at all with Rinaldo, perhaps not long enough to suspect how vanquished his departure from this world would leave her.

Rising from my stool I dared to share the sight of the cleansing flames of the fire with her. But the heat hurt my face, since I was short, and therefore much closer to the funeral pyre than she was. She seemed to guess this without even looking my way that I was aware of and put her hand on my hot cheek for the first time, cooling and protecting it.

I wondered if she would speak, and dared not do so myself. I was so glad she had not given Rinaldo to the SPCA but had taken charge of his transfiguration herself, that I put my arm around her as far as it could go, which in any case was not very far. We were saying good-bye really, that is what we were doing, and his ashes were good to smell, not dry and cindery, but sweet.

"You c'n go now," she said, her voice gruff and her speech countrified Irish. "You c'n broadcast to the world how you left your grandmother crushed, how you feared bein' with her through the night now, afther what she did."

"I won't," I said, "really I won't."

"Yes you will, and I won't blame you if you do. You'll get up in the middle of the night in obedience to a voice you're always talkin' to."

"I am?"

"Sure you are. Talkin' and talkin' to whoever it is, though I know his name well enough."

"You do?"

"I do."

"What — is it?"

"His name?"

"Yes, its name."

"Why, I hear you talkin' to him. You must have gotten it from your mother. Now what do you think of that?"

"Why, nothing. What am I supposed to think?"

"That you'll leave me, especially now, since you can't stand what has happened, or abide by it, or support it."

"I'm glad you didn't go to the SPCA."

"So you approve of me."

"Oh yes."

"Of what I did, the savagery of it, you'll tell someday."

"I won't. I promise."

"You will, but not before you're ready, not before you have crossed your Atlantics and suffered yourself. Now promise."

"I promise. But — how will I know when I am ready?"

"Ripe?"

She laughed and put the lid back on the stove and sat down, drawing me to her. It seemed a long time to me before I disentangled myself from her embrace, for we had slept in one another's arms.

It was a long way home through dark streets, but no harm could come to me, I felt, so long as I kept walking. My bag grew heavy, and my sled, and my feet too, but heaviest of all were my eyelids. All my mother said when she saw me was "Well, I've been having some time with the truant officer over you."

383

"And not a word about my mission," I told Aunt Frances next day.

"A prophet," said Aunt Frances, "is not without honor except in his own country."

In the following summer my father arrived home from work early one morning while it was still dark outside and stood at the foot of the stairs:

"Kate, Mom's dead."

I heard a twang reverberating through the house.

The silver cord had broken.

I slipped out of bed, got into a pair of pants, and left the house for the swimmies, where I waited until the sun rose. When the swimmies opened I swam in the blue water as if it was the sea, or Galway Bay. For she had taught me to love many waters, and to feel at home everywhere, the world being her country, as it is mine.